THE CITADEL
OF
SOULS

Emma Bradley

For all the different kinds of Fae in Faerie:

You are valid and perfect exactly as you are.

CHAPTER ONE

TALIE

"It's going to be fine, stop fussing."

Talie smiled as she shovelled Molly along the lamplit lane spiralling up the citadel tower and towards the door to Selene's bar. Molly had spent ages choosing a pair of jeans that looked like the other two pairs she had, and a hooded sweatshirt from the tiny pile of clothes still lurking in the back corner of her old workshop. She'd brushed her blonde curls out to tie them back so many times that they were almost completely flat.

Talie had strapped on another dagger to her belt, but other than that her dark hair was flat already, and she didn't need to be seen in anything other than black trousers, t-shirt and coat.

"I mean, we can come back tomorrow," Molly tried. "What if they all stop talking because I'm there, or leave?"

Talie sighed. "It's been two weeks of you wandering the levels and waving at people. Now you have to actually talk to someone besides me."

"I've talked to people!"

"About the citadel, and what needs to improve. This is your chance to show them you're still you and not all royal and stuff."

She shoved the door open before Molly could protest any further, and the spill of laughter and conversation danced out.

Molly sucked in a breath as Talie hustled her through the door.

The entire bar looked up and fell silent, from the Fae gathered amid clusters of chairs and tables to the long bar counter at the back. Molly tried to reverse but Talie pinned a strong hand against her back.

Selene lifted her head from behind the bar and she wasn't smiling.

Talie tensed. *Maybe it wasn't such a good idea.*

"We didn't expect to see you among us," Selene said, her tone even.

Talie bristled instantly but she had to let Molly be seen leading the situation.

Molly grimaced. "I don't see why. I'm still me."

"You're the ruler of the tower now," someone else said warily. "Probably shouldn't be seen slumming with us."

Talie pushed up her sleeves, ready to intimidate or fight, whichever came first, but Molly laid a soft hand on her arm.

"Seen by who?" she asked. "You lot voted me in, kind of. I'm as much a part of everything as any of you. I can leave if me being here makes you uncomfortable though."

"We thought you'd be whirled into the mores of the elite," Steve muttered.

Talie settled into the strange warmth of pride in her chest as Molly straightened and held herself steady like a true leader.

"Why?" she asked. "I mean, I'll have to deal with the nobles in order to make sure we're still standing and people don't go hungry, but our tower provides grain and fibres for clothing. We grow cobnuts on the upper levels and raise Arumpii on lower ones. Just because I have to play go-between more than the rest of you, it doesn't mean my job is any different."

It wasn't exactly a lie, but Talie knew most of them wouldn't see it like that. The stilted silence swelled as everyone looked at everyone else, and Molly took a small step back.

"Let the girl drink," a woman hollered from the back. "She's no more a noble than I am, not where it counts."

Talie sought through the crowd and caught Fern's eye. Fern gave her a tiny nod, a recognition, but there was iron in Fern's tone and several other people started nodding in unison.

"She's got a point," someone muttered. "A noble wouldn't have known how to fix my old clock."

"Molly grew up as one of us," Merry shouted from the back. "She's earned the right to be here as much as any of us have. Can't help who you're born to."

"We did sort of hire her to lead us to be fair."

Talie shook her head wearily at the mutterings that followed, but it was an acceptance of sorts, enough that Molly took the necessary steps to reach the bar.

"Best not tell them you have an appointment with the

fashion houses and frippery merchants tomorrow," Talie murmured.

Molly groaned. "I don't want to. You do it for me."

"You got me in a dress once, Princess. Don't hold your breath."

Molly rolled her eyes as cups of *Beast Lite* thudded in front of them. Molly fished in her pockets before Talie could get to it and dropped some *pesanas* in the dish on the bar.

"There should have been some perks to this whole responsibility thing," Talie muttered.

Molly smiled. "I offered you the best rooms in the Menagerie."

"I wasn't talking about fancy rooms."

"I gave you a salary."

"To spend on what?" Talie sipped her drink. "You already insisted on paying for food."

"You could get new…" Molly hesitated. "New hand wraps for fighting."

"My normal ones are fine."

"They have holes in them."

"Thumb holes, strategically worn through."

"Thumb holes halfway up your arm?"

Talie grinned. "Scared I'll embarrass you, Princess?"

"Worried you'll get bored more like."

"And leave all this?" She waved her half-drunk cup between them. "Now you're in charge, it's just a case of running everything."

"Oh yeah, great."

Molly bit her lip but Talie caught the smile lurking

there.

In the two weeks that had passed since the fight in the labyrinth beneath the citadel and Molly's appointment as ruler of their tower, Talie had made herself impossible to shake off. They shared the little two-room house next to Molly's workshop, walked everywhere together while Molly was busy being seen by people to keep reassurance high, and she would be at Molly's side when she had to face meeting the delegations from the other towers along with their own nobles in the morning.

With Demi's assurance that the well of power and the Omens were contained for the time being, Molly's sole focus was on how to rebuild the citadel. The other towers had sent missives in the form of veiled demands to be seen and acknowledged, and insistences that they would decide if they recognised her rule. So far though, Molly hadn't made any attempt to raise the wards that contained their tower from the rest of Faerie again, or to find out how it might be done.

The air froze and silence fell, not the wary silence they'd received on stepping inside the bar, but a stunned tipping point of tension that had Molly swinging around on her stool.

Talie leapt to her feet before Molly was fully rotated and her gut twisted. She threw out an arm across Molly to stop her from standing and raised a protection warding over them as a familiar voice that filled the air.

"I've been looking for you."

Molly's warding curled around hers, hesitant with shock as they stared at the boy standing in the doorway, his black hair swept back and jewel blue eyes dancing in the bar's flickering faelight.

"Ru?"

His name burst out of Molly's mouth as a strangled whimper.

Ru hovered in the pub's doorway like a spectre back from the dead, all the worse because Talie had seen him die when he was pretending to be her during one of Celeste's attacks.

Unless that was all part of the greater plan. What if he was working with Phoenix all along, keeping Celeste on side?

"Molly." His voice rasped across the silence.

Talie cocked her head and squinted at him. There was a strange emptiness about him, something to do with the lack of depth on his face and in his tone.

Without another word, he turned and retreated out to the lane again. The door banged loudly and the low hum of whispers started up as Molly strode after him.

"Orbs," Talie muttered, already a pace behind her.

They charged out onto the lane to find it deserted, and Talie winced as the cold bite of the artificial wind from the tower's vents hit her face.

"Where'd he go?" Molly asked.

Talie folded her arms and made sure her warding was firmly around them.

"What does it matter? It's clearly a trap."

"But he's supposed to be dead!" Molly hissed. "Then he comes strolling back in to say hi and disappears again. How?"

Talie shrugged. "Not a clue, but he wasn't on your side before so I doubt he's changed tune now."

"But... he's meant to be dead, and now he's disappeared again."

A flicker of hesitation had Talie stalling. Molly had been best friends with Ru for years, and Talie was almost certain there had been some kind of crush there at some point. She shook the unwelcome thoughts aside.

"Can't you use your new status to find him?" she asked. "This princess and leader stuff has to be good for something eventually."

"Oh I'm sorry, the crown didn't exactly come with a manual!"

Talie would have laughed at the sheer horror on Molly's face, but Ru lurking was a bad sign all round.

"He probably isn't going to do anything with you lurking either," Molly added.

Talie frowned. "Meaning?"

"Well, tiptoe off a tiny bit and-"

"No."

"But it's the ideal way to-"

"No."

"At least let me-"

"No."

"I'm the one who's leader here!"

Talie bit her lips together to stop the twitching, and the ready retort.

"It would be unwise to leave you unguarded, your royal obstinance."

Molly rolled her eyes. "Oh, nice. Seriously though, how

are we going to find anything out otherwise?"

Talie eyed the lane and lifted her chin.

"I'm not leaving her, so you might as well show yourself," she called out.

Molly winced as a couple of sets of curtains shivered in nearby windows, but a shape in the shadows solidified as Ru appeared again.

Talie dropped one hand to the dagger it her wrist.

"Molly," he said.

Again that emotionless voice, the expressionless face. He moved with no fluidity either, no sense of personality.

Almost as if he's not all there. She shuddered. *Resurrections. Surely even Phoenix wouldn't...*

But he would, and she knew it.

"What happened?" Molly demanded.

Ru blinked. "What happened?"

"Where have you been?"

He said nothing for several seconds, and Talie inched closer to Molly. If she had to use the new orb in her pocket to call in Kainen and Demi and all the royals in Faerie, she would do it.

"In darkness," he said slowly. "Then light. It burns sometimes."

"Something's really not right there," Talie muttered.

"Why have you come here?" Molly demanded. "Tell me who sent you."

"I am here for you," Ru said.

Talie scowled. "Why?"

He turned his head and his vacant stare fixed on her.

"I was told to."

"By who?"

"By Ru."

The tiniest hint of personality marred his brow, the suggestion of a frown. Before Talie could think of a way to force more information out of what was clearly a completely addled mind, he rotated and disappeared down the nearest alley.

Talie tensed, ready for Molly to dart after him, but she didn't move.

"You're right," Molly said.

"Wow. What about?"

"Something's not right. He's not Ru."

"I did wonder…" Talie hesitated. "We shouldn't be talking about this out here."

Molly nodded and set off along the lanes. Talie kept pace with her, wishing she had thought to pocket one of the many bags of Sticky Sap sweets that Molly had strewn around her bedroom.

She didn't say a word and Molly didn't either until they were safe in the house with the door shut and a shaky bubble warding doming around them, a technique Molly had learned from Demi but still hadn't got the hang of yet.

Talie eyed the hints of moss grew over the walls, a side effect from her splurging storm gift that tended to toy with the moisture in the room at random and inconvenient intervals. She was clearing it away as often as she could, but at least it hadn't reached over the bed at the far side of the room yet.

"Phoenix was talking about resurrections as one of his end goals," she said.

Her nerves jangled inside her restless limbs so she jumped straight into it, but a brief moment of regret clenched her chest tight as Molly's face paled.

"You think Celeste or Phoenix… so when Ru was pretending to be you, and he died, you think they used him as a test for this whole undead process?"

Talie started pacing beneath the small dome of the bubble warding.

"No way of knowing for sure, but it's a possibility. We need to consider him the enemy. It's not worth letting him roam around like that either."

"What can we do when he keeps disappearing?"

"Set a net," Talie said grouchily. "Trap him. Put him in the cells."

"We have no guarantee of anything. We can't exactly confine him to a cell if he hasn't done anything wrong yet."

"Not done anything wrong?! He helped Celeste imprison you!"

Molly settled onto the bed and tucked her legs beneath her.

"And was supposed to have died since. If he hasn't, doesn't that give him some kind of second chance or a reprieve or something?"

Talie kept pacing the same infuriatingly small patch of floor as her fears of lingering emotions on Molly's side wrapped thorny tendrils around her throat.

What if he's not undead and manages to convince her he's on her side? What if she still loves him?

CHAPTER TWO

MOLLY

Molly sat on the bed in the centre of the main room of the house as Talie paced back and forth like a fury-filled spinning top.

"That's just great," Talie seethed. "Two weeks. Two orbing weeks and now that orb-muncher comes strolling in like nothing could possibly be orbing wrong, and you're just happy to orbing forgive him!"

"That's a lot of orbs, even for you," Molly muttered.

"*Forgive* me, Princess, but I didn't expect to have to deal with my- the-"

She huffed and paced away again.

"Why don't you stand still a minute?" Molly tried.

"Oh I'm sorry, do you want the pacing space for yourself instead given it's your ex, or almost ex, or could-have-been-an-ex-given-enough-time that's come back?"

Molly bit her lips between her teeth because irrationally dramatic Talie was one of her favourite vibes and it took all her effort not to smile.

"It doesn't change anything," she said.

Talie folded her arms and stopped pacing.

"It changes everything."

"Does it?"

"Doesn't it? We thought he died. We didn't even get a chance to interrogate whoever it is. It might not even be him."

Molly nodded. "I know, I've considered that. I've got options too."

"Such as?"

"If it is him, the wards are down. I can invite whoever I like and trust in to question him if I really want. I know enough about him to ask the right questions too."

"And if it isn't him?"

"If it isn't him, then we should be expecting this to happen from now on. Veiled attacks, attempts to throw us off balance, to trick us. I never wanted to rule this place but I do want to help it run properly."

"And…" Talie hesitated. "If it is him?"

Molly smiled wearily and held a hand out.

"It doesn't change anything. If it is him, then he can tell us where he's been all this time. If he's done nothing wrong, he can rejoin the citadel and be part of it like everyone else here."

She meant it but Talie eyed her outstretched hand warily.

"Oh sure, as if he won't be championing his place at your side," she muttered.

As if he even has one. Is she really worried about him somehow taking her place even now?

"Talie, he doesn't have one, not before what happened

to him and not now."

She waved her hand insistently, but Talie grumbled under her breath the whole way to her side. Molly slid her fingers firmly around Talie's as she sat down on the edge of the mattress.

"Promise?"

Molly nodded. "Promise."

"Okay." Talie frowned. "You're taking this surprisingly well."

"I've seen so many weird things I don't even question it much anymore. It simply is until it isn't. I'm not that kid anymore."

It technically wasn't a lie, that innocence was long gone, but she didn't want to admit she still felt like a scared kid trying to survive deep down.

"So, we question him," Talie said doubtfully.

"Yeah."

"Right now?"

"Well…" she smiled. "Not right now necessarily."

A loud hammering noise lasted all of two seconds before the door swung open.

"Sammy!" Talie seethed. "In the name of Faerie and the nether, wait to be asked inside!"

Sammy strode in, her brown eyes dancing even as she pulled a sulky face. She came to a stop at the end of the bed and wound one of her braids around her finger.

"This arrived in your office," she said, holding out a stiff pale pink card edged with dark green.

Molly groaned. "I think I know what that is."

She took it, aware of Talie trying to look without

looking like she was looking, and read the short script of swirly green.

"Anything to worry about, Princess?"

Talie's shoulders hunched the second she saw the name signed at the bottom with far too many looping swirls.

"It's from Violetta, angling for an invite." Molly announced it anyway.

"Oh lovely. As if this day can't get any worse."

"Don't jinx it then," Sammy suggested cheerfully. "Who's Violetta?"

"A friend," Molly said, at the same time as Talie retorted, "Molly's fancy ex."

Molly threw the card onto the bed and stood up with a huff.

"She's not my ex! Ru is not my ex. I have no exes, let's get that clear, okay?"

Talie scowled. "Fine."

"Fine!"

"FINE."

Sammy rolled her eyes. "Stop it both of you. Molly has no exes and Talie has no manners and everything is aggressively fine."

"Fine." Molly smiled the tiniest bit.

Talie's lips twitched. "Fine."

That was another thing she loved about Talie; she never stayed mad for too long.

"Aah, I've missed her Molly smile," Sammy said.

"Her what?"

"Her Molly smile. Normally it's just a slight lift of the mouth, barely even a smile. Then she sees you and both sides almost reach her ears."

"Stop it," Talie muttered.

Molly laughed. "Let's all stop it. We have bigger issues to deal with."

"What bigger issues?" Sammy asked.

"Ru's shown up," Molly said.

Sammy's eyes grew wide. "As in the tall man who used to follow you about?"

"Wouldn't put it like that but yeah, him." Molly sighed.

"Where is he?"

"He found us in Selene's bar, dropped a couple of vague statements and left again," Talie muttered. "Faerie knows where he is now, probably spying on us."

"You need to be careful then, both of you," Sammy insisted.

Molly nodded wearily. "Until I know he is who he says he is and what he's suddenly shown up for, I'm not trusting him an inch."

Talie slouched on the bed as Molly pulled her orb out of her pocket and swiped the surface a couple of times.

"What are you smiling at, Princess?"

Molly didn't look up, too amused by the nonsense on the orb-cast.

"I'm in the royals orb message chat."

"The... what?"

"Yeah. Taz set it up. I mainly lurk to watch the fireworks. He kicks Kainen out at least six times a day, then we work on a rota to invite him back in again. I know it's weird."

It was strange in a way, but in another it was exactly

like the new generation of royalty who weren't traditional in the slightest.

"It's not entirely weird," Talie conceded. "It's your family and it's kind of sweet."

Molly smiled wickedly and tapped the orb a few times.

Talie frowned and dug a hand in her pocket to retrieve her own orb.

Molly has added Talie to Royals Chat

"What did you do that for?!" Talie gasped. "I barely know them."

Molly rolled her eyes. "Kainen's one step away from adopting you as his heir for Faerie's sake, it's fine."

Both of them looked down as the next notification burned in.

~Royals Group Chat~

Taz: Did I authorise this? No offense Talie, but until you two are at least engaged, you don't count.

Kainen: Rude. I claim her as an honorary member of our court's nobility with no binding.

Taz: Still, it's more of a family thing.

Kainen: ...I'm family? I'm so touched!

Taz: Barely. But it's not the same, no offense Talie.

Kainen: I'm still in awe of our relationship status. We need to get matching bracelets, or necklaces or something. We could get matching piercings. Anyway, Talie and Molly are courting.

Molly: Let's not start flinging labels around.

Talie: Yeah, and I'm not nobility, honorary or otherwise. Who even came up with this mad chat anyway?

Taz has removed Talie from Royals Chat

Kainen: Rude! And unbecoming of a king.

Taz: I knew she was too much like you. Bye.

Taz has removed Kainen from Royals Chat

Demi has added Talie and Kainen to Royals Chat

Demi: Play nicely or I'm revoking the group entirely.

Taz: You can't, it's my group. I started it. I'm the admin.

Demi has changed Demi to admin

Kainen: Queen behaviour. I approve. If it weren't for our perilous past and the fact I love my wife more than living, I'd say it's a shame you ended up with such a fastidious example of royalty instead of me.

Demi has removed Kainen from Royals Chat

Taz: HA.

CHAPTER THREE

TALIE

"Why do I have to do this again?" Molly groaned.

Talie sighed as she swept Molly along the lanes toward the Menagerie with a firm hand on her shoulder.

"Because you're leader of this crumbling wreck and you need to hold your own with the other leaders of the other less crumbling wrecks."

"Important people make fashion statements all the time. Look at Demi, and she's an actual queen! Why can't my statement be trousers and climbing shoes?"

Talie decided not to answer that as they walked through the Menagerie doors and into the entrance hall. She still hated the sight of the place, but reminded herself often that it was technically where she and Molly first kissed, so tearing it down would be a slight overreaction.

A tall woman bowed her head as they approached, her black hair wound into an ornate bun, but the look she gave them was pure critical purpose.

"Princess. I am Selene, a seamstress from the Tailor's Guild." She frowned. "I understand your only stipulation when enquiring with the Guild was for someone from the citadel who hadn't worked for Celeste Elverhill previously?"

"That about covers it, yeah. I need to be certain that nobody I deal with is in alternative employ."

Selene's ruby lips pursed as she smoothed down her sleeveless beige suit.

"I have no prior link to the nobility or the other towers."

"That's okay then. I want something casual, none of these huge trailing skirts or big ruffles."

Talie frowned. "She still needs to look like them though, the nobles."

Molly folded her arms across her chest and gave her an acidic look.

"Who appointed you my personal dresser?"

"Well it's important. Even Kainen said you're well overdue choosing your own colours as princess, and these noble types will kick off if you don't play along."

Molly scowled, but whatever sulky retorts we're brewing on her tongue, she didn't vent them in front of Selene.

"If you'll forgive me, your friend is right," Selene said. "So much can be said without speaking where clothing is concerned. It sounds like we have some work to do yet, so where can we set up?"

Talie risked letting go of Molly's shoulder as she nodded with a grimace.

She didn't correct the 'friend' bit either.

"We might as well go upstairs," Molly said. "There's probably something in there you can salvage from the last lot of frippery."

She turned toward the wide curving staircase and missed Selene's miniscule wince at the word frippery, but Talie caught it.

They traipsed upstairs and along the corridor of doors and large plants to the bedroom Molly used at the Menagerie. It had originally been hers during the imprisonment during her mother's rule, then Talie's during Phoenix's brief occupation. Since then it had been gathering dust as Molly insisted on staying at the house near the workshop.

The moment they got into the bedroom and Talie closed the door behind them, Molly pointed to the half-open door that led into the walk-in room full of dresses.

"The clothes are through there."

Instead of going to look, Selene snapped her fingers and a table overloaded with fabrics thudded into the centre of the enormous room. As her critical eye passed over Molly, Talie kept a wary watch on her in return.

"Hm... you would do well in satin," Selene suggested. "Perhaps ruched skirts, no ruffles, and you have ideal shoulders for suits."

"You can tell all that already?" Talie asked. "She's wearing two layers."

After Phoenix had kept the vents at a hostile temperature for months claiming they were broken, Molly had listened to the pleas that they reinstate the seasons. She agreed instantly but it would take time for whatever mechanical sorcery managed the vents to re-regulate.

Selene snorted and picked up a roll of deep blue fabric.

"It's as much about how you carry yourself as your size

and shape. Any fool can don a dress and suck in their gut, but clothing needs to take the strain after the gut has un-sucked and the shoulders have slumped. Now, down to the underwear please."

Molly hesitated. "Um, I'm not wearing a bra though."

"Why not?"

"I don't. They're uncomfortable."

"Well, it's about time you started. Hm... try these then."

Another click of the determined fingers and a pile of bras that looked more like the fight-wear kind Talie sometimes trained in appeared.

Molly took them with careful hands like they might bite.

"Okay, I'll just... yeah."

She retreated into the dress room and Talie tensed as Selene gave her a once over.

"You have good posture. A proud bearing bordering on arrogant. I could make a noble out of you easily."

"Well, I'm not one." Talie shrugged. "Think of me more like a bodyguard."

Selene's lips curved up as Molly came out with her torso twisting. Talie sighed and reached behind her to pull the straps straight.

"Stop wriggling," she muttered. "There."

"Are you sure you don't want to do something with all the dresses in there already?" Molly asked.

"Tell me, Princess." Selene advanced. "Why do you need the Tailor's Guild if you already have dresses?"

"Because I don't want those ones, but it's a waste. Why not just modify them?"

Selene sighed. "I am not in the habit of modifying creations for royalty or nobility. I can however relieve you of them and have them redistributed for a nominal fee."

Talie panicked and held a hand up as Molly's eyes widened hopefully.

"Define a nominal fee."

Selene laughed. "Okay, I see. Well, we are all independent creators as part of the Guild. Being able to say my creations are being worn not only by the leader of our tower but the princess of Faerie, well... throw in some free fabric to repurpose for those in the citadel that are going without, you could say everyone wins."

Talie held her tongue as Molly's head tilted to the side, the slight narrowing of her eyes suggesting that the puzzle-solving part if her mind had pinged on.

"So, you'd take all those fancy dresses, cut them down and make clothes for charity?" she asked.

Selene swung the fabric she was holding under her arm and pulled out a lime green orb. She swiped her thumb over the surface a few times until an orb-cast image of a leaflet appeared in the air between them.

"Not charity, but affordable clothing markets, yes. The Tailor's Guild understands currency of the item over the arcane, much like the Grain Guild does. We do what we can to repurpose and redistribute."

Molly nodded. "Then absolutely take them, no debt or trade needed. Urgh, fine. Let's get this over with."

"Ah yes, what every artiste trains their gingers to the bone to hear when they're called to create," Selene said drily. "Arms up."

Talie slouched across to the bed and sat down, revelling in the irritable look Molly gave her.

Molly's moods were nothing some quiet time and a pastry wouldn't fix, but she still revelled in being the one allowed to see the moods and fix them. Aside from tiny grumbles, Molly was sweetness and light with everyone else.

"We'll fashion a spring line to start with as we're said to be heading into the new season soon," Selene said as she began draping Molly in the blue fabric. "I think for you some effortless, flowing ambers and midnight blues maybe? I wouldn't say too much adornment or embellishment, but there will need to be some. Do you have any statement jewellery you're known for?"

"I have a crown," Molly said.

"What notes does it have?"

"Um… it's a crown, it doesn't sing."

"Notes, Your Highness, colour palettes, shades."

"Oh, well it's kind of pale gold with pink stones. Also, please call me Molly."

"If you wish. Hmm. Pale gold and pink will not be the best with the colour set I'd choose for you. Let me think. I have some silk-spun cloth in a more muted gold, that could work. It's a tad more expensive, but let's have a look."

She bustled to the table and Molly gave Talie a helpless look.

"Perhaps we steer clear of the excessively expensive fabrics," Molly suggested. "We're still in the process of solidifying what our tower can provide, and I will not spend it on myself when others need it."

Talie smiled as Molly folded her arms across her bare middle and slouched extra low. She might not want finery, but she already sounded like a leader when it came to defending the citadel.

She never wanted to stay here but perhaps that can still change.

Selene pulled a lump of gold fabric with a slight glittering sheen to it from the table and held it up with a frown.

"An admirable notion, but consider that you still need to represent us to the other towers. You wouldn't want them to assume we're suffering. Everyone outside sees us through you, and if you're well dressed, they'll be curious as to why. Oh, they'll talk about how you're going to be just like the rest but that's just gossip. Let your appearance do the talking and your actions make the decisions."

Molly sighed. "I suppose, but I was sort of guided into the pink and gold, I guess because it's similar to the Oak Queen's summer colours."

"Well, you are princess of the summer court," Talie offered, purely to be inflammatory.

Molly pulled a face and stuck her tongue out as Selene dropped the fabric and twitched her fingers. It wriggled in midair and a pair of scissors leapt up unaided to start cutting it.

"I'm leader of the Citadel Sunset tower first," Molly insisted. "I should choose my own colours."

Selene stopped the scissors mid-cut with a twirl of her finger.

"Very well. What colours would you choose?"

Molly frowned. "Muted amber, maybe hues of gold. Or possibly green tones, like leafy green not bright. Charcoal and silver, but not too much, more like trim here and there. Then deep red, like this."

She held up her hand to show the *Akiai* charm on her thumb and a tumble of emotions fizzed in Talie's gut.

She could just like the colour.

Even so, Talie let her grin flare freely for a few seconds before biting it down again. If Molly was using the tiny gift she'd given her a while back as a colour base, perhaps it did mean something.

"That… could work." Selene eyed the table. "Hm… Actually, yes. Bold colours. Let me reassess a moment."

Talie lounged back on the bed as Molly looked her way.

"You're enjoying this," she muttered.

Talie nodded. "Kind of. So, amber gold and green, red and I'm guessing silver and dark grey like the Illusion Court?"

"Yeah. Demi's got bold colours because of her court, so why can't I have bold for mine?"

"It sounds similar to Demi's colours. Green and red is very Yuletide."

"Not always. There are red flower fields at the top of the Illusion Court that only bloom in summer, and green doesn't have to be evergreen. Summer sunlight can be golden too."

"Wasn't criticising, Princess. You can go for different shades. It does show an allegiance though."

"Good."

Talie smiled at the prim irritation in Molly's voice as

Selene draped her in multiple bits of different coloured fabric.

"How about some spider-silk?" Selene suggested.

"As in…"

"Spun by spiders yes. Again, it's more expensive-"

"I do not need ridiculously extortionate cloth made from the butts of spiders," Molly huffed.

"It's the best though, maybe with feathers-"

"No feathers!"

Talie couldn't help the snort of laughter that bubbled out.

"Just think, when you're all dressed up and striding around, at least you'll look the part," she said.

Molly's ferocious glare upended into a smile. Suddenly. Sweetly. Dangerously.

"She's going to be accompanying me," she said. "You'll need to attire her appropriately too."

Selene nodded. "If you wish it. Now, I think I've got enough measurements to be going on with, and a head full of designs."

"But you didn't measure me."

"No need." Selene waved a dismissive hand. "I'll have samples of the finished pieces to you for review in the next two days, if that suits you?"

A brief knock on the door had Molly dashing toward the dress-room.

"That's fine, thanks," she called over her shoulder.

Talie pushed off the bed as the bedroom door swung open without invitation.

"Sammy, for the millionth time, what have we said

about knocking?" she groaned.

Sammy strode in waving a piece of card. Selene gave Talie a firm nod as she finger-clicked away the table and left the room, but Talie had her attention on the black card dangling from Sammy's fingers.

If Molly has more admirers wanting to visit, I'm going to scream.

Molly hurried out again in her normal jeans, sweatshirt and black climbing shoes to give Sammy a weary smile. She noted the card and her entire body stiffened.

"That's the Night Tower's calling card," she said.

Talie couldn't fathom how she knew that, but it was black with light yellow writing scrawled on it so it fitted their aesthetic.

Sammy nodded. "It's a summons from the other towers. Also you have a visitor."

She glanced over her shoulder before Talie could lecture her about reading other people's mail, and someone else filled the doorway. Someone she'd never met before but couldn't forget the face of even if she wiped her own mind.

"Hello!" Even the nauseatingly lyrical voice was irritating. "Sorry to barge in, but I did send a calling card. Then some of my friends were coming to your lower levels so I thought I'd chance a journey up."

Talie clenched her fists at her sides, unable to move her feet as the tall redhead swanned into the room like she owned the place.

She headed straight for Molly, who stood frozen with a look of absolute panic on her face.

"Hi." Molly grimaced a smile. "That's fine. I should have answered. Um..."

She swung around, but Talie had the sense to shove her fists in her pockets and hide him.

The other woman also looked her way with a calculated narrowing of her eyes.

"I take it by the arctic vibes, you must be Talie," the woman said. "I'm Violetta."

CHAPTER FOUR

MOLLY

Molly stood utterly helpless as Violetta introduced herself to Talie, and given the mutinous look on Talie's face she was moments away from grabbing the dagger she kept on her wrist and throwing it at Violetta's head.

Orbs, we haven't even had the conversation yet but I can't let Talie think there's anything going on.

Aware of Sammy ogling the whole thing gleefully, she moved across the room to stand at Talie's side.

"Sorry, Violetta, that's Sammy, and this is Talie, my… girlfriend. Welcome to the citadel, and the Sunset Tower. I'll ask them to find you a room here if you're staying?"

She couldn't take Talie's hand when they were shoved so deep into her pockets they were almost level with her knees, but the girlfriend bit didn't seem to have made a dent in the mood.

Violetta blinked for a moment before rallying with a bright smile.

"Of course. I'd love to stay a while if you're okay with it? I remember mention of a promise to show me your workshop too."

Molly bit her lip. She remembered Violetta mentioning promises, but the woman had also been extremely helpful when needed so she couldn't be rude.

"Okay. Sammy, could you check with Dillia and have a room arranged please?"

Sammy grinned. "Sure thing. Follow me… Violet, was it? Are you a lady? We don't use titles here, but I will if Molly says I should."

Violetta gave Molly another bright-eyed smile instead.

"If you're available I'd love to invite you for dinner sometime?" she pressed.

Molly half-nodded, half-shrugged helplessly.

"It's a bit busy at the moment I'm afraid, and I have a meeting with the other towers, but we can do a mini tour now?"

She risked resistance when she slipped her hand around Talie's wrist and tried to pull her hand out of her pocket. Talie let her, but her expression still remained clamped down tight.

"Of course." Violetta laughed with a flirty bow of her head. "I'd be happy to, and as always I am at your disposal."

Sammy disappeared, hopefully to get the room sorted, and Molly clung to Talie's hand as she led the way out of the room.

"How's things at the Flora Court?" she asked in absence of anything else to say.

Violetta made sure to walk right at her side so their arms brushed, and Molly clung to Talie's hand as they started down the stairs.

"It's ticking along," Violetta said. "Lady Lolly told me to send her regards and gratitude for speaking with the queen on her behalf."

"I didn't do much, just said a few things about leniency being sweeter than restriction, and how the courts need to see it from both sides, not just Demi's."

"The Holly Queen certainly does seem pro-reform. Ah, your struts need replacing up there."

Molly nodded. "They do, and we have people working on it."

"Including you," Talie said. "Even with everything else. Do you get your hands dirty much then, Violet?"

"It's Violetta, and technically it's Lady too, but I'll let it slide."

"How noble of you."

There was nothing genuine about the bright chuckle that followed.

"Well, some of us do have standards to adhere to."

Molly grimaced as they set off along the lanes toward the workshop, but in a way it was an addictive horror show that she couldn't stop herself watching.

"I'm sure you do. Swanning around fanning yourself takes a lot of practice."

Violetta sighed. "I do actually do most of the engineering and mechanics from day to day at court. We build all sorts."

"All sorts of what?"

"Well, all sorts of things. Do you do anything useful?"

It was worse than a horror show. Molly increased the pace as the turning of the workshop alley came into view.

"I have a couple of uses," Talie retorted. "Being able to stab things is one of them. Want to see?"

"Here we are!"

Molly hurried into the alley but stopped dead outside her workshop. A woman stood outside the door to the house, the *open* door, bent over a ridiculously enormous pile of stuff.

Molly walked forward slowly, the uneasiness of change settling heavy on her chest.

"Um, Beryl?"

"Molly!" Beryl lifted her bright purple-haired head along with a hand that almost released a bag of nappies at the wall. "Oops. Alright if I take my old place back? I need some peace and quiet. Hiya, Vi. Didn't realise you'd be here as well."

Molly stood with her mouth open, unable to say a word as it looked like Beryl was mostly moved in already.

"Let it go a bit with the damp," Beryl added. "But no matter. Hutch and my sister are coming tomorrow with Aurora too."

She bustled into the house and Talie grimaced.

"Oh, are you letting Beryl stay?" Violetta asked. "It'll be lovely to have more familiar faces around."

Molly frowned. "I guess. I wasn't expecting her but sure."

"Is this wise?" Talie asked.

"Wise?"

"I'm just saying, maybe keep an eye on her, what with the history. She could be a loose cannon looking for revenge."

Molly couldn't imagine it, but then Beryl was the volatile kind from what she'd seen and heard.

Violetta went one further and rolled her eyes.

"She's in the Holly Queen's inner circle, I doubt she needs monitoring. I'm surprised you didn't know that considering you've labelled yourself the princess's guard dog."

The dig slid sharp beneath the bright smile, but Talie only shrugged, although her shoulders went up and didn't come back down again.

"I don't keep track of the queen's acquaintances," she said. "Workshop is back there, then there's a lot that needs doing."

Molly took a couple of steps back as the two of them continued locking eyes. She couldn't do anything about Beryl, although she'd need to rescue her own things from the house.

She still had the workshop as a safe space too, and grabbed the key hanging around her neck. A quick tour for Violetta, then she would need to find some way of convincing Talie there was definitely nothing to be concerned about.

"So, the workshop is in here. It's not the same as the one at the Illusion Court but this one is mine." She babbled on as she swung the door open and hurried inside.

The scent of dust hit her nose and she tensed as Violetta followed next, then Talie with her arms folded across her chest.

"It's homey," Violetta offered.

Molly shrugged. "It's home, one of them anyway."

She scanned the workshop to check nothing was out of place and her chest squeezed at the sight of the threadbare screen around her bed in the far corner, and the empty plates stacked in a heap on the kitchenette counter.

"I suppose you won't have much time for visiting now," Violetta said. "The courts will miss you. Has the queen visited?"

"The Oak Queen? No, and I'm dreading when she does."

"I wouldn't admit that out loud."

Molly smiled. "Maybe not."

She flinched as a loud clang echoed through the air.

"Sorry." Talie shrugged. "Foot slipped."

Molly looked at the metal bucket by the door, unpainted with several dents. It also wasn't hers.

The skip-way.

She glanced around but couldn't see anything else out of place. Reyan still had her workshop door key, but there was a skip-way somewhere in the workshop that they'd set up as a failsafe before the wards came down.

"Anyway, it's not much to look at." She headed back toward the doorway. "I should be getting back to work, what with the meeting tomorrow."

"What meeting is that?" Violetta asked as she followed them out.

"Citadel business," Talie retorted. "Don't let us keep you, Viena."

Violetta blinked, then another bright smile swept across her face.

"Of course. I'll be in touch, Molly. We can have tea."

Molly nodded, helpless in the face of Talie's blatant rudeness to give anything other than a weak smile.

Instead of turning toward the main lane, Violetta walked the few paces to the house and the open door. Beryl's stuff was still piled outside, but Molly didn't wait to see if she started helping or not.

She strode down the alley and turned onto the main lane heading downward.

"That was rude," she said.

"I prefer pre-emptively un-diplomatic," Talie muttered. "She's probably here as a spy."

Molly sucked in a breath to deny it, then hesitated.

"Maybe, but even more reason not to antagonise her."

Talie huffed something under her breath.

"What was that?"

"Nothing. You didn't lock the workshop either. Maybe you should."

"I don't have the key."

Talie frowned. "Why not?"

"Long story. I had to give it to Reyan. She-" Molly glanced around and lowered her voice. "She set up a skip-way shortly before we came in to get you from the labyrinth. I'm guessing that bucket is it, considering it's the only thing I don't recognise in there."

"So anyone can just stride in?!"

Molly grabbed Talie's arm as they approached the Menagerie and dragged her into the nearest alcove behind one of the stone pillars.

"No, because hardly anyone knows it exists. I trust Reyan, and Taz. I imagine Kainen knows too, and Demi, but they're the only ones. And now you."

"Oh, how delightful that you've finally trusted me with it too."

Molly hemmed her lips between her teeth to hide her smile.

"I forgot, or I would have told you. Come on, we have to wade through all this meeting stuff yet. Are you going to sulk all evening?"

Talie scowled. "No."

"Just most of it?"

"I'm not sulking. I'm concerned. Bad enough she's turned up all fluttery, but your Ru's still lurking around somewhere as well."

"He's not *my* Ru. We don't even know if it's really him either. One problem at a time. If you don't want to help…"

She left it hanging but Talie rolled her eyes and stomped toward the Menagerie doors.

"I never said that. Fine, but I'm not being nice to her."

Molly grinned as they walked up the stairs toward the bedroom.

"I wouldn't expect you to. Maybe just keep it to glowering though, for the sake of inter-realm relations."

She swung open the door to her room and a thought occurred to her as she saw the bed. Talie stopped beside her and sighed.

"Beryl's taking the house back."

Molly grimaced. "Yeah."

"Which means we have to hole up here now."

"I guess. I mean, there's the workshop, but the bed will be all dusty and I should probably be here."

Talie hesitated, reluctance scrawled across her face.

"Okay, well, I should go and see if there's another room down the hall or something I guess."

"Yeah."

Molly shuffled further into the bedroom as Talie shut the door and left her alone without another word. Neither of them had once mentioned out loud that they ended up sharing the bed in the main room of the house, but it kept happening. First it was easier because of the late nights sorting out citadel issues. Then it was a convenient issue of not enough clean bedsheets. Talie's storm gift soaked the bed in the smaller room. Eventually, it was just a wordless agreement.

She tensed as the door swung open and bounced into the wall with a loud bang.

"You shouldn't be alone right now," Talie announced, her face set with grim determination. "Your nightmares."

Molly forced her lips downward when they insisted on tugging up. They hadn't once mentioned the nightmares she'd been having occasionally, but each time she woke with Talie's hand around hers and a comforting arm settled around her middle.

"I haven't had one in days," she said.

Talie tilted her head to one side, a tiny upward flick at the corner of her mouth.

"How do we know it's not because I've been sharing the bed with you? Besides, it's not safe here for you alone. Best I stick around."

Molly made a show of frowning and considering, even though her insides were floppy with relief.

"I guess this bed is the size of a house almost anyway, plenty of room."

Talie shut the door and started pulling off her boots.

"You sure you wouldn't rather be sharing with Viola?"

Molly rolled her eyes. "It's Violet. Orbs, no, I mean Violetta. Stop it! You know what her name is. And no, I wouldn't."

She didn't comment on Talie leaving her boots lying on the floor in a heap, just moved toward the adjoining bathroom.

"What gifts does she have then?" Talie's voice floated after her. "In case she tries to swap us out in our sleep?"

Molly hesitated. "I haven't asked."

"Hmm."

It was another thing Molly hadn't thought to find out, but she added it to the mental list of issues getting longer by the hour and focused on brushing her teeth instead.

One problem at a time.

CHAPTER FIVE

MOLLY

Molly rubbed her bleary eyes and sat up in bed, not entirely sure why people were striding into her bedroom. Talie was already on her feet with one hand ready on the hilt of her blade, even though she hadn't properly opened her eyes yet either.

"Apologies for the early hour." Selene's rich voice followed a procession of clothing rails into the middle of the room. "The tower is a-buzz with news of your first official communal meeting and I figured you'd want something suitable in your new colours to wear."

"Should I make some kind of rule about knocking?" Molly asked Talie grouchily.

Talie shrugged. "You can do. Nice colours though."

Molly blinked as she eased herself out of bed and grabbed the first pair of trousers she could reach on the nearby chair.

"No need for those," Selene added, holding up a pool of fabric.

Ignoring Talie's wicked smirking, Molly dropped the trousers back on the chair and stomped across the carpet in her cotton shorts and sleeveless top. She folded her arms across her chest as Selene's staff hurried out again.

"Hopefully these are up to standard," Selene continued. "The dress has a detachable skirt with trousers underneath for ease of use- actually, they all do. Some sensible suits as well for the less formal meetings. I've erred on the side of caution and mixed the gold and the earthy green as your base colours, with the red and silver you asked for as trim."

Molly stared. Beside her, Talie uttered a soft "wow". Selene swept the fabric up to show off a corseted dress, strapless with an amber underskirt over-layered by swathes of lighter gold and red that curled over the dress like a sunset sky.

"I have taken the liberty of adding some dark muted pinks, but they're a minor addition, barely noticeable."

Molly moved through the various styles of dress, then the suits. She stopped in front of a more sports casual rail and Selene grinned.

"I also took the liberty of assuming you at your word, so those are for your bodyguard." She winked at Talie. "Any immediate alterations to sizing will of course be free."

Molly bit her lip. "And the cost of all this would be…?"

The meagre remnants of the tower's coin funds that Phoenix had left when he fled were trickling away, and she still had to consider repairs to the tower alongside the grain and production levels needing support.

"The clothes you so kindly donated were sold yesterday. As it turns out, many a noble will fight to the last tooth to own a piece of royal merchandise. They are of course yours to spend as you see fit, but should you still wish to donate some of those funds, I'm sure we can let these clothes here go with our goodwill."

Molly brushed her fingertips over the soft oak green fabric of the nearest sweatshirt.

"That's kind. Is there a lot left for the donations if I accept these?"

Selene chuckled. "Considering the goodwill part, most of it is left. I took what I needed for materials of course, and labour, but given that these are based on the latest fashion templates it wasn't too much of a bother."

"Then yes, I'll accept these and donate whatever's left with my compliments to the speed and elegance of your craft."

"Are you sure?" Selene frowned.

"It's a considerable amount. If I might be bold to suggest, you could take forty percent and that would still leave plenty for donations."

Molly nodded. "Okay. Whatever I keep goes straight back into the tower anyway at the moment, so I'll accept. Thank you."

"You are most welcome. I will of course be claiming the credit for the creations, unless you object?"

"Of course, they're absolutely beautiful. If you need an introduction anywhere at any point, consider me good for one."

Selene's smooth confidence faltered, her smile frozen for several moments.

"That would be very kind." An almost awed smile crossed her face. "The citadel doesn't often get introductions anywhere these days, and especially not this far up the levels."

Molly nodded. "Something I'm planning to change, but progress has to be gradual."

She left the rails and went to her dressing table to pick up the tiara the Oak Court staff had given her.

"Would it be a huge insult if I replaced the stones do you think?" she asked. "It's gold but I think the pink maybe doesn't match?"

Talie pulled a face but Selene laughed.

"I don't imagine so, but the pink will still work fine with these colours. If you wish to have matching jewellery though, I imagine the jeweller's branch of the Artificer's Guild would be extremely keen to offer you one."

"Another guild I haven't had time to meet with yet," Molly muttered. "Anyway, thanks for this, Selene. They really are stunning."

Selene bowed her head and left the room with an amused farewell.

"You can have clothes if you want," Talie said.

Molly frowned. "She made them for you, and it'd be good to have someone else in our colours. You don't have to wear them if you don't want."

Talie quirked her mouth wryly and grabbed one of the darker outfits. While she went into the dressing room with it, Molly scrambled into the golden dress with the colours that flowed like a sunset. The skirts went halfway down her legs but even with the corset it was like wearing a soft blanket.

She tugged at her hair with her fingers until Talie

walked out, head to toe in black boots, trousers and a flexible long-sleeved shirt. The fabric wrapped around her limbs like a second skin and seemed to shimmer gold and green as she moved.

"I kind of really love these," she admitted. "The movement is amazing. I might buy some new hand-wraps after all to match."

Molly stopped gawping as a knock came at the door.

"At least someone around here knocks," she muttered.

Before she could cross the room, the door swung open and Beryl charged in with Reyan behind her.

"I did knock," Reyan said apologetically as she swiped a hand through her short blonde hair.

Beryl rolled her eyes. "And I didn't. Whoa, those are nice. New colours?"

"Sunset Tower colours now," Molly said. "Ready for the meeting later."

"Good, good. Don't let them beat you down either. Stand up for yourself. Ooh, I'd love me one of these."

Molly caught Reyan's eye and stifled a laugh as Beryl strode through the clothing rails.

"Figured you might need some moral support beforehand," Reyan said. "Taz offered to pop by but Demi said it might be seen as interference as it's a citadel meeting and not an official event sort of thing."

Molly frowned. "I guess so. By the way, I'm probably going to start using my workshop for bits. Is there anything in there that might need clearing out of the *way*? You still have my workshop key."

"That would be a Taz question." Reyan shrugged.

"Beryl, put that down!"

Molly eyed her crown now askew on Beryl's bright purple hair, then pulled her orb out of her pocket.

Molly: When I was staying at the Illusion Court, we set up something in the workshop here. Does anyone know where or what it is?

Kainen: Cryptic, I like it.

Demi: ?

Kainen: What, I can like cryptic stuff.

Demi: Not you, although if something's gone wrong it's probably to do with you.

Kainen: Unfair! True, but unfair. Besides, your exploits could fill the Book of Faerie.

Demi: I'm queen. When I do it, it's stylish.

Molly: No, a way of passing to and fro? Taz knows.

Demi: Ah, I'll ask him in a bit.

Kainen: ... I'm stylish.

Molly shoved her orb back in her pocket as Reyan managed to remove the tiara from a pouting Beryl and slip it back on the dressing table.

"I want to get back soon," she insisted. "Kainen's had another delivery of the oia berry pies and I can't seem to stop eating them. I swear, he's trying to bankrupt us."

Beryl sighed. "Oh orbs, reminds me of my pregnancy cravings, but it's not like you're pregnant is it?"

Molly eyed the nearest rail until the silence registered.

"I SAID IT'S NOT LIKE YOU'RE PREGNANT..." Beryl repeated. "Orbs alive! Are you?!"

"No! And I don't intend to be anytime soon. The court is more than enough to manage." Reyan huffed.

"Are you sure? You've gone bright red."

"Because I'm exhausted. You try managing an entire court of squabbling nobles with no help whatsoever."

"Does Kainen know that?" Talie asked.

"Does Kainen know what?"

The voice came from the doorway amid a flicker of shadows. Kainen grinned as he leaned with his shoulder against the doorframe. He had his brown hair swept back from his face, his eyes glinting with amusement, and didn't look much like the lord of a Fae court in ripped black jeans, t-shirt and a worn leather jacket.

"Do I know what? Is it about my birthday? Don't tell me."

"We'll leave you to talk." Beryl hurried toward the door and shunted past Kainen. "Family matter clearly."

Molly gave Reyan a helpless grimace and headed after

Beryl. As Talie closed the door behind them, Molly bunched up next to Beryl to eavesdrop.

"All I hear is muttering," Beryl grumbled. "I could probably move a bit of wall, but the foundations looked a bit shaky on the way in."

A loud thud cut off any chance Molly had for a defensive reply as the door swung open again. Talie caught the full weight of Kainen's back and steadied him to the floor, while Beryl grinned wickedly.

"Oh orbs, he's fainted!"

Molly glanced over her shoulder as a disgruntled huffing noise came from the region of the ground.

"I have not," he said. "If someone hadn't left all those clothes for me to fall over, I'd be fine. What's all the fuss about?"

"Beryl thought I was pregnant," Reyan said wearily.

Kainen choked. "Are you?! Orbs, that's amazing! I'm going to make an *excellent* dad."

"Not if you keep falling over random stuff you're not," Beryl retorted.

"Technicality. Wait until Taz hears about this! Orbs, wait, does anyone else know? How far along are you? Thats a thing, isn't it? I hope we have girls, but I wouldn't mind otherwise either. Is it healthy?"

"I'm not pregnant!"

Molly crept into the room to slip her feet into the nearest pair of slipper-shoes, then she caught Talie's eye and looked meaningfully at the hallway. Talie nodded and together they tiptoed toward the staircase down to the entrance hall, the sound of Beryl and Kainen arguing floating behind them.

"I reckon he would be a good dad," Talie said, her gaze fixed on her fancy new boots and her tone distant.

Molly nodded. "Insufferable, but good. You said you've met the delegations from the other towers before?"

"Not met exactly, but I was in a meeting with them all before. There's one from the night tower, Argon I think, and he's one to watch out for."

"Okay, good to know."

They descended the staircase as Sammy skidded up toward them.

"Oh wow, you two look amazing!" She grinned. "So matchy-matchy. The kitchens are ready for your guests and I've seen to the meeting hall personally. Why haven't you brushed your hair?"

Molly pulled a face. "Talie hasn't brushed her hair."

"I have actually," Talie retorted. "While you were being dressed."

Sammy grinned. "Yeah and hers just sits in a flat ponytail all her life. Here."

Molly stood irritably while Sammy prodded and pawed at her hair then swept down the rest of the stairs. As she crossed the entrance hall toward the archway that led into the adjoining reception hall, she sighed loudly.

"We shouldn't have slept so late," she said. "I don't feel at all ready for this."

Talie shrugged. "We were either getting up early or staying up late. You've got this. Promise nothing and insist you'll need to consider everything."

They slowed to a halt as a woman approached, wearing

a sharp black suit with her blonde hair pinned back tight and large glasses. The only jolt of colour was the single teardrop red gemstone hanging from a golden chain around her neck as she offered a genteel head bow.

"Good day to you."

Molly hesitated. "Um, hi?"

"Selene suggested I might be open to approach you on the subject of your jewellery. I am Rosette, Head Jeweller of the Jeweller's Guild. I have twenty seven years of experience in the craft and it is my absolute delight-"

"Her majesty has an audience to deal with," Talie interrupted. "Now's not a great time."

The air shivered in the centre of the hall and Molly eyed the four Fae that realm-skipped in, two men and two women immaculately dressed in finery.

"Of course," Rosette continued. "My apologies. I am available at your earliest convenience. I would be delighted to fashion you an entire vault of new jewellery for the occasion. It would be my honour-"

"Good, we'll be in touch," Talie insisted.

"And what trade or cost would jewellery be?" Molly asked, conscious of the delegates of the other towers massing in ominous clusters.

She didn't much care about the jewellery, especially as she had so little free to spend anyway, but she needed a minute to gather herself before facing the councillors from the other towers.

Rosette rubbed a finger over her bottom lip.

"I heard tell of a tiara, gifted from the Royal Oak court itself. Also of your amenability to trade."

"That was a gift I'm not yet desperate enough to part with." She couldn't stop the snap filtering into her voice. "Name a price and I'll consider it. Now, if you'll excuse me."

She set off toward the group but after few steps, Talie settled a hand on her arm.

"I'll sort her out," she murmured. "Go greet the guests and promise nothing. They're basically a bunch of berries without a basket but be careful."

"I know, I know. Wait, you're not going to threaten her or anything are you?"

Talie smiled. "I'm just going to talk to her."

"Talie..."

"I'm just going to talk to her."

Molly took a deep breath and faced the waiting group as Talie walked back toward Rosette.

"Welcome everyone. Please come through to the meeting hall."

She took two steps before one of the men blocked her path with a curl of his bearded lip. Tall with swept back chin-length blonde hair and sharp green eyes that matched his three-piece suit, he clearly didn't want to be there.

"You're even younger than we were led to believe," he said.

Molly tensed as Talie appeared beside her, stance easy but with one hand loose over the dagger always strapped to her wrist, ready for battle.

I can do this. It's either I pull it together or Talie's going to stab someone.

She tilted her head and made a show of looking the man

up and down.

"Oh, really? Who led you?"

A beat of silence stretched taut between them and the cooling slip of Talie's warding weaved around her own.

"Well, I have no problem with young blood," one of the women called out. "Wasn't too keen on the royal part, but as long as your lot keep clear, then fine."

Her knee-length blush pink dress was the least ostentatious outfit among the councillors, with long sleeves not quite covering her bright red fingernails. Molly wondered if she might be a potential ally, but she had no idea who the woman was or which tower she governed.

"We haven't even done introductions, Tulip, honestly," the other woman said. "Molly, as Representative Official from the Sunrise Tower, I must warn you we have very stern concerns about your appointment."

Talie had told her enough about the councillors from Phoenix's time as leader of their tower, so she could at least sort the women now by name.

Molly nodded. "Betula, of course. I'm sure you have, and I'll answer that I can. I was voted in by the various guilds and holding nobles of this Tower and I intend to do my best by them all. That starts with trade."

She took solace as the first woman, Tulip, grinned.

"She's even more formal than you, Argon."

The dour-faced man winced as she jabbed a deceptively not-delicate elbow into his arm. Argon, leader of the Night Tower and the one Talie had warned her against before.

"Formality is the least we should be able to expect," he muttered.

Tulip rolled her eyes. "So, no hint of your royal family deciding to interfere? Celeste might have held the line in terms of trade, but she was a slippery one."

Molly ignored the swoop of uneasiness that settled in her gut at the mention of the woman who'd given birth to her.

"And yet even she got herself caught," she said lightly. "I have assurance from the Holly Queen herself that she won't interfere in my running of the Sunset Tower. More importantly, we need to find a way of cohabiting our towers in harmony, so if there aren't any more objections about me or mine?"

The second man with short silver hair and matching goatee sauntered forward, not quite as tall as Argon but with brawny arms that hinted he might pitch in with the work around his tower on occasion. He stood with his hands in the pockets of his dusky blue velvet jacket and nodded at Talie.

"Her," he announced.

Molly followed his gaze in time to catch Talie's eyes narrowing back at him.

"This is Talie. She works alongside me," she explained. "You must be Oak, from the Morning Tower."

"I am. She served Phoenix before you."

"She did, but I trust her."

"My loyalty is to Molly, whatever role I had to play before now," Talie said, her tone sharp as jagged ice.

"Not to the citadel? To the Tower?"

"No."

Molly fought the urge to smile and groan at the same

time as darting glances circled between the councillors.

"Either way, Talie stays," Molly insisted. "My loyalty is to my Tower and hers is to me, apparently." She gave Talie her weariest look to mask the sudden urge to laugh. "Any more questions, or should we sit down?"

She set off toward the archway that led to the meeting hall, her pulse thudding for several fraught moments until the rest of the group followed.

"We'll keep this brief," Argon said the moment his shiny black trousers were in the orbit of his chair. "We've been led to believe that you're able to access the fabled well of power that lies beneath the citadel."

He stared expectantly but Molly drew strength from Talie lounging on the chair beside her and channelled her inner Kainen.

"You do seem to be led to things a lot." She smiled sweetly. "I can only assume you must have come across Phoenix in the recent weeks if you're asking about wells of power? Either that or perhaps you have informants meandering about my Tower?"

Argon stiffened in his seat, his clasped hands rigid on the table.

"That is a dangerous thing to accuse a fellow Tower Leader of. Perhaps you-"

"Perhaps you're not understanding me." She held her nerve and pressed her hands to the tabletop to hide the shaking. "You're talking in trickery and I'm matching it, but if you'd rather talk in truths then I'll expect you to be led- forgive me, to *lead* by example."

She caught the utter glee on Tulip's face and a hint of

renewed assessment in Betula's pursed lips.

Oak it seemed was still fixated on Talie and sat frowning at her instead.

Argon appeared to be struck silent in his indignance, so Molly forced her tensed shoulders down and took a steadying breath.

"I'm sure you know what lies beneath the citadel, the rumours at least," she continued.

"You'll have all kept yourselves informed of recent events too," Talie muttered. "Different faces in certain chairs but the meetings are the same."

Molly nodded. "Sure. I'm not in a position to discuss any wells of power yet, not when you're all no doubt going to tie future trades to its supposed existence. That is what this meeting's really about, isn't it?"

The swamp of exhaustion hit so suddenly she almost slumped in her seat. Talie tensed beside her, but whether it was obvious or she was just responding to Argon muttering something foul under his breath, she wasn't sure.

"We it need to consider though," Betula said.

Tulip nodded. "True enough, but I won't be hanging any trades on it. Assuming you've no changes to make to current deals between Sunrise and Day, Molly, then I'm fine plodding on."

"I'll claim the same then," Oak agreed as his gaze flicked back to Talie again. "But that's on the condition that Morning Tower isn't left out of any discussions, movements or decisions about what's beneath the citadel."

Molly held herself upright, fighting the growing headache as it gnawed behind her eyes.

Betula sighed. "I'm fine with that, but you will need us, Molly. Sunset tower is hanging on by a thread as it is."

Molly nodded but held her tongue. They did need the recycled metal that the Sunrise Tower mined to reinforce part of the damage to the tower structure, wood too which meant Oak and the Morning tower would have a stake in future decisions and deals made.

"I'm aware we all need to work together to keep our towers safe," she said carefully. "I still have nobles to settle and our current trades to handle, so I'll appreciate your patience as we navigate our way through this."

She looked at Argon, but his tight-lipped glower didn't give her much hope.

Should I be relieved that at least Phoenix sorted out fixing the glass before turning traitor and running off?

"You do come highly recommended by one of your nobles," he said reluctantly. "An old friend of mine who I owe a favour of sorts to. For her sake alone, I'll abide by the council's decision to honour our current deals."

Molly opened her mouth to ask who but almost choked on it as he leaned forward, hands braced on the table.

"I will not be denied for long though. That well belongs to all of us and we will decide how to use it."

Talie leaned forward to match his stance, but before Molly could put out a hand to calm her, Tulip laughed.

"You want the Omens roaming around the citadel bouncing off the glass? Or are you going to chase them through the cracks when they inevitably suck the place dry? Please don't tell me you're still arrogant enough to assume anyone can channel them?"

Talie snorted loudly and Argon flew to his feet so fast just chair slammed to the ground.

"Watch your tongue," he hissed.

"Can't," Tulip retorted. "It's not long enough and I have better things to look at."

She winked at Oak who raised his gaze to the ceiling in disbelief.

"Is it always like this?" Molly asked.

Betula nodded. "Yes, welcome to the torment."

"We should invoke the Rose Tournament."

It was said so calmly, Molly couldn't be sure for a moment. Then all eyes turned to Oak.

He shrugged. "Molly is new. The Rose Tournament is her chance to honour our traditions publicly. I vote we invoke the Rose Tournament."

Betula cocked her head. "The idea has merit. Once, long ago, the Rose Tournament was the initiation for new councillors taking over a tower."

"What is it?" Talie asked, her arms folded across her chest as she slouched in her seat.

"The Rose Tournament is a competition of skill that all citadelian nobles can enter."

"What's that got to do with Molly though?"

Betula smiled and Molly almost shrank from the sudden wolfish gleam of wicked intent in her eyes.

"Well, that's how new councillors honour the tradition," she said smoothly. "They offer themselves as the prize for the winner of the tournament."

CHAPTER SIX

TALIE

Talie stared around at the four amused faces. Argon was still stewing but cheering up fast, and the other three were smug as anything.

"Suddenly they all think they're funny," she said.

Molly shook her head. "I'm not selling myself in any tournament."

"It wouldn't be selling yourself, nothing so vulgar," Tulip said, although her grin intimated otherwise.

Talie folded her arms across her chest so she could slide her dagger out in one swift swipe.

"What would it be then?" she challenged. "She just offers an arm or a leg?"

She kept her gaze between the two women. They were all awful, but Argon was a complete orb-muncher and the other one kept staring at her.

"It would be an audience of sorts, little more," Betula said. "It will be open to all nobles of course, as is tradition, those that live in the towers at least. Granted, some patronise without owning actual holdings here, but who knows? Maybe it would encourage them to buy some."

Tulip nodded. "It's simply an audience, a meeting, a date if you will. Arranged unions between towers have been a great plus of the Rose Tournament in times past as well."

"And if I refuse?" Molly asked.

If. Talie's insides turned icy. *Like she's actually considering it as an option.*

Talie stood when the guests did, Molly a second behind her.

"Right now we're humouring you," Betula said, all signs of any humour long gone. "Life gets dull when your tower is thriving but there's no right to rule, it's not like royalty."

"If the four of us agree, we can assume command of your tower," Tulip finished.

Argon smiled. "You'd be best remembering that."

Talie waited but Molly was frozen with shock.

"I'll organise the tournament then," Betula announced into the taut silence. "We'll host in the central gardens of course, been a while since the nobles have seen it opened to all. We'll send you an invitation, Molly, but don't bother making too many plans for the next few days."

Talie had no words either, stunned as the four of them realm-skipped away.

"I- that's-" Molly shook her head then clutched both hands to her head. "What in the name of Faerie and the nether just happened?"

"You agreed to this Rose Tournament."

"No I didn't!"

"Well, you didn't not agree."

Molly hurried toward the entrance hall and Talie tailed her, mindful to keep the warding around them. It didn't keep their conversation private as such, but she added the tiniest hint of thunder from her storm to distort the truth just in case.

"They said they'd take the tower away if I didn't do this," Molly muttered. "Orbs, this is such a mess."

"You're not going through with it though, right? It's clearly a trap to get you under their heel."

"What choice do I have? Maybe I can get someone from the tower to compete, someone I can trust."

Talie scowled. "How many citadel nobles do you know then, Princess?"

"None, because I spent the last few weeks with the people and fixing things. There's Glennoria, but she wouldn't put herself out for me."

"Then what's the plan?"

Talie hunched tighter into her folded arm stance as Molly stopped at the base of the stairs. She couldn't see a way out that didn't involve disappointment or danger, but she couldn't stop snapping either.

"Maybe Beryl... but I don't think she's actually nobility."

"Kainen? He'd do it for fun."

Molly shook her head and Talie's insides twisted at the devastation on her face.

"He's done more than enough for me already, and he's close enough to count as royalty which would probably be considered interfering. The covenant is still in place with the other towers, even if it isn't here."

"Then who?"

Molly hesitated, and Talie's blood burned in her veins. Her stomach flipped like acid hitting a wall and a fierce rumble of thunder cracked overhead.

Molly winced, but Talie couldn't contain the fury.

"You're going to ask *her*?"

She didn't need to wait around for Molly to confirm it, but the grimace and the long pause sold it.

She turned on her heel and stalked out of the Menagerie as the precipitation brewing furiously over her head dropped down in one lashing torrent.

There was one person she might be able to trust owing a big favour to, even though she wasn't entirely sure how she was going to go about asking for it.

She stomped up the lane to the workshop, grateful that Beryl wasn't anywhere to be seen and that Molly hadn't been able to lock the workshop up.

She pushed the door open and stepped inside to stare at the metal bucket. Molly had mentioned it but nothing had happened when she kicked it the day before.

"So how is this a skip-way?" she muttered. "Is there a password or something?"

Something flickered inside the bucket, a wisp of purple smoke. She bit her lip and stuck her hand in. The smoke grew around her skin, a massing cloud of grey and purple that billowed up her arm and cloaked it from view.

She gulped down a shriek as the workshop and all sight disappeared, only to fade away moments later.

Rocky walls lined a corridor lit by flaming torches with

stone underfoot. A long, dark grey carpet covered the middle of the floor, lined with silver and light purple, but the tapping of shoes nearby drew her gaze upwards.

"Who are you?"

She jumped around at the demanding voice and found a tall, stern woman frowning down at her.

"I'm looking for Kainen."

The woman's eyes widened. "Is his lordship expecting you?"

"No, but I need to ask him for a favour."

"You need to ask Lord Kainen Hemlock of the Illusion Court for a favour."

"Yeah, kind of a big one."

"Just like that."

"Yeah. Is he here? I don't really want to trouble Reyan. I can wait."

She couldn't wait for long, not after storming out on Molly when she looked like she had a bad headache brewing.

I'd rather be in serious debt than let her choose that bat-eyed harlot to save her.

"Does he know who you are?" the woman asked doubtfully.

"Oh, yeah. I'm Talie, from the citadel. I'm Molly's..."

She called me her girlfriend to Vulgarletta, but then said I work with her to the other towers.

"Hmm. Wait here."

The woman vanished and Talie bit her lip as she looked up and down the hall again.

A door opened in the wall nearby, a door that she was

almost certain hadn't been there a moment ago.

"Talie?" Kainen peered out. "Is everything okay?"

"Yeah, I need to ask something."

He frowned but stepped back and held out his arm to invite her through the doorway. She stepped into an office, suitably grand for a lord despite the bare rock walls, and hovered as he perched on the edge of his desk.

"What's going on?"

"So, Molly had the meeting with the other towers, and they tricked her into this Rose Tournament. Apparently, nobles compete for a date with her? It's some kind of tradition but I've never heard of it. Nobody mentioned Phoenix having to do it."

Kainen sighed. "Ah. Classic first move. Why didn't you just say she's already promised elsewhere?"

"That would be a lie."

Orbs, what if she is and hasn't told me? Or doesn't know?

The thought of a certain red-headed noble sniffing around turned her insides sore with jealousy.

Kainen eyed the tiny droplets of water sneaking out of a glass on his desk to bead above their heads as her storm gift broke free.

"Well, technicality maybe, but you two are dating, right? That counts as promised in a way."

"I don't know what we are," she muttered. "But we need a noble to compete and win, but Molly doesn't want to ask any more of you."

Kainen sucked in a breath, hesitated, then sagged.

"Yeah, tournaments can be tough. It's got to be

someone who patronise the citadel though, and I doubt me buying a few pastries in the next day or so would qualify me."

"How do people go about becoming a noble then?"

She fought to keep her voice calm. Too calm, as his gaze turned pitying.

"You either trade for land to give you a title or get awarded it by royalty, and no, Molly titling you would be a conflict of interest."

She scrunched her muscles tight.

"If I were to give something, service or, I don't know, a big favour..."

"I can't." He grimaced. "Trust me, I would if I could but I've got nothing to spare here that I can risk letting go of without angering others. Lots of things are tied up in trade or safety leverage-"

"It's fine. I shouldn't have asked. I just need to know how to get back home then."

She headed back toward the door, and the prickle around her eyes did nothing to help with the subtle drip of her gift from above.

"Tell you what, I'll take this to Taz and see if there's anything he can do. If you wait outside for me for a few minutes then I can take you back."

Talie opened the door and walked out into the hall, biting back the retort that she couldn't exactly say no considering she still had to get home somehow.

Kainen disappeared and she leaned back against the wall.

Not only have I stormed off in a tantrum, I've

embarrassed myself by all but begging and it hasn't even solved anything.

She tensed as smart taps of heeled shoes drew closer and someone rounded the corner.

"Oh." The woman stopped in front of her with a frown. "I recognise you."

Given the abundance of feathers in her dark red hat and the ruffles of velvet all over her matching dress, she was one of the richer nobles, but Talie couldn't find it in her to bow, or worry about not bowing.

Talie nodded. "I'm Molly's..."

Yeah, that about sums it up.

"And your name is?" the woman demanded.

"Talie."

"Ah. I am Lady Featherdown, a friend of hers, of sorts. What brings you to the Illusion Court?"

Talie froze, icy fear crawling over her skin as a wisp of sour coated her tongue. She'd only experienced it briefly before, but it was enough to have her panicking. In her grouchiness, she hadn't even thought to ward.

"I wanted to see Kainen."

"Why?"

"To ask him a- question."

"My, you are stubborn. And which question would that be?"

"If he'd compete in the Rose Tournament so Molly wouldn't be at the mercy of the other towers having someone win."

The sour taste faded and Talie pulled a face as Featherdown rubbed a forefinger across her lips.

"Interesting. There's not been a tournament there for a long while. Of course, his lordship has no holdings there, doesn't patronise the place, but I do."

Talie wrapped a warding around herself with her cheeks burning from embarrassment.

"I'm guessing you don't want to enter on her behalf," she muttered.

"Orbs, no. I have much simpler methods of gaining social standing thankfully." Featherdown shuddered. "I could however be persuaded to part with some more pointless parts of my vast wealth for a worthy cause."

"Huh?"

"Well, there's a portion of land, barely an acreage, far from court and my other holdings. Won it in a card game, riddled with cerasus trees, whatever they are. I could be convinced to donate it for a fair trade."

Talie let her mind race over the words, torn between panic and desperate hope.

"I doubt I know anyone who could have anything you'd consider a fair trade."

"Nonsense. Social standing is everything, young lady, and whether you know it or not, you hold a particularly desired stance."

"I do?"

Keep her talking. Either she's going to give me a title, or Kainen will come back and save me.

Featherdown sighed. "Molinia is the youngest heir to the oldest dynasty in Faerie. Given the way the Oak Queen is running things lately, she may be the only heir left in good standing. As the first, and currently only, grandchild of Queen Tavania, she is also given allowances most royals couldn't even dream of. She is still a teenager and yet she rules one fifth of the Faerie citadel. Her social worth is all but infinite, and you stand beside her, not just emotionally but publicly."

"So she's special, and she puts up with me, so what?"

"Well, she is the future." Featherdown sighed. "Most nobles would very much like to keep their proximity to such a person."

Talie lowered her shoulders and pretended to be considering.

"So, you'd essentially bring me into the happy clappy stabby noble circus, and in return I put in a good word for you with Molly? Be specific."

Featherdown laughed. "How delightfully intransigent you are. You remind me of his lordship in younger years, although your charm needs a lot of work. Perhaps that's not to be where your strengths lie though."

"Yeah, I'm more of a fighter than a flirter to be fair," Talie agreed.

"Very well. In exchange for me gifting you the acreage previously mentioned and therefore a noble title in name only, you agree to use your sway with the princess to help me get the prime noble spot at the Sunset Tower."

Talie frowned, searching for pitfalls. Featherdown sounded too nonchalant about it for it to be a good thing.

I don't have any other choice though.

She nodded. "Okay."

"No no, you need to repeat the agreement back to me for it to be binding. Dear me, what do they teach you nowadays?"

"Mainly how to avoid getting punched." Talie scrunched up her nose and took a deep breath. "Okay, I agree to use my sway with Molly to help you get a top noble spot at the Sunset Tower, if I can, to the best of my ability, and in return you give me this acreage and a title."

She flinched as something tingled over her skin and lifted the hairs, but she couldn't see any difference when she looked down.

Featherdown smiled and adjusted her hat.

"Excellent. I shall enjoy being her number one noble as well as his lordship's."

"Well, technically her number two." Talie shoved her hands in her pockets with her heart pounding. "If anyone's going to be top noble, to her at least, it's going to be me. I did say 'a top spot', not 'the top spot'. Also, I don't know how much sway I have really, like I suggest stuff and off she goes the other way."

The words tumbled out but her mouth was so dry from sheer panic and adrenalin that she couldn't tell if Featherdown was compelling her or not.

"My word." Featherdown tilted her head slowly. "I think you're going to make a suitably devious noble after all. I'll have the title deed for your land sent care of the Menagerie. Until we meet again then."

Talie got the sense Featherdown was suddenly eager to escape, but she had to ask.

"Wait! What is the actual title? Am I just Lady Talie now?"

Featherdown waved an airy hand over her shoulder as

she continued walking away down the hall.

"Some take their last names as family pride, but whatever you choose will be fine."

She disappeared and Talie crashed back against the wall with shaking knees.

I can't believe I just did that. Nobility. It's madness. I have to choose a title too. Lady Talie sounds awful but I haven't got a family name to use. Would I have to go by Lady Talie Talie if all I've got is my name?

"There you are." Kainen appeared before her hysterical laughter could bubble free. "Sorry it took be a while, and sorry I can't help more. I really wish I could."

"It's fine, I sorted it."

He stared in amazement. "You what?"

"Got myself a title."

"How?"

"Traded for it." She shrugged.

"I've only been gone ten minutes! Who was it?"

"Featherdown."

Kainen's eyes popped impossibly wide.

"She did what? That's unlike her. You didn't promise anything irretrievable did you? Like your soul?"

"Social contacts and potential influence, nothing more."

"You got off lightly." His surprise upended into a wicked grin. "That's… I have to admit that's impressive. She's devious at the best of times. Still, I would have done the same for love."

"It's not- that's-"

He waved her inability to lie aside. "Never mind that. I can't promise she won't try and use you for further gain, but as lord of the court she's sworn to, I can put some protections in place."

"Don't need protecting thanks. I get a tiny spit of land in some far-flung part of the realm apparently, but it's the title that matters. If she asks any more of me she can have it back. I only need it to get into the trial."

"Don't be so quick to cast a title aside." He frowned. "It may come in handy in the future, and not just for you. What is the title I should be calling you now then?"

She frowned. "I don't know. She said to pick one, but i don't have a family name or anything."

"Well, until then I shall call you Lady Rain." He bowed ridiculously low with a wide grin.

Lady Rain. Maybe that could actually work.

"So, Lady Rain, do you need me to see you back to the citadel?"

She did, but first she had to ask him something and her nerves twisted in her gut.

"Stop with the bowing. But I do need..." She hesitated.

"A tissue? Advice?" He lifted an eyebrow. "A favour?"

She nodded and wedged her hands deeper in her pockets.

"I need to learn to... dance. There's probably going to be one after this tournament, right? Assuming I survive I don't want to disgrace her."

Kainen stared for several seconds like she'd just grown a second head. She scowled at the hesitation and took a step back while he tried to keep the smile off his face.

"Okay. No favour though, call it a gift. You are technically one of the nobles who owns land in my realm now, so let it be a goodwill gesture between us."

She nodded. "Yeah, fine, thanks."

"I won't get a dancing master at this short notice though," he added. "You'll have to make do with me. Luckily for you, I am an excellent dancer."

Talie followed him back through the door to his office and glowered at his amusement as he cleared the desk to the side of the room with a flick of his hand. She bit down the urge to ask if anyone could get to clear solid objects so easily, and hovered at the far end of the office as he held out a hand.

"Oh, come on," he huffed. "I mean you no harm, if that's what you're worried about."

"It's not. I don't know what to do."

"Obviously, but you won't learn if you don't unclench once in a while."

He held out the hand again and Talie forced herself to take it. Warm and smooth, no workworn calluses unlike Molly's.

Wrong wrong wrong.

She gritted her teeth and forced her other hand onto his shoulder.

"Now, I know this is a disastrous notion for you, but relax and follow my lead."

She did, even though it was impossibly awkward and she kept stepping on his toes. Neither of them noticed Reyan standing in the doorway until she cleared her throat.

Talie flinched back, Reyan only smiled.

"I have to say, you move really well," she admitted.

"Surprised?" Talie frowned. "Dancing's not much

different to sparring when it comes to controlling movement.”

“Only slightly less stabbing and punching,” Reyan retorted.

Kainen grinned as he grabbed Talie’s hand and whirled her into an effortless spin.

“You’d think so,” he said. “Never underestimate the danger of dancing. A neatly concealed blade, a carefully placed fist against a kidney mid-dip.”

Talie nodded. “A swift kick hidden underneath a skirt.”

“Have you ever worn a skirt?”

“Once.” She pulled a face. “Useful for hiding bigger weapons I guess.”

“Stick to a stiletto, I would.”

“What’s a stiletto?”

Kainen stopped mid-spin. “What’s a- Orbs, we have *so* much work to do.”

CHAPTER SEVEN

MOLLY

Molly wiped a hand over her face as Talie stormed out of the entrance hall. A few Fae milling around watched her go, some of the Menagerie assassins that Molly still hadn't worked out how to handle yet, and she groaned as Sammy skidded towards her.

"You've got visitors," Sammy announced. "The smiley one Talie's jealous of is waiting in the office, and the other one left when I said you were busy."

"Other one?"

Sammy pulled a face. "Your friend who we thought was dead, the tall one? I told him to go away but he laughed at me."

Molly sighed. She still hadn't figured out what to do about Ru either, assuming he was even really him. Where he'd been the whole time she was thinking he was dead she couldn't be sure, but Talie hadn't mentioned him being around during Phoenix's short reign.

"Oh, there you are!" Violetta trotted down the stairs toward them. "I got bored waiting, but you're done now, aren't you?"

Sammy rolled her eyes while her back was still to Violetta, but Molly couldn't be rude and managed a weak smile.

"I am but I've got tons to do. There's… the other towers have insisted I submit myself as a 'prize' for the winner of some tournament that only nobles can enter, and I have people to see still and a tower to fix."

Sammy grimaced. "A tournament? That sounds ominous, but also fun. Let me know if I need to do anything. Otherwise, can I take the rest of the day off?"

"You're not in my employ, you can do what you want."

"Yeah, you should change that," Sammy retorted. "If Talie comes stomping back in, I'll send her to you."

She sauntered off toward the doors leading out to the lane and Molly tugged at the body of her dress. The perfect fit still wasn't a suitable replacement for comfortable trousers and a well-stocked sweatshirt.

"I'm going to go up and change," she said. "Sorry to fob you off, but maybe we can catch up later?"

Violetta waved her hand and shook her head.

"No need, I can attend you. I used to attend the previous Lady of the Flora Court before she retired."

"Um, I don't need attending."

Violetta laughed. "Okay, well then I shall keep you company."

Unable to tell her to go away without being rude, Molly set off up the stairs toward her room. She bit her lip as she grabbed a sweatshirt, t-shirt and her favourite pair of cotton trousers with all the pockets from her dressing table chair on the way past, determined to put her foot down if Violetta followed her into the dressing room.

She didn't, but Molly heard the rustle of bedsheets as Violetta sat down.

"I must say, a tournament does sound exciting," Violetta said. "Are there any stipulations for entry?"

Molly hauled her t-shirt over her head with a grumble.

"Only that it's open to any of the nobility that have patronised the citadel."

"Ah. Well, I'm not sure about patronised as yet, but I did manage to secure a small holding on the lower levels this morning. Perhaps I shall go and purchase some drapes later."

Molly misjudged the proximity of her foot to her trousers and thudded against the nearest clothing rack with a startled grunt.

"You did?"

She righted her balance and hauled the rest of her clothes on.

She's got a place here. In the same tower as Talie. Who hates her. Orbs alive, this is a disaster.

"Mm-hmm. Nothing grand of course, but it is sensible to own something outside of the court you're sworn to. Who knows? If you're keen, I could even throw my hat into the tournament."

Molly took a deep breath and fixed her expression before venturing out to find Violetta lounging comfortably on the bed.

"Oh, you don't have to do that. I'm sure it's bound to be dangerous."

"Best way to live," Violetta grinned. "I'll consider it."

A knock on the door saved Molly from having to answer, but the thought of yet more people demanding things from her had her trudging across to open it.

"Now's *really* not- oh."

She stared up at Ru's almost vacant smile as her heart plummeted down to her toes. He looked exactly the same as he had the last time she'd seen him, tall with his black hair finger-raked back, but absolutely no sign of the Ru she remembered in his expressionless eyes.

"I need to talk to you," he said.

Molly glanced from him to Violetta, then back again. She did need to talk to him, to find out who he really was and why he'd chosen now to drift in, but she hadn't imagined having to do it without Talie's unerring confidence beside her.

Perhaps it's for the best. She'd probably gut him before I could ask anything.

"Sorry, now's not a good time."

She gave Violetta a somewhat apologetic smile, and the responding one was the tiniest bit brittle as Violetta eased off the bed.

"Of course. Please don't let me take up any more of your time for now. I'll send an invite next time that you can accept at your leisure."

With a polite bow of her head and a quirked look of intrigue at Ru as she passed him, Violetta disappeared and Molly wrapped a protection warding tight around her.

"Well then." She called her compulsion gift forward. "Are you really you?"

Ru cocked his head. "Compulsion? I have a memory of deserving that. Yes, you have known me for years. We parted on shaky terms but I promised to keep you safe."

Molly took a tiny step back as the compulsion did nothing to force a full answer out of him. He sounded as though he was reciting a distant memory where the details were fuzzy.

"What's best for me is having friends around that trust my judgement," she said. "Not people who assume they know better than I do. I need people I can trust not to sell me out to the enemy as well. I have that now."

"You are moving in the highest circles now."

She let her compulsion spool through the air in case it might still work somehow as anger climbed up through her chest and into her voice.

"Who have you heard that from then?"

"People."

"What people?"

"Ones I've seen."

"So trickery," she scoffed. "You won't tell me a thing, yet you want me to trust you? Not going to happen. Why bother coming back now anyway?"

He leaned his shoulder against the doorframe like she'd seen him do so many times before and nostalgia crunched her insides tight.

"You don't want me around, but I promised to keep you safe. Are you banishing me?"

"I- what?"

"Are you banishing me? This is your domain now, as it always should have been."

She clenched her fists at her sides.

"Why did you come back now?" she demanded again.

"I promised to keep you safe. You need me."

"For what?"

For a split second, he gave her a look that she remembered, the one that had often fondly pitied her innocence, and his blue eyes flooded with emotion.

It dissipated just as quickly, but there was a hint of the old him inside whatever sorcery was containing him.

"I promised to keep you safe," he repeated.

She stared in astonishment as he pushed away from the doorframe and disappeared.

"Come back here!"

She stormed to the door and peered out both ways, but he was already gone. She had no idea if he had been given a speed gift since they'd been apart, but either way she was exhausted and her head was pounding enough to make her queasy.

"Orb-muncher," she muttered under her breath.

Then for good measure she slammed the bedroom door, because she could. The real Ru was still inside there, she'd managed to drag that much out of him, but that wasn't exactly good news. He had an agenda, one he wasn't telling her, and she would find out what it was.

Until then, she had to focus on the issues the tower was facing. She scraped her hair away from her face and headed to the dressing table to grab a ribbon, only to find a pale gold and black card in the centre. She picked it up and read the swirling purple script aloud.

"The Citadelian Council cordially invites Molinia

Acorn to attend the Rose Tournament, and congratulates her on her donation of an audience with the winner. Nobles only, central garden, tomorrow at- *tomorrow*?!"

She dropped the card like it might bite and spun around to stare at the door. The one person who might have considered helping her was probably halfway down the levels already.

"I can't ask her," she muttered. "Talie would kill me. I'll have to take my chances with whoever wins and refuse to agree to anything."

It was an audience with the winner, and nobody had said she couldn't take protections or guards in with her.

She pulled her orb out of her pocket and swiped to the Royals orb chat. As she considered what to say, she started pacing.

Bringing them into it isn't an option either. They're not nobles that patronise the citadel, so they can't enter. But I don't know any other nobles yet.

She slipped the orb back into her pocket and headed toward the bed. There was still part of the day left but after a late night and no food, she couldn't face leaving the room again. Someone would come to disturb her soon enough either way.

The many situations she had to deal with tangled and twisted in her head as she lay down and stared at the wall.

Ru returning was worrying.

Violetta hanging around was a pain.

The council were an absolute disaster.

The Rose Tournament was a trap and she had walked right into it.

By the time she heard the door ease open, she'd reached a stage of inner contemplation that had disconnected her awareness from her body almost entirely.

The bed creaked behind her and the faintest hint of Talie's normal smell wrapped around her.

"Where have you been?" she mumbled.

The sheets rustled. "Needed to calm my head, sort some stuff. Did something happen?"

"Oh. Only Ru coming back, but he didn't say anything useful, only that it's definitely him. And Violetta, but she went away again."

"Small mercies then. Are you mad at me?"

"For what?"

Talie sighed. "For disappearing. For being jealous."

"No. Could have done with you here though."

"Sorry."

"I don't like her like that, you know that, right?"

She held still as Talie's arm slipped around her waist over the covers.

"I know. I'm not going to be nice to her, but I'll stop being mean to you, okay?"

"Fine. You can be mean to both of them."

Talie laughed softly and a weight crumbled away from Molly's shoulders.

"Done."

"The tournament is tomorrow though," she added. "I'm going to have to accept an audience with whoever wins."

Talie sighed. "Yeah, probably. Maybe it won't be so bad in the end."

"That all depends on who wins, but I'm a princess,

right? And a tower leader. I should be able to take guards into any audience I have to give."

"True. Do we have anything else to do today?"

"Loads." Molly didn't move. "I'm hungry."

"Alright. Five more minutes, then I'll get us something."

Molly smiled and closed her eyes. With Talie back at her side and not mad at her, it all seemed less frightening somehow.

CHAPTER EIGHT

TALIE

Talie watched until Molly's breathing deepened to tiny snores. Even though she was wide awake, she didn't move away.

Kainen had warned her that the tournament would likely happen immediately, both to excite the nobles into attending and also to stop Molly having any time to find a way to back out. He'd also given her a whole host of advice that was still jangling inside her mind, but he wouldn't be able to follow her in and help her once the tournament started.

Just before dropping her home, he'd orbed Taz and explained. Taz had told Demi, who insisted she would find the time to come and spectate somehow. Knowing the queen would be there had its merits, but the other nobles were far more gifted and experienced than she was. She didn't have anyone to ask any favours of either.

She stifled a laugh as Molly's stomach growled disagreeably, but even then Molly didn't wake.

She's exhausted. I'll let her sleep a while longer.

The subtle warmth and glow of Molly's sunshine gift

spilled free, so Talie inched closer until her nose was wedged in puffs of Molly's hair.

It took all her effort not to focus on the fact that it might be her last chance if the tournament was as dangerous as Kainen seemed to think.

She inched herself free after a couple of minutes and tiptoed out to the hall in her socks. Molly would need food when she woke up so she set off toward the kitchens, but a familiar face was coming up the stairs toward her so she stopped to wait.

"Hi, Nia."

Nia smiled. "Hello yourself. I came to ask Molly if she could sign the lease on the gym as it's due in the next three days and the warehouse next door are waving their grubby fingers for the space."

Talie eyed the paper Nia held out.

"I'll do what I can," she said carefully. "She's got a lot on at the moment.

"So I hear. Rumour's going around about her signing up for a Rose Tournament? I remember one from when I was a kid, dangerous stuff. Even Butch gave it a frown when he heard."

"So much for keeping things quiet."

"Flyers have gone all over the place, black and yellow ones."

"Orbing Night Tower."

"Yeah, that's the consensus." Nia sighed. "What's Molly going to do? I'm guessing she knows nobles now who can compete on her behalf?"

Talie hesitated. "She's… considering options."

"Well make it quick. The Rose Tournaments can be anything, gift combat, melee fight or one on one, bare knuckle boxing, first to the post-"

"I get it." Talie grimaced as her stomach twisted with nausea. "It's the audience she has to give after I'm more worried about."

Nia looked back down the stairs at the few people milling about. The entrance hall was always occupied by someone, but all Talie could focus on was getting food for Molly then finding a quiet place to panic. Possibly to be sick too.

"That's the tricky bit. The official win of the Rose Tournament is an audience, but the unofficial expectation? Favour and concession. Whoever wins will be given the opening to set their cap at Molly and request her hand in marriage."

"She doesn't have to accept though surely?"

Nia frowned. "Well, no, but can you imagine what a refusal would do to inter-tower relations? Nobility reputations have been dashed and wars started over less. Anyway, if she does have a chance to sign the new lease, it'd be a huge help."

Talie took the paper from Nia's hand without seeing it, her skin flushing as moisture leapt into the air above them. She ignored the soft pat Nia dropped on her shoulder, and stood there at the top of the stairs long after Nia left.

So it's either win, or risk Molly being deposed by the rest of the councillors.

She bit her lip and forced her feet to take the necessary steps down to the entrance hall and across to the kitchens.

They couldn't refuse now, even though deep down Molly hadn't even been given the chance to refuse, not really.

She had her mind wipe gift, her storm gift and she could ward well enough.

As she pushed the door to the kitchens open and came face to face with a shiny row of knives, she chose determination over doubt.

Can't hurt to order a couple more daggers too with all this money Molly's paying me, just in case.

CHAPTER NINE

MOLLY

Molly stood in the entrance hall of the Menagerie with her arms folded and her leg bouncing from nerves. Talie was absent when she woke up, but the messy bed suggested she hadn't been gone long. The time to realm-skip to the central gardens and the tournament was fast approaching, and only Sammy had been around to help her sort her hair out.

She smoothed down the strapless, ankle-length golden dress that flickered with hues of green and starlit silver when she turned, then flinched when the hidden pocket against her thigh grew warm. She pulled her orb out and swiped to the group chat, too nervous to smile at the new chat name which had exceeded the character limit.

~Royals Group Chat~

Demi: I'm on my way, Molly. You need to officially invite me though I reckon.

Molly: Sure, please attend the Rose Tournament as my guest, and guest of the Sunset Tower, and all that

Kainen: "As long as you mean no harm to me or mine." Honestly, I need to write all these down for you.

Demi: Milo will be thrilled. I'll let him know you're beginning a bibliographical work of great literary importance.

Kainen: What! NO!

Demi: Incoming, Molly.

Molly looked up as the air shifted to deposit the Holly Queen of Faerie in her entrance hall. Demi's messy black curls were twined around her silver holly crown, and her smart red sweatshirt and black jeans had been chosen to match.

"Hi," she said with a nervous smile. "We need to realm-skip to the central gardens, but I haven't actually done realm-skipping before."

Demi nodded. "Hold your hand out."

Molly did as she was told, then flinched with a shriek as invisible pressure closed around it.

"That'd be me," a familiar voice said. "Um, Milo, in case that wasn't clear."

Demi grinned. "You can't be seen to be not knowing things, but I figured some small measure of personal help was okay."

"Thanks."

"Any more?"

Molly hesitated. All she'd had when she woke up that morning was Sammy insisting that Talie said she would meet them at the central gardens. That was before Molly realised she would need to leave Sammy behind as the one she trusted most. Sammy had taken it with grace, but Molly realised she'd have to make up missing the big event to her somehow.

"No."

Demi lifted an eyebrow, but she didn't comment. With her holding Molly's hand, Milo realm-skipped them through the swirl of purple-grey nether and a clamour of noise swelled up.

Thick-trunked trees towered over the circular garden to create a perimeter, with a stone walkway and hedged mini gardens around the edges and most of the centre laid to grass. Tents had been pitched at one end in the various tower colours, and Molly bit her lip to see the councillors and many nobles already assembled.

"This is pretty," Demi commented loudly.

Those nearest them turned in alarm. The effect rippled outward across the crowd until the silence was deafening.

Demi sighed. "Something I said?"

Molly smiled awkwardly and let go of her hand as Milo's grip disappeared on her other side.

"Probably. I don't know anyone here I don't think. Oh

actually, there's Lady Featherdown."

She smiled as Lady Featherdown bustled up in a deep red velvet dress complete with actual bustle pushing her skirt out at the back as she bowed low.

"Your Majesty." She flicked a look up at Molly next. "Princess."

Molly caught the deliberate hesitation and tried not to roll her eyes.

"I'm not sure if you two know each other," she said. "Lady Featherdown is sworn to Kainen's court and patronises my tower often."

Demi nodded. "Cool. Kainen's mentioned you before I think."

Lady Featherdown's eyes narrowed the slightest amount as she straightened up. The rest of the crowd had fallen into a deceptively casual chatter but Molly would have bet they were eavesdropping on every word.

"I believe your box is prepared for you and your guests, Princess," Lady Featherdown added. "Allow me to accompany you."

"Oh, that's thoughtful, Lady Featherdown."

She wasn't entirely sure she needed escorting with an actual queen already in her entourage, but another familiar face was better than none.

"Call me Glennoria, please. With such short notice, I took the liberty of checking it would be ready. The small girl in your employ was extremely short with me."

"Small girl- tall with braids? That's Sammy. She's practically family and she's taking her new role very seriously."

She definitely had to make it up to Sammy on several accounts, especially when Glennoria inclined her head a minute amount to indicate which way they should go.

Demi trailed behind them, which Molly was almost certain broke several types of protocol, but the mutterings were all but inaudible as they passed.

Five small marquees with different awnings lined the far end of the gardens, and Molly bit her lip as she recognised the now familiar gold, green and red colours on the fourth one along. She'd had her tower's colours chosen for barely forty-eight hours and yet there they were.

Sammy wants a job, she's got it.

"The colours are nice. You can be gold and I can be silver, summer and winter, works well," Demi said.

Molly searched for any hint of mockery in her tone but she couldn't find any, so she lifted a hand to direct Demi into the marquee ahead of her.

Glennoria cleared her throat.

"I'll take my leave then, Princess," she said, her tone flat.

"Would you like to join us?"

It slid out before Molly could stop herself, but if it came to it she'd blame Kainen for the kind of courtiers he kept.

Glennoria smiled. "I would be honoured, Princess."

She left the seat in the middle free and smiled with innately Fae smugness at those clustered nearby as she sat down. Molly thumped onto the chair between them and flinched as a loud fanfare echoed across the garden.

"Here come the competitors," Glennoria announced. "Have you seen a tournament before, Your Majesty?"

Demi shook her head. "Not a citadelian one, no. We have puzzle towers and contests, but I'm sure this will be just as eventful."

"Do we actually know what they'll be expected to-" Molly blinked. Squinted. Gasped. "What the-"

Demi leaned forward. "Is that Talie?"

Molly pressed a hand to her mouth as her pulse sped up and her insides tumbled. Talie stalked through the centre of the garden with the rest of the competitors, about fifteen in total. She was dressed in one of the fighting outfits Selene had commissioned for her, arms bare, hands wrapped and several blades belted to her sides.

"Did you know she was doing this?" Demi asked.

Molly shook her head. "No. She disappeared yesterday but I had no idea. I'm going to- she is so- *argh*."

Glennoria chuckled. "She's fierce, I'll give her that."

"Did she come to you?" Molly asked Demi.

"Nope. Kainen did tell Taz that Talie had approached him to ask, but he had to refuse and so did we."

"How is she able to do this if she isn't nobility then?"

"She is."

Molly turned to face Glennoria with her jaw hanging open.

"What?"

"His lordship wasn't in a position to part with any land to use for a title, but I have plenty," Glennoria announced smoothly. "It's only a tiny slip of land, more a token than an actual ascension, but it's enough to give her status. She won't be sworn to the Illusion Court either, not unless she chooses to be."

Molly gripped both arms of her chair until her fingers throbbed.

"You… but she…"

Talie lifted her head and caught her eye. Molly raised both hands and gave her an incredulous glare, determined to get as much fury across the distance as possible.

Talie winked at her.

"Welcome nobles!" Betula stood in front of her marquee as her voice boomed across the crowd. "We are honoured to host the Rose Tournament, and commend our potential new councillor Molinia for offering herself so willingly!"

A smattering of laughter rolled across the crowd and Molly forced an awkward smile.

"Okay, that was painful," Demi muttered. "I can't smile at will either, but maybe keep your mouth closed while you do it."

Glennoria waved that away. "Nonsense, but maybe sit up straight, Princess. Square the shoulders, chin level. Remember your standing far outweighs everyone else's. Oh, except yours of course, Your Majesty."

"Nope." Demi shook her head. "Citadel's outside royal control so technically Molly does outweigh me here. It's extremely liberating."

Molly had no time to assess that as Betula's strident voice continued assaulting everyone's ears.

"As we all know, the tournament is a mystery until the time comes, and now is that time! Today we will be having a battle of wits and giftery, with the last competitor standing in possession of the rose glass spear. The spear will be unreachable until all but one competitor remains able to reach it."

Betula lifted a long shard of glass with roses carved along the length of it and lethal points at both ends as it caught the light.

"The tournament will begin very soon," she finished. "But first of course we have the preliminary meet and greet. Nobles, you will have half an hour to meet the entrants and bestow any favours. Then we begin."

Molly wasn't prepared for the immediate swarm of nobles to crush in toward the competitors, and given the scandalised expression on Talie's face, she couldn't either.

"Favours?" Molly shot to her feet. "What favours?"

Glennoria lifted a hand to block her from leaving the marquee.

"The councillors can't interfere," she warned. "I, however, can join the swarm. I trust that suits you, Princess?"

Molly nodded. "I'm sure my gratitude will be sought in some form or other soon enough."

Glennoria laughed as she left the marquee and carved a path through the crush toward Talie, who was still standing alone.

"Why in the name of Faerie has she done this?" Molly hissed.

Demi shrugged. "Do you want the honest answer or the reassuring one? Actually, it's not that reassuring, but still."

"She's already got a target on her back and they know who she is as well, so they'll probably do anything to stack the deck against her!"

"Yep, that's definitely the way these things are done. I once had to complete a puzzle tower as a fairy with nothing but my wit and Taz."

"Then we stop it! Or I'll burn everyone standing between us."

"You don't want to mock their traditions," Demi said. "Fae are weirdly territorial about that. It's the one thing they all agree on."

"You say that like you're not one of them."

"My human side is vastly unimpressed. I just don't get it. All this progress and they want to still in trickery and deceit and, and..."

"Ego?"

"Yes, that. So no, breaking the rules won't go down well. Neither will incinerating all of them, unless you're planning to set your reputation as following in your grandmother's and your mother's examples."

Molly folded her arms and slumped down in her seat.

"She's defenceless and only there because of me, and because she's a total idiot-"

"For you, yeah. It's cute." Demi frowned. "Besides, who says she's defenceless? She's in the competition as a noble. I can't be seen to get involved but why do you think the rest of the Fae courts are here? Look, there's the Word Court, and Flora, although Ty is technically from the Revels Court, but they're merging. Why do you think they're here?"

"Bloodshed?" she groaned.

"Friendships not favours. Talie has to make her own debts and trades, but Taz and Kainen have called in favours, so she may find several clumsy people dropping hankies for her to pick up in exchange for kindness in return, that sort of thing."

Molly stared at her in horror, and her mind whizzed through the calculation of how far she'd get if she tried to strangle the queen of Faerie.

"You think she's going to stop to pick up someone's hanky?!"

Demi hesitated. "Well, that was an example, but-"

Molly hissed a feral noise and shoved her hands into her hair.

"I don't have anyone I can ask either."

"Nope, nothing to be done now." Demi settled back and snapped her fingers to summon a basket of oia berry puffs. "Want one?"

Molly shook her head and watched Glennoria say something that made Talie scowl.

She's got herself into this mess, probably for me, and I have no way of getting her out again.

CHAPTER TEN

TALIE

"You could at least smile a bit."

It took all of Talie's resolve not to strangle Lady Featherdown with her stupid feathery hat.

After a brief stop to pick up some blades from the gym, along with a promise to Nia that she would explain why she needed them later, she'd started the long walk to the central gardens entrance. Now her legs were twinging and she wondered if she should have risked realm-skipping in with Molly after all.

She'd have found out somehow and compelled me not to enter.

The waves of vulnerability washed over her skin and focused on breathing through the chill to keep her gift calm.

A tinkle of laughter brought her gaze up and the uneasiness turned sour.

Violetta had her hand on some man's arm, laughing along with him. She also had blades, two across her back, and her all-in-one green suit looked like the fancy ones advertised on the orb channels that did something technical to remove sweat.

A loud clamour rose up and the crowd parted as a large silver cat thundered between people's legs. The moisture on Talie's skin chilled almost enough to crystallise as the cat zipped closer.

"Stop her!" someone shouted.

Talie ducked without thinking and shot her arm out through her warding. The cat careened right into it almost like clockwork, and she hoisted the scrabbling creature against her chest. Tiny ice crystals in the fur bit against her skin as a tall woman with brown hair reached them.

"Sorry! Thank you! I told my girlfriend not to bring her, but she's off visiting her sister and I got lumbered with Frostypaws here."

Talie lowered her warding enough for the woman to step through and scoop the disgruntled cat from her arms. The moment the woman stepped back and snapped her fingers to summon a cat basket, Talie reformed the warding.

The cat yowled as it got bundled in, but Talie was more intrigued by the ice already melting on her skin.

"Sorry, I'm Tira," the woman gabbled. "Lady of the Word Court. I can see Demi's turned out, and I've only met Molly in passing."

Talie eyed the meaningful look Tira gave her.

Is she trying to suggest we're allies?

She managed a tight smile. "Word Court, what's that, stories?"

"Stories, histories, fables, and more. We don't actually have much about the citadel, but apparently these Rose

Tournaments are often gift heavy."

"Great, I guess at least I have one or two of those," Talie muttered.

Tira gasped. "Where are my manners? I can't imagine how distraught Meryl would have been if I'd lost the cat. Let me see your hand a second?"

Talie lifted her hand between them and cautiously let it slip past the boundary of her warding again. She flinched as Tira grabbed it and gave her knuckles the faintest touch with her lips.

Orbs, I can't let Molly see people kissing me!

She was halfway through looking frantically toward Molly's open-fronted tent when realisation dawned on her. The subtle rush of a new gift tingled through her bones, roiling up through her chest to radiate like a soft breeze across her face.

Tira leaned close.

"Stealth at will, best I can offer. Imagine yourself invisible and it should work. Ah!"

She made a show of sidestepping the large man that stumbled past her, but Talie was still reeling at the new gift and didn't move.

The man bounced off her warding and staggered back as a small glass vial dropped from his hand.

"Sorry! I'm so clumsy," he muttered. "Thanks for blocking the way."

Talie reached out to pick up the vial with a shaking hand and held it out.

He shook his head. "No, kindness where it's due. Keep it. I have more."

Talie lifted the vial to her face and inspected the dark grey sand inside.

"What is it?"

"Iron filings," he said quietly. "Special. I hear from our queen that you were down in the core with them, so you should know what it does."

The fancy iron. Talie stilled. *The same iron as the royal sword that can cut through wardings.*

"Thanks, um..."

"Tyren. I'm from the Revels Court. Watch out for the one with the red hair and the green suit. She's one of ours so I'm not taking sides, but she's been training hard."

Talie eyed Violetta and squared her shoulders with bitter determination. That was one fight she was almost looking forward to.

She pocketed the vial as Betula's voice swelled over the crowd.

"The time has come. Can all nobles please venture behind the borders so we can raise the fences please?"

Talie nodded her gratitude to Tira and Tyren as they slipped away, and Glennoria was already long gone. Then she looked up at Molly, torn between gratitude and guilt that Molly at least looked as frantic as she felt.

A grumbling sound cut through the silence as wooden fencing rose from the ground to hem them in. She firmed her warding and lifted her hand in front of her. With all her effort, she visualised it disappearing the same way Molly had taught her to imagine control over her rain gift.

Her skin paled, the solidness becoming a mere outline she could see her boots through. Then a loud bang rattled her bones and the effect faded as shouts went up from the crowd.

The fourteen other Fae leapt at each other like savage animals, but a flash of shining white atop grey-brown dropped from the skies before she could figure out how to join them.

"Orbs, what are they orbing thinking," she cursed.

She barely got her warding parted in time as Aurora sailed overhead to drop Arrow at her feet and arced back into the air. She had no idea if she was allowed animal helpers, but she reset her warding as Arrow shot up her leg and arm to her shoulder.

"Bad idea," she told him. "You should have stayed safe. Next time we get into trouble, go protect Molly instead."

Arrow chittered irritably at her and clung on as she broke into a run to swerve two Fae slinging what looked like spiky balls at each other.

Talie pulled Tyren's vial out and flipped the cap, sprinkling liberally as she ran past. The screams were confirmation enough so she didn't bother to look back and dodged the fringes of the carnage.

Three were unconscious already, or worse. One was standing in a large red square marked on the ground that had 'Forfeit' hanging above it in big red letters.

Nine more. If I let them pick each other off, I'll only have to face one or two.

Arrow barked a warning and she twisted seconds before a savage jolt crashed against her warding. It sagged under the sheer force, enough for the man attacking to not only reach her shoulder but injure it as her legs staggered to keep her upright.

In that tiny slip of time, her warding fractured and Arrow darted through it.

Talie lifted a hand to her shoulder and seethed through her teeth as pain sliced along her back. Panic gripped her chest and a breathy chill swept through her bones.

The man halted with his gaze unfocused. He looked around as Talie stared down at where her body should have been. Cloaked with her stealth gift in the sheer panic, she crept away from the man and the chaos toward the boundary fence.

The man turned to find his next opponent as Talie searched her pockets, only to find Tyren's vial gone.

Two more competitors were out cold with white smoke curling above them, stasis protection she assumed, which left her facing seven others.

Not exactly facing if I'm not even fighting.

She eyed the weird glass spear thing, set up on top of a vast fountain in the shape of a large marble rose. No doubt with her luck one of the others would have a levitation gift and grab it when they were done fighting.

She couldn't see Arrow or Aurora anywhere, and she couldn't bring herself to look at Molly when she wasn't even fighting, but Violetta she could see clear enough.

Even with the ripple of jealousy giving her a shot of determination, she had to admit the woman was well placed.

Violetta fought with swords in each hand, and the sheer onslaught she was putting her enemy though had the man stumbling back toward the forfeit box. The moment he crossed the red line and sagged in defeat, Violetta whirled around, fiery hair flying, and stormed after her next conquest.

I still don't like her. Talie rolled her shoulder and winced. *But only six more to go.*

She pulled her storm gift forward and crept toward the remaining six, now tracking each other as they formed a tense circle.

A flash of brown moving fast and low caught her eye, as did the glint of glass in Arrow's mouth. He raced toward the wardings of her enemies, as if he knew exactly what was in the stolen vial between his jaws, but one of the women spotted him. She lifted a hand and a vine shot out of her sleeve like a whip.

Talie lunged forward and caught the whip in hand. The woman stumbled at the resistance and a loud crack of thunder tore the skies overhead as Talie yanked it, pulling the woman forward. Her shoulder throbbed and she was pretty sure catching the vine had ruined her hand, but as the last reserves of her emotional strength spiked, her stealth gift faded.

The crowd roaring was a dull, distant echo, but her sight was clear. Arrow darted a circle over them, using the resistance of their wardings like springboards, with particles of iron flowing like glitter behind him.

He was giving her an opening, and she dropped any pretence she had of being accomplished at using gifts.

She swung her good arm through the shattered warding of the nearest man and flipped the dagger under his chin. He dodged but she twisted and kicked his hip to send him stumbling toward the forfeit box.

He found his footing mere inches away from it but she gritted her teeth and shunted her shoulder against his chest to push him over the line. He spat at her, fury turning his cheeks purple, but she twisted out of the way just in time.

Nothing like a tournament for making enemies. Five more.

She winced as Violetta's sword went clean through some woman's thigh, and the other remaining three were flinging clouding potions at each other.

Talie eyed the fountain with the spear as Violetta appeared in front of her. She warded warily and eyed Violetta's footwork.

Deep in the leading knee. Left-handed. I could probably catch her out in a fair fight, but I'm injured and Fae never fight fair.

She didn't plan to either but her gifts were depleted, the iron was gone and so was Arrow again.

Molly will probably get all huffy if I just stab her pet noble and be done with it.

In the end, she cocked her head and went for sheer irritability.

"Surprised I wasn't the first enemy on your list."

Violetta shrugged. "It's not personal."

"It is for me, considering you're sniffing around what's not yours."

One of the trio behind Violetta crashed into the fountain with an almighty splash and didn't get out again, but Violetta didn't even turn to look.

"We'll see. Molly's social gold, so I'd get used to it if I

were you. Unless I manage to charm her first of course."

"Charm?" Her snort of incredulous laughter sounded unusually loud. "That's what you're leading with? She's totally immune to it so good luck with that."

"I can be extremely persuasive."

Talie smiled as a rivulet of haziness curled across her face and through her chest. Betula had tried a charm gift on her before, and Violetta's was even stronger.

"Won't work," she said. "Nice try, but charm won't work on me when my heart belongs to her."

Violetta's eyes widened even as Talie opened her mouth to warn her.

The last man standing, the one with the powerful force, charged into Violetta and sent her flying across the garden.

Talie reached for her stealth gift but her Fae connection barely flickered awake. She cursed under her breath and set off at an awkward run.

Her vision blurred as her head swam from exertion, her hand burned, and her back throbbed with each step. She wouldn't be able to climb the fountain one-handed but she had to try surviving first anyway as the sound of feet thudding close behind had her spinning around. The man charged and she dodged, able to make out Violetta on the ground with white smoke above her.

"You've got no hope," the man crowed. "I wonder if the princess will be fun to chase."

Talie froze as anger flared white-hot in her chest.

"Say that again with your warding down," she snarled.

He splayed his arms out with a loud laugh.

"As if I need to waste energy on a kid with a barely there

title. Wardings are for real fights."

Talie nodded. "Thanks for the opening then."

The dagger was out of her wrist strap before she'd even finished speaking, and he barely had time to twitch before she embedded it deep in his shoulder.

"That's close enough to an artery that you probably shouldn't wait or you'll bleed out." She twisted the metal until he yelled. "That was for the chase comment. You come near her, ever, and next time I'll carve out a rib."

She shoved him onto his back and pulled the dagger free. He tried to get up again, but a white cloud fell over him and all that was left was the silent mimicry of him shouting behind the protection.

It was then that she heard the silence.

She still couldn't bring herself to look Molly's way and faced the fountain instead. With the dagger sheathed, she reached up for the nearest stone level. Her legs burned as she used them to push upward, and her shoulder was fast solidifying her arm at her side. She winced as something flashed overhead and braced for the inevitable fall that would no doubt come next.

A soft crooning noise echoed overhead. She forced her head to tip back and saw Aurora nudging the spear with her beak at one end, and Arrow barrel-kicking the other with his back legs.

A sob tore past her lips as she forced her bad shoulder to yield and inched her throbbing hand up to catch it.

"And we have a winner."

The announcement filled the arena with all the ceremony of a death sentence.

She clamped her fingers around the middle of the spear all the same and clutched it awkwardly to her chest as she somehow slithered back down to the ground.

Arrow landed on her good shoulder but Aurora took off elsewhere.

I owe them both so many treats.

Talie limped away from the fountain, not even sure where she was heading.

"Talie!"

Her senses were dull but she smiled weakly at the sound of Molly's voice. She opened her mouth to protest, or make excuses, but Molly kissed her fiercely before she could do more than draw breath. She rocked on her feet under the unexpectedly welcome onslaught until Molly pulled back.

"I am so beyond furious with you!"

CHAPTER ELEVEN

MOLLY

"I can't watch, where is she?" Molly peered through her fingers.

"It is a bit tense," Demi agreed. "Oh, that was savage!"

Molly crunched lower in her seat as Talie materialised out of thin air and slipped her dagger beneath someone's chin.

"Orbs, she's hurt, look at how wonky her steps are. I'm stopping this!"

She launched out of her chair only to be blocked by Kainen walking into the marquee.

"She's not doing too badly, all things considered," he said as he slid smoothly onto the seat Glennoria had never returned to.

"Not doing too badly?!"

"Yeah, look at that body slam! Poor man never saw her coming."

Molly hugged her middle tight as Violetta approached Talie. As if by design, the air stilled and a crackling sound echoed over the garden.

"It's not personal." Violetta's magically magnified

voice carried closely across the expectant crowd.

"It is for me," Talie snapped back. "Considering you're sniffing around what's not yours."

Okay, she's really mad.

Molly lifted a hand to cover her mouth, horrified and unable to look away as someone crashed into the fountain behind them.

"We'll see. She's social gold, so I'd get used to it if I were you. Unless I manage to charm her first of course."

"Charm?" Talie snorted. Loudly. "That's what you're leading with? She's totally immune to it so good luck with that."

"I can be extremely persuasive."

Molly pulled a face at that. Violetta's attempts were entirely one-sided but Talie didn't know that.

"Won't work," Talie said, her voice smug beneath the exhaustion. "Nice try, but charm won't work on me when my heart belongs to her."

Molly sank lower on her chair.

Kainen grinned. "Well, can't say clearer than that. I did tell you a while back she's besotted with you."

The crowd was silent, then a loud roar rippled up as the man who'd attacked Talie in the beginning sent Violetta flying. Molly winced as the white smoke descended but her attention stayed on Talie.

"Do we know who he is?" she asked.

"That would likely be the favourite to win," Kainen announced. "And absolutely not someone the rest of your towers would ever consider admitting they plan to win with."

She didn't ask how he knew. The other towers had an agenda and right now, she was the only one blocking them from finding the well of power in the core.

"You've got no hope," the man announced. "I wonder if the princess will be fun to chase."

Molly groaned. "She won't take that well."

"It's a threat," Demi muttered, her face speckling with a hint of icy blue magic.

"Say that again with your warding down," Talie goaded.

Molly pressed her hands back to her face as the man laughed.

"As if I need to waste energy on a kid with a barely there title. Wardings are for real fights."

"Thanks for the opening then."

Moly saw Talie's hand move before she'd even finished speaking, and a second later the length of it was deep in his shoulder.

"That's close enough to an artery that you probably shouldn't wait or you'll bleed out," Talie taunted, twitching the knife until he yelled. "That was for the chase comment. You come near her, ever, and next time I'll carve out a rib."

Shocked whispers swept through the captivated crowd.

"Yeah, okay, she's my official favourite," Kainen said with awe. "Sorry Molly."

She ignored him as Talie turned to the fountain and started to climb.

"I feel so orbing useless," she muttered.

Demi nodded. "Me too. Once this is over, get yourself

back to your tower. We can't rule out retribution here."

"We'll all go back together," Molly insisted.

She grimaced as Talie almost slipped halfway up the fountain, but a flicker of white and green had her heart lifting.

"See, this is why I said let the animals in," Kainen grumbled. "I tried to bring Betty but she's about to pop out an egg."

Demi wrinkled her nose but Molly clung to the edges of her chair as the spear slipped into Talie's grasp.

"Thank Faerie!"

"And we have a winner."

"Sound more excited, why don't you," Kainen grumbled, the amusement draining from his face.

He and Demi swapped wary glances as Molly clambered past him and shot across the grass. Even before the fences were fully down, she hurtled over the nearest one.

"Talie!"

She called out loud mainly to stop Talie walking over an unconscious competitor, but Talie looked her way with a pained smile.

Molly stopped in front of her with a hundred thoughts flitting through her mind, but the hush of the crowd accompanied the words dancing round in her mind.

Once the heart belongs to someone else.

She stared into Talie's unfocused hazel eyes almost devoid of their usual gold hue, then covered the distance between them.

Talie's lips were dry from using her storm gift and she

was wobbling on her feet, but she still had enough awareness to smile as she kissed back like it was the most natural part of her world.

Molly pulled back and finally found words that tumbled out in a rush.

"I am so furious with you!"

Talie nodded violently. "I had to. Think she deserves to have you? Or any of them? You're precious like sunny, shiny gold."

Molly blinked, her frustration diverted by the lyrical lilt in Talie's voice. Her gaze was still unfocused and she looked like a drunk on too much *Beast*.

"I think you need to rest," she said.

Talie pouted. "But I won, right? No Vienettas or bad men taking you away."

"Er... yeah, you won."

"I did? *Wooow*. Hey, Princess?"

"Yeah?"

"I think I need to lie down now."

Molly looked out at the fast dispersing crowd, and at the other competitors already cleared from the field. Talie's last opponent was standing with Betula and Argon and none of them looked pleased.

It was a set up. They gave him the kind of gift that would move anyone into the forfeit zone.

She slid her arm around Talie's waist as Demi and Kainen approached.

"Congratulations, Talie." Demi held out a small cup full of purple liquid. "Drink this."

Molly froze and her cheeks burned as Talie collapsed

against her.

"Should I drink it?" she whispered loudly.

Molly nodded. "Definitely drink it."

Talie kissed her ear and swiped the cup from Demi.

"I'd do anything for you," she announced, then downed the cup.

"Yeah, I'm getting that impression." Molly waited a few moments until Talie's gaze sharpened. "Better?"

Talie winced. "Orbs, I feel like I've fought an entire tower."

"You might as well have! What were you thinking?"

"That you wouldn't have been safe otherwise, and I was right."

She was, but Molly selfishly didn't feel like admitting it as Kainen strolled toward them with a wide grin.

"Lady Rain. You have no idea how delighted I am that you'll now be affiliated with the Illusion Court. Do let me know if there's anything we can do to help facilitate your new lodgings."

"It's a tiny strip of land, no lodgings," Talie muttered.

"And you are lady of it, and as always, welcome at our court anytime."

Talie rolled her eyes at Kainen's delighted face, but she froze when Demi fixed her with a determined look.

"Can I have a word, Talie?"

"…sure?"

It sounded serious but Molly could almost hear Talie's sarcastic voice in her head saying something like 'as if I can say no'.

"Allow me to escort you home, Molly," Kainen offered.

He held out an elbow and she joined his side as Talie gave her a wary look and followed Demi a short distance across the grass.

"Is it something bad?" she asked. "I know Demi's a queen but Talie doesn't take threats well."

Kainen snorted. "No, she doesn't. Maybe Demi just wants a chance to get to know her a bit better, get her into the orb chat, that sort of thing."

"Maybe, or more like you know what it's about and you're not telling me."

She folded her arms across her chest but Kainen's gaze moved past her. She twisted around before realising his hand was headed for her shoulder.

An iron arrow sailed through the air before the shout could leave her lips. Talie turned toward the danger even as Demi lifted a hand.

"Don't!" Kainen shouted.

The arrow pierced through whatever protection Demi had, and only her outstretched hand stopped the arrow carving right through Talie's chest.

Molly stumbled over the grass, legs flailing in mid-air as Kainen's arm came around her middle.

"Let me go!" she screamed.

He clung on as four unknown Fae stared around and found them instead.

"Go," Demi insisted.

"Don't you dare! Talie!"

Talie's gaze narrowed as the group fractured to attack from both sides, then the air around her body rippled as she glamoured into Molly.

"Get her out of here," she yelled, her voice sounding scarily familiar for all the wrong reasons.

Molly stared at the vision of herself now standing next to Demi and tried to get her elbow into Kainen's gut as he clung on.

The enemy slowed at the sudden change, but Molly screamed as a swathe of darkness wrapped around her. She fought as Kainen's shadow mingled with the purple-grey of the nether and the entrance hall of the Menagerie materialised around them.

She rounded on him the moment he let go and stepped away.

"Take me back!"

Her fist landed on his warding and sent her reeling backwards.

"I can't do that." He grimaced. "Why do you think Demi was there with you today? This was never about a competition for your favour. They were never going to let you rule a tower on your own with royal connections in play."

"But Talie-"

"Is with the queen of Faerie, and she's not stupid either. Rash maybe, and argumentative… she's actually quite like Demi now I think about it."

"That's irrelevant!" Molly snapped. "Demi they can use, hold hostage, ask for money or the tower or something. What use is Talie to them?"

"If she's smart, she'll continue pretending to be you. I gifted her with glamour a while back so she should be able to hold it easier than most. They won't risk hurting you until you concede the leadership of your tower or they take it by conquest."

"No orbing chance!"

"Exactly. Even if they have Demi, and trust me Taz and their court will be on the offensive as it is, Talie pretending to be you also brings the Oak Queen into play too."

Molly rubbed both hands over her face. She had to be sensible but she wanted nothing more than to charge through each tower and tear them down until she found Talie.

"What do we do then?"

CHAPTER TWELVE

TALIE

Talie watched Kainen fighting to hold Molly back and her exhausted heart twisted. The four people charging toward them would take Molly over Demi as punishment for her ruining their plans, and to secure some level of instability in their tower so they could swoop in and demand control.

"Go!" Demi shouted, then out of the corner of her mouth she muttered, "Don't do anything dim."

Talie dredged up the last dregs of her glamour gift, the one she'd barely had time to practice with, and made the change to looking like Molly with pure gritty determination alone.

Demi groaned. "That would be something dim."

"I'm not letting them take her." She lifted her voice in a shoddy imitation of Molly's voice. "Get her out of here!"

Molly screamed as Kainen wrapped shadow around them and they disappeared.

"Can't you do something fancy?" she asked, still getting used to the awkward crunch of Molly's figure compared to her own.

Demi shrugged. "I could, but you seem to be making

the decisions here. I'm just visiting."

"Seriously? You're a queen. Can't you blast them off the edge of a tower or something?"

"It's because I'm queen I *can't* do that. Imagine if queen's went around blasting everything all the time. Bad publicity, Milo would have a fit."

"Are we even warded?"

Demi cocked her head. "I have an arrow in my hand, so I'm a bit indisposed at the moment."

Talie stared down and seethed through her teeth as Demi turned her hand with the arrow still pinching the thin skin between her thumb and finger.

Even then, she lifted her chin like a queen and smiled at the enemy as they stopped a short distance away. Talie struggled to pull a protection warding over both of them and swayed with the effort. Whatever was in the purple tonic was wearing off fast.

"We seem to be at an impasse," Demi announced, as if they were having a friendly conversation in the lane. "How about you let her go and we can talk properly?"

The hovering Fae parted and Talie bristled on her wobbly legs as all the councillors minus Molly, who she was now supposed to be, approached.

"Not a bad catch, all things told," Argon crowed.

Betula flicked a despairing look at him.

"You'll forgive us, queen, but you've caught yourself up in citadel business," she said.

Demi shrugged. "I don't have to forgive you, but I get the sentiment. It seems to me that you've caught yourselves up in family business here, and it's arrogant to assume your business with her outweighs mine. Or hers with me, she's technically in control here."

Talie glanced sideways. She couldn't remember the last time she'd thought of Demi as anything other than a sort-of relation of Molly's, even after the fighting down in the citadel core over the well of power. There was no obvious change in her, just black jeans, a smart red sweatshirt with holly stitched on it and a small circlet of silver, red and green on her head. But the bright blue eyes, those were sharp as ice, and it was the Holly Queen of Faerie staring down an adversary with astonishing wickedness.

"Let us have a little chat with Molly and you can go," Argon said.

Demi laughed. "You know I'm not going to do that. Let's move this along, shall we? You say you want to let me go, I say no, you say I'm risking the whole 'royals not interfering in the citadel' thing, then I say you started it by throwing an arrow in my hand- oh, hang on."

She lifted her hand and closed her eyes. Talie winced as she pulled the length of iron out and blinked in pain several times, but she didn't hand over the arrow, only clicked the fingers of her good hand and the arrow vanished.

"We weren't aiming for you," Oak said.

His gaze was on Demi now, but Talie remembered the frank staring he'd done of her in the meeting before and fought against the shudder that rippled through her.

Demi pretended to frown. "You were aiming for Molly? Why? She's one of you, or a councillor of one of your towers at least."

"We were aiming for her girlfriend, actually," Tulip

said. "I'm still not happy about that."

"Yes, good point. Which one are you really?" Betula asked.

Talie said nothing.

Argon rolled his eyes. "What does it matter? Even queens aren't immune to iron, and that wound will have her incapacitated for a short while yet."

"He's right, we can't waste time here," Oak said.

Demi eyed Talie. "Are they always this unorganised?"

"Yeah. Talie called them a bunch of berries without a basket once."

Talking about herself in third person felt unusual, but it didn't trouble her any so she tucked that as a tiny extra strategy she had to use. Word-tangling wasn't her skill, but she had to pretend to be Molly for a while yet.

Amid the indignant huffs from the councillors, she caught the subtle flicker of amusement at the corner of Demi's mouth. If she could convince them she was Molly, they wouldn't look too closely at who was in the Sunset Tower calling out for reinforcements.

"We can do this the easy way or the hard way," Betula warned.

"What's the easy way?" Demi asked.

"You come with us willingly."

"Oh. And the hard way?"

"You can't do anything with that wound, Argon's right. Talie, Molly, whoever that is, can't fight four of us on her own." She pushed a hand out and pressed against Talie's warding. "That protection won't last long either."

Demi sighed. "Easy way or hard way?"

Talie hesitated as Demi looked her way. If she chose the easy way, she could give Molly time to make herself safe, or more likely give Kainen time to stop Molly doing anything mad. If she chose the hard way, they might force her to answer questions immediately, and Demi needed time to work the iron out of her system.

"Easy way." She bit her lip, doing her best to fake some hint of Molly's endless compassion. "Taz would never forgive me otherwise."

Demi rolled her eyes. "Probably not. Alright then, lead on. What's it to be by the way? Is there a bed, or are we going for the dungeon-keep vibe?"

She flexed her hand and all four councillors flinched.

"Drop the warding then," Betula said.

Talie shook her head. "No thanks. You want us to do it the easy way then you'll have to do the rest the hard way. Better start walking."

"No need."

Tulip pressed a hand to Talie's warding and she felt the faint threads of her strength give under the pressure. She thought Tulip would push right through it, but she only closed her eyes and the nether whisked around them.

The moment the purple-grey haze cleared, Talie eyed the room around them. It was simple, one bed, stone walls and no windows. Only one door too, so no bathroom.

"This room is laced with iron, so don't bother yourselves about escaping," Argon said gleefully.

Demi smiled and lifted her good hand. He twitched backwards and flung open the door, but Talie couldn't take any satisfaction in it. Even if Demi got her power back fast, an iron room wasn't something they were escaping easily.

The councillors filed out and Tulip gave them an almost regretful look before she closed the door. A key scratched on the other side, then silence.

Demi ambled to the bed and eased herself on it with a groan.

"Okay, that really hurts," she muttered.

Talie bit her lip and let her warding drop. She needed rest and her head was rolling around like a bucket tumbling down the lanes, but she couldn't exactly tell a queen of Faerie to get up and let her have a lie down instead.

Demi bit her lip as she pulled out a tiny vial full of swirling purple.

"How bad are you feeling right now?" she asked.

Talie shrugged. "I've been better."

"Not helpful. Broken bones? Dislocations?"

"None. My head is shot and my gifts are on empty." She rolled her bad shoulder with a wince. "My back is probably jarred."

Demi nodded. "Okay, here goes."

She poured the vial's contents over the wound on her hand, the dark greenish grey impact point on her skin smoking on contact. Talie waited while Demi grimaced through the process and eyed the empty bottle.

Could have maybe saved me a drop though.

She didn't voice it but froze when Demi's gaze snapped up. Demi flexed her hand and pocketed the empty vial, then pulled her legs up onto the bed.

"You couldn't have done that while we were arguing with them?" she asked.

Demi shook her head. "Would have escalated too quickly. That was quick thinking though, talking about yourself in third person."

In all her imaginings about being praised by people, Talie thought she would have expected to feel more pride when it came from a queen. She didn't.

"Molly's safe," she said. "I need to remember that. If I can keep this glamour up, it'll give her time to send out for help. Your lot won't leave you here long before tearing the towers down anyway."

Demi laughed. "They have orders and protocol to stop them doing exactly that. Doesn't work often because Taz is an idiot who never does what he's told, but still."

"They'll still come for you."

"Eventually. Kainen knows exactly what to tell the nobles, who will then go and tell Tavania. She's fond of Molly, sees her as a second chance at moulding the future, so she'll issue threats."

"What good are threats?" Talie scowled as she strode to the door and inspected the lock. "Orbs, Molly would have had this open in seconds."

"She's very resourceful. Threats are everything in Faerie. They're the balance to gifts and deals, but it took me a fair while to figure that out. Imagine Tavania tells the nobles she's going to take all their realmly goods if they don't pull their support from the citadel."

"She can do that?"

"She's queen, of course she can. Remember what happened when your tower came down? The nobles fled. The other towers probably lost some of theirs as well, which is why they let that Phoenix bloke resume control. Put on a happy face and the money turns up again."

"While the rest of the people starve and freeze."

"More often than not, yeah. The real problem is-"

The sound of a key in the lock had Talie hurrying across the room to stand at Demi's side. Demi didn't bother to get up, but she did flex her hand again with a grimace.

"Are you-" Talie whispered.

Demi shook her head firmly as the door swung open and Talie's gifts sputtered inside her limbs, fighting to flare awake as fury clawed to life in her chest. The man standing in the doorway was smiling at her, and she clenched her fists to see his silver hair freshly washed and tied back from his face, with no sign of tiredness or strain around his eyes.

"Warding," Demi muttered.

Talie almost didn't bother, but when she glanced Demi's way she saw Molly reflected back at her in Demi's eyes.

Oh, right. I'm not meant to be me. Although Molly would probably punch him too.

She raised a warding over both of them as Phoenix eyed her up and down.

"A princess and a queen," he said. "You'll forgive me if I don't bow."

CHAPTER THIRTEEN

MOLLY

Molly stood in her bedroom with Kainen and Reyan on one side, and Taz being held back by the arms by Ace and Milo on the other. The moment Molly had mentioned a plan, Kainen started communing with the shadows. She couldn't bear the thought of having to answer questions from anyone in the Menagerie, so she went up to her room with him following.

It was all she could do to change into comfortable clothing before the sound of shouting drew her from her dressing room.

"We need to be sensible about this," Ace insisted, running a hand over his cropped black hair.

"They have my wife!" Taz snarled.

Molly took a step back as his fiery wings flared out and scored a singe mark through the doorframe. With the wings, it looked like his honey blond hair was on fire too, but beyond the hair Molly still wasn't sure she could see much of a family resemblance between him and her.

Kainen frowned, apparently less intimidated by Taz's wrath than Molly was.

"She's the queen of Faerie, and not exactly the fluffiest happy clappy people person. I'd say she probably has them."

"They learned from the iron in the well though," Molly added. "They've somehow managed to get hold of metirin iron to-"

Kainen shot her a warning look.

"To what." Taz raised a hand into the tense silence and icy blue fire lit his fingertips. "I swear, if you don't tell me…"

Kainen sighed. "They shot her with an iron arrow. It barely grazed her hand though, and she was fine when I-"

"YOU LEFT HER!" Taz swore under his breath. "She's all but defenceless and now I'm the one having to manage all this because she's run off to play hero again!"

"She knows how to fight well enough in any capacity," Kainen soothed. "They won't harm her before asking for ransom or similar. We'll think of a plan and-"

"They might not harm a queen but they have Talie as well," Molly snapped.

Kainen nodded. "Yes they do, the absolute orb-munchers."

"She's who you're worried about?!" Taz exploded.

"Considering she aligned herself with the top dog noble at my court to get herself into this ridiculous contest, yes. Besides, she has a habit of punching first and asking questions not very often."

"So are we going in for them or not?" Ace asked. "It is basically a declaration of war."

"Oh we're going in," Taz muttered.

Ace let go of him and turned to whisper something to Milo, who straightened his knitted sweatshirt with a firm nod and vanished.

"Absolutely." Kainen clicked his fingers and summoned his leather jacket and a similar one for Reyan. "You know, if I have a daughter, I imagine she'll be a lot like Talie. I probably shouldn't have kids."

"So I should start interviewing if I ever want kids?" Reyan asked wearily.

Kainen hesitated as she took the jacket and slipped it on.

"Only if you want a row of dead men, sweetheart."

Reyan rolled her eyes and took the jacket.

"You don't need me, do you?" she asked. "There's so much to do at court still and I'm up to my ears as it is."

Kainen hesitated. "No, we'll be fine."

Reyan shadowed away but Molly was out of patience.

"What are we planning then?" she demanded. "I doubt they'd come to a meeting if I summoned them."

"They hopefully think she's you." Kainen shrugged his jacket on. "That was really smart on her part, because if they believe it, they won't be looking too closely here. They'll either try to marry her off or get her to resign control of the tower."

Molly pulled a face. "She'd probably decapitate them in their sleep, in either scenario."

"Exactly, she'll be fine. I've put some threads out among the nobility that things aren't great here, and that if called on they'll be asked to pick a side. They won't want to anger the crowns so they'll be withdrawing on principle any moment now."

"I've told my mother," Taz muttered. "Or told Marthe to tell her. She won't care about Demi but if she thinks it's Molly that's been taken she'll do something."

Molly set off out of the bedroom with Taz a step behind and Kainen at her side.

"That's why we have to hope Talie keeps her glamour up as long as possible. From now on, you need to pretend to be Talie, Molly."

"I can't hold a glamour long though."

"I gift you with the ability to hold a glamour any time you choose, easily as possible." Kainen shrugged and grabbed her hand to kiss her knuckles. "On the condition that- why does everyone keep pulling faces when I do that! On the condition that Taz, Demi, Talie, me and Reyan can see through it."

Molly barely noticed the sudden rush of energy rippling through her limbs. She didn't want to pretend to be Talie, she wanted the real one stomping around and glaring at her. Then she'd be able to yell at her properly without feeling guilty.

"Can't you give me power to confine her to the tower or something?" she muttered.

Kainen sighed. "I swear, nobody pays any attention. Your compulsion gift can do that if you really want. I wouldn't though, not nice to confine people."

"You would know," Taz retorted.

"Unfair!"

"Absolutely fair, and we're wasting time. Where are they likely to hold them?"

Molly frowned. "I don't know, but Talie mentioned some maps in the vault downstairs. They might have schematics of the other towers. I don't think our library does."

"Right, you do that. I'm going back to court to get the FDPs."

"Yay!" Kainen grinned. "No tower will be left standing once they're done."

As Taz growled under his breath and disappeared with Ace, Kainen clapped his hands with a determined air.

Okay, I'll go and get Beryl. She'll be able to hold the fort and support Sammy while we're off doing what we do best."

"Is that wise?" Molly asked.

"Why?"

"Well… Sammy's great but she doesn't know all that much about running the tower yet, and Beryl is… Beryl."

Kainen laughed. "She is indeed Beryl, but she was trained to be a court aide at the Flora Court before she followed her sisters to Arcanium. She knows far more than she lets on. I'll be right back."

He disappeared into the shadows and Molly continued along the hall toward the stairs.

Okay, Talie. I can do this. She stopped in front of a mirror and closed her eyes. *I just have to glower at everyone and threaten them a lot.*

It took her a couple of tries, but when she opened her eyes the third time, she found Talie staring back at her. With a catch in her throat, she focused on changing her clothing to match Talie's style, but she couldn't manage to invent any arm-wraps.

"That's good, well done." Kainen's voice brought her round. "Where are these maps then?"

Molly led the way down the stairs to the entrance hall and along to the corridor at the back that led to the vault. She hadn't had a chance to go in there before, but Talie had told her.

She pushed the door open to reveal a square room full of large glass cases and wooden trunks nailed to the wall, all dusty. It had an air of forgotten chaos to it, with each section encroaching on the one beside it.

"Wow, this is messy," Kainen said. "And I thought I was disorganised."

Molly moved through clustered heaps until her gaze landed on a glass cabinet. Memories of Talie telling her about a recipe, something to do with the gift replication, filled her head.

"Look at this," she murmured. "Last known recipe for enervation. Three days' infusion and shock and enervation is complete. Ensure the body has no decomposition- *eww*. Ensure no decomposition and check on resurrecting that inner decay in minimal."

Kainen appeared beside her. "That's… chilling."

"Talie said Phoenix was dealing with something to do with undead Fae, but surely that can't be possible? I haven't even had time to think that far yet."

She thought of Violetta lurking around and Ru randomly reappearing. He hadn't answered any questions yet, like how he was magically alive after Celeste killed him while he was pretending to be Talie. She shook her head and pressed a thumb to her forehead to ease the pressure building.

"There are ancient myths," Kainen said, his tone drenched with disgust. "Whether they're true, nobody knows. I'll send this to Milo in the meantime. Any luck with the maps? Taz will start chopping heads if we don't find anything."

Molly bit her lip and surveyed the mess, but she couldn't see anything remotely map-like.

"There is one person I can ask, someone Phoenix trusted. He doesn't like me much though."

Kainen smiled. "Oh, well he'll be very, *very* friendly to me, don't you worry."

Molly didn't doubt it as she led them back to the entrance hall and locked the vault behind them.

"Ches, any idea where Mulberry is?" she asked a passing girl from the kitchens.

Ches nodded. "He's been lurking behind the double doors a lot. Think he's probably shirking, but please don't tell him I said it."

"I won't don't worry."

She strode toward the large doors at the far corner of the hall that led through to the labyrinth. Hauling one of them open, she stepped inside with Kainen close behind her and squinted past the firelit doors lining each wall ahead.

With her sight gift she caught the flicker of movement ahead and strode forward.

"Mulberry, a question for you," she called out.

The movement stilled and her irritation spilled over.

"Come here."

Her compulsion gift sprang from her lips and she revelled in the contemptuous scowl on Mulberry's face as he stomped toward them with belligerent feet.

"Yes?" he snapped.

She smiled. "Where are the maps?"

"Maps?"

"Phoenix had you sort some maps shortly before he left. He'd have trusted nobody but you I imagine. Where are they?"

His lips contorted as he tried to keep them pinned shut, his bulky shoulders shaking under the effort.

"I've got them."

"Hand them over."

His hand spasmed as it fought its way into his pocket and pulled out an orb.

"Unlock it."

He turned away to whisper his password, but she only needed the maps.

"Send the maps to me, all of them."

His thumb swiped across the surface of his orb but the hatred in his eyes was fixed on her.

"You're not to tell anyone about this conversation," she said, thinking fast. "You're forbidden from coming down here. You're not allowed to pass any knowledge or hint of this to anyone, unless it's someone I trust."

"More specific," Kainen said. "Use names."

"Unless it's the King Consort, the Holly Queen, or Lord Kainen here. Oh, or Sammy. Or Talie." Her chest squeezed at the thought of Talie stuck somewhere. "My Sammy or Talie, you know who I mean."

His head nodded against his will and she gave him a final warning glare as she turned away. He had to follow them to leave the labyrinth, but as Kainen closed the doors behind them, Mulberry stomped off across the entrance hall.

"That's going to come back and bite me, isn't it," she said.

Kainen nodded. "They usually always do in some way. Still, let's see those maps."

Molly swiped her orb and picked up the maps to project them into the air in front of them.

"Ah, here. See the centre, and those pathways branching off." Kainen frowned. "We'll have to make a show of calling the other towers to a meeting first to demand Demi and Talie's return. It's expected."

"Why waste time?" Molly asked.

"Appearances. If they think we're doing things by the right channels, they won't expect us to be storming their side from the tunnels underneath."

"They won't fall for it, and Taz won't stall much longer. I won't either."

"Either way, it has to be done first. We'll make it quick." He noticed her scowl and grimaced. "Yeah, and I think I'll let Ace and Milo convince Taz. I reckon some part of him still really wants to see my head mounted on his wall some days."

CHAPTER FOURTEEN

TALIE

"No need for the hostilities, Molly," Phoenix said. "There's little you can do to me, but there are ways we can mitigate the disaster all this has caused."

Talie clenched her fists tight. She still had her wrist strap on and her arm-wraps, but if Phoenix had any misgivings about who she really was then he was pretending well.

"The disaster you caused," she said.

He sighed. "It's been a mess all over. Your mother certainly set the ball rolling by being too greedy too quickly, then of course you insisted on finding the well before any of us could."

Talie kept her gaze welded to his face. She didn't have much chance of fighting him, but if he let her outside the room then she could maybe dredge up enough rain to scare him.

That's his big fear, except I'm meant to be Molly and I can't lie either.

"Celeste isn't any concern of mine," she tried. "The citadel though, the tower, they matter."

"I couldn't agree more. Talie didn't get my vision but perhaps you might if you see the range of the plan."

"I doubt it."

He smiled. "Let's see if we can swing those doubts to maybes then. Give the queen time to rest."

"Don't drag her out on my account," Demi said, her tone deceptively sunny. "We don't have secrets among family."

Talie inhaled deeply against a sharp prick in her chest. Demi was playing the part to perfection with the whole family thing, but Talie couldn't help wondering what it would be like to be properly part of Molly's family one day.

Even with her title, which was all but pretend anyway, she wasn't Molly's equal.

Even with all the tradition and hierarchy swept away, she was the darkness and Molly was the light.

"How nice." Phoenix's tone disagreed with his words as his trademark habit of getting distracted struck. "We can do this the easy way or the-"

"The hard way, I know. What's the easy way?" Talie grumbled.

"Let me put iron cuffs on you to remove any risk of you using gifts against me, and I will show you what we're working on here."

Demi rose from the bed, her shoulders square and her blue eyes flashing.

"I'll have your word that she'll be returned unharmed," she said.

Phoenix glanced her way. "I don't see what position

you're in to be demanding anything, queen, but I won't be harming her. You seem to have gotten yourself caught easily, but I imagine the Oak Queen won't be quite so weak."

Talie tensed at the obvious insult. For one charged moment, Talie thought Demi would strike somehow.

"Okay." Demi shrugged and sat back on the bed. "As long as you're not hurting her."

"He can't do anything anyway," Talie said. "He and Taz had a deal, isn't that right?"

Phoenix's gaze brightened with hostility for a moment.

"We did and that does have to stand. I can't however guarantee that the others won't overpower me. The deal was to not harm or try to coerce you, but there was nothing about not letting others do as they will."

Demi nodded. "Got it. Have fun then."

It wasn't entirely gratifying to see the subtle narrowing of Phoenix's eyes, but as Talie put her wrists out for Phoenix to cuff, she took the tiny comfort that Demi's dismissiveness had rattled him.

"These are Talie's," he said, tapping the dagger strapped to her wrist and the arm-wraps.

She flinched her hands free before holding them out again.

"So? It was necessary."

He nodded. "I imagine so. I did wonder when she entered the field how she'd managed it, but of course she hasn't got a noble title. I knew then it had to be you fighting for yourself. It worked too."

She held still as he cuffed slim lengths of iron around

each wrist like bracelets, then pulled a face at his back as he turned toward the door.

"I won, if that's what you mean. Nice to see the friends you keep don't stick to their honour though."

He shrugged. "Why would they? The plan was to have you taken during the audience but you ruined it."

Talie gave Demi a last look and followed him out into a dimly lit stone hallway.

"Good," she muttered.

"Not for us but no matter. Follow me."

She did, guessing they were somewhere under the levels of another tower. They passed a few people while turning this way and that, but none of them lingered to stare.

"So, what is this grand plan you're so keen to share then?" she asked.

Phoenix slowed to keep pace with her.

"How about I start by offering you a goodwill gesture? There are those who are determined to kill the queen." He ignored her gasp. "She matters very little to *my* plans though."

"So what, I agree to whatever plan you've cooked up for me, and you help me get her out?"

"Of course not. I've told you their plan, so what you do about that is up to you. Ah, here."

He opened a door and jostled her through onto a stone balcony high up above a cavern. Bare fires pitted with slabs of stone lit the edges of the vast space, but Talie stared in horror.

Flashbacks of sneaking through the labyrinth under their tower with Molly filled her head, of Fae strapped to tables being tested on. There were still several steel vats strewn around the space, along with tables full of papers and vials. Crates stacked in random piles, but she couldn't see any sign of torture below.

"This is… similar."

Phoenix nodded. "I did wonder how much you'd seen. I'm sure Talie's also been embellishing how awful I am, but then I did have to take drastic steps to get her on-side, and still she refused to see the vision."

Talie held her muscles taut even though they were screaming. The purple tonic had worn off, her back and shoulder throbbed and her thoughts were scrambled.

"Not one to exaggerate," she muttered. "I suppose you're the one who sent Ru back as well. Wasn't he a favourite of yours as Marcus? How did he even survive?"

"Ah yes, Ru. I'm surrounded by irritatingly soft hearts. That is what I wanted to show you, the wider plan I mentioned. Watch."

He pointed down as a thud echoed up and a small group carried in a struggling man. Talie didn't recognise him, and a flicker of panic raced through her mind as she wondered if Molly was meant to.

Phoenix eyed her carefully as she watched them strap the man to a table. He stammered protests and pleas, but as a woman nearest his head passed a blade to someone else, Talie closed her eyes. She'd seen death before, but somehow in her weary state, she couldn't bear it.

"Ru was particularly tricky." Phoenix's voice circled in her head like a nightmare. "Memories need to be distilled back into the host body, but he seemed to be clinging on to some remnant of emotion. I'm not sure yet whether it was some lingering hold Celeste put on him or just stubbornness, but the progress will evolve as we continue. Different Fae, different gifts, varying results."

The awful sounds went still and Talie risked opening her eyes.

"Now watch, this part is brilliance in motion," he insisted.

Talie risked a glance at him and almost resurrected the last dregs of her meagre breakfast. His enraptured gaze was fixed on the scene below, but she knew what was going to happen before it did.

"This is what it's all been about, isn't it?" she said quietly. "Let Celeste experiment with gift extraction while you work toward creating an army of undead Fae. What's the plan, take on the whole of Faerie?"

"Eventually, but think about what this means! The nether chose me to impart this wisdom to. Celeste heard it speak first of course, but once Talie led me down there I heard it talk to me too. I knew it would."

"It talks to all of us."

"Maybe so, but it gave me the method for resurrection. Imagine the citadel reigning over the whole of Faerie, a seat of power that none could rival. Cut down our fighters and we'll send them back the next day. They gift their forces, we steal them."

Talie stared at the tubes being tunnelled into the dead man's bare chest, neck and face.

"Does it always work?"

Phoenix nodded. "We've had minimal casualties, and a

few undesirable results that needed to be removed permanently, but the general numbers are growing steadily. With more time, more resources, we can grow immeasurably."

"So Ru is definitely one of them?" She managed to keep the revulsion out of her voice, too sick at heart to be anything other than faint. "That explains the vacant tone and dead eyes."

"Like you said, he was one of my favourites. We've worked hard to sever the last of his emotions but sending him back to your tower was the final test. Thankfully, he's returned completely unmoved. Talie was a favourite too but her treachery I can't forgive."

"Why his and not hers then?"

She expected some kind of emotional pain at the rejection, even for nostalgia's sake, but none came. She kept her gaze welded to the sight below her as some kind of murky brown concoction pumped through the tubes.

"You have a certain poise that seems to turn hearts," Phoenix said. "Ru, Talie, they gravitate toward you. Likely the result of countless generations of royal blood, but Ru was still mouldable, even by Celeste. Talie… she's too stubborn."

She nodded. "I can agree with that."

And you'll die by it or I'll die trying.

"That's about the extent of the demonstration. He'll be like that for the next three days, then he'll wake. We put them through a holding process to ensure they're amenable, but so far it's been a great success."

Talie followed him through the doorway and along the

hall with her pulse pounding.

"And the councillors, they all know?"

"Betula and Oak have agreed not to ask too many questions. Tulip is another soft heart so we tend not to let her in on the wider plan, but her tower is extremely useful and she doesn't ask questions either when she benefits so much from the trades."

"And Night Tower, Argon, I bet he's well in with all this."

Phoenix laughed. "Where do you think we are? Argon and I have been in conversation for a very long time, among other more secretive powers. Now, I'll let you consider the offer a while."

He unlocked and swung a door open, standing aside to let her pass. Demi sat up as she walked in, but she turned to face Phoenix.

"You haven't given me an offer," she said.

"I can't give you anything. The King Consort saw to that, but the rest of the councillors? They can do whatever they like to you. You could agree to join their cause, work with it, be amenable, and they'll likely reinstate you to ruling your tower."

"That's it?"

"Well, what else were you expecting? You have nothing they want beyond your royal blood. That could open up all sorts of alliances with the Oak Queen until it's time for fates to change."

He shut the door and Talie eyed the iron cuffs still on her wrists. As she slumped and pain radiated across her back, Demi beckoned her over.

"I've had a test of the room and I can't do much to get us out. I tried a hairpin on the door but it's the wrong kind of lock. Lie down." Demi waved an awkward hand at the bed. "No offense but you look awful."

"Molly never looks awful," she grumbled as she clambered onto the bed.

Demi opened her mouth to say something but the door swung open again. They shared a startled glance, because clearly Phoenix hadn't bothered to lock it and neither of them had noticed, but Talie inched off the bed again as Ru walked in.

"Molly, are you okay? Has he hurt you?" Ru asked.

Astonished at the flicker of emotion in his voice, Talie folded her arms across her chest.

"What do you care?"

"I'm holding on but everything is so scrambled. Big patches of time I don't remember. There's so much you don't understand as well. I know he's shown you what he's working on here but he's got other plans for you. He intends to make a claim on you and take Sunset Tower back through me, and I... I can't disobey him."

"Because you're undead?" she asked.

Demi flinched beside her but said nothing.

"He told you? I never wanted... well, it doesn't matter. I made a promise once that I'd protect you, and I mean to stand by it."

"What..." Talie hesitated. "What is it like, being undead?"

He lifted his gaze to hers and she almost stumbled back at the sheer torment in his eyes. There was a vacancy, a wideness that seemed unfocused, but in the very depths was a pit of fractured emotion.

"It's living torture. My memories are there but they don't feel like mine. I'm not meant to have emotions, just memories but even they don't attach to the right parts. I remember you though. You were always so bright. I can't see it now, you don't look like you used to through dead eyes, but I remember it."

Talie winced. She had no idea if it was his eyes or her glamour that was at fault, but he thought she was Molly and she couldn't tell him the truth without dooming herself as his eyes grew fully vacant again.

"Ru?" She drew his wandering attention back to her. "We need to get out of here. Can you help us?"

He shook his head slowly.

"I promised to keep you safe."

She bit her lip.

"Okay, can you take these off for me to start with?" She held her cuffed wrists out. "That would keep me safe. Then telling me how to get out of here will keep me even safer."

Ru closed the distance between them and she sucked the disgust down deep as he pulled out a few keys on a small ring.

"Only room for one."

Talie frowned. "How though?"

"Through the darkness." He freed the first cuff, then the second, his attention solely on the task until he was done. "I go where I'm told. But I promised to keep you safe. I can show you."

"I'm not leaving anyone behind," she insisted.

"Just leave the door open," Demi said. "I'll sort myself out."

Footsteps echoed along the hallway outside and Ru looked over his shoulder. His head rotated too far to be normal and Talie shuddered.

"We can take our chances in the tunnels. You just need to show us where to go."

Ru shook his head. "The darkness is all he can offer."

He loped out and shut the door again. This time, there was a telltale clunking in the lock.

Demi lifted one eyebrow as Talie ambled to the bed and collapsed.

"Well that was stubborn. Not that I don't appreciate it, but still."

Talie sighed. "She'd never forgive me if I left you. No guarantee what kind of darkness he's talking about either. Any sign of your fancy queen powers returning?"

Demi sighed. "They're trickling back slowly, but they're of little use while the room is warded. I even tried to pick the lock the human way. So, unless you have a magic immunity to wards, I'm guessing his by the strength of them-"

Talie sat up with a pained squeak and held up her arm.

"I am! Because of this."

"Your armband thingies?"

"No!" She tore the arm-wraps free to reveal her wrist tattoo. "This. He put permissions in. I bet if you teach me how to pick the lock, or we do it together, we can get through. Assuming they're his wards and not Argon's."

Demi frowned. "How did you end up with that then? It

sounds very convenient."

"That's him all over. He gets side-tracked. I used to do it all the time when I was trying to keep him away from Molly, talk a lot so he gets distracted and goes back to his default state of issuing orders and wandering off to the next thing. Fiendish mind but scattered."

Demi still didn't move.

"Oh." Talie sighed. "I get it. This isn't some kind of trick. I'm not working against anyone, except him. Molly's enemies are mine, and since you're not one of hers, that puts us on the same side."

"You want what's best for her," Demi said quietly.

"Yeah. Are we doing this or what?"

Demi pulled out a ridged pin and a wicked smile dawned across her face.

"You know… you remind me a lot of Kainen sometimes."

Talie huffed. "Why do people keep saying that?"

CHAPTER FIFTEEN

MOLLY

"I still don't get why we have to have a meeting with them at all," Taz growled.

Molly nodded. "Seconded."

They stood in the Menagerie entrance hall waiting for the councillors from the other towers to arrive.

"Because we've got no proof the other towers had anything to do with it," Kainen said. "Because Demi told Milo and Ace this should be the first action in event of something like this, and because it gives us the upper hand to rattle them."

"Which is why Kainen is going to do the talking," Reyan added.

Taz's scowl deepened, but he didn't argue. As the air rippled and the councillors appeared, Molly shuffled closer to Taz's side.

I'm Talie, I need to remember they think I'm Talie. She folded her arms. *Which means I can be as horrible as I like.*

"Took your time," she snapped.

Kainen groaned under his breath and approached the group. Betula and Oak were as impassive as ever, but Tulip looked concerned. Argon had his hands clasped in front of his chest and could barely veil his glee.

"We're all concerned, as you can tell." Kainen gave her a warning look. "We won't keep you, but as Molly's been taken, and the queen, we need to treat this as a move of hostility and an incitement to war. As such, we'll be expecting a full investigation."

"Of course," Betula said. "We'll find out the truth immediately. Such a worrying business to have two royals taken so easily."

Kainen nodded. "So true, especially now the nobles have word of it. You know how these things are, and so many of them will be worried about the citadel's safety. Last time they were this worried, they all pulled their holdings, didn't they? I think the harder we work on the return of the missing, the better for all involved."

A glance passed between the councillors, shadowed with doubt. Molly had never taken Kainen for a diplomat, not really, but now she realised why he had the almost nervous respect of his court and so many others.

"Yes well, as we've said, we'll find out the truth immediately," Betula replied.

"Yeah, before we end up with an undead queen," Molly retorted sweetly. "That would go down great."

The flinch was satisfying enough, but also telling that only Tulip looked confused.

"A what?" she asked.

Molly smiled. "Oh, funny thing about rumours. With Fae, they have to have at least a grain of truth, and we know all about grains and truths in our tower. Given the reactions of three of you, there's more than a grain. Probably an entire silo of little truth grains. I mean, Phoenix had to end up somewhere, right? So one of you knows exactly what he's up to. Maybe even three of you."

The glances passed around again but Kainen and Taz flanked her, one on each side, letting her lead.

"You seem to have a lot of far-reaching ideas for someone who has no real power here," Argon said.

"No real power?"

"You're not a noble, not one of our council, not one of the royal family."

Molly leaned forward. "I am hers though. For that reason alone, I'd keep one eye over your shoulder if anything happens to her. Besides, you don't have to admit anything. We all know what's really going on. Are you all really so arrogant though that you think you're the only one not getting played? Please. Ask him one day. Ask him and watch how he twists the truth."

"I don't think-"

"Go on, ask him. Phoenix's gift is truth and he can weave it into pretty little knots to trap you with easier than breathing."

"You're upset, we understand," Oak said.

Molly frowned at him, until she realised exactly why his gaze hadn't shifted from her since he'd arrived. She clenched her fists inside the sleeves of her sweatshirt and narrowed her eyes back at him.

She strode up to them, using their assumption of her arrogance to find the edge of their warding. She lifted her thumb and subtly swiped it through the edge, quick to retreat her hands behind her back before anyone saw the spiked iron ring on her thumb. She angled one thumb up to Kainen as she surveyed each councillor in turn.

"If anything happens to her, everyone's going to be upset. Trust me on that."

"So, where are they being kept?" Kainen asked.

"At my tower of course, it has the most reinforcements," Argon scoffed.

His hand slapped to his mouth and horrified looks passed around.

Before Molly could taunt them, Taz's hand wrapped around her wrist and drew her back between him and Kainen.

"Compulsion? You dared use compulsion on us? The covenant-"

"Isn't in effect in Molly's tower," Kainen replied with a shrug. "You're free game here. Where exactly are you keeping them, and what's the plan?"

Nobody answered, and given the feral looks now, their wardings were locked down tight. Molly took a step forward and they veered back.

"No point chasing them all over the tower," she said. "If you're going to run around pretending to investigate, then do it."

She made a shooing motion with her hand and revelled in the indignant scowls as the council disappeared.

"That was…" Even Kainen struggled for words.

"A tiresome necessity now done," Taz said. "Let's go."

Molly bit her lip and looked up to find Sammy lurking at the top of the stairs. When she beckoned, Sammy all but slid down the banister.

"We're going after her," she said. "I need you to hold the fort. Keep any communications from the councils and other towers tied up, and if anything happens, defer to Butch and Fern, okay?"

She froze as Sammy hugged her tight, then gently patted her on the back.

"I will. Bring her home safe, Molly, please?"

"Um… how did you…"

"I know my sister." Sammy pulled back with a roll of her eyes. "She wouldn't have been here still talking if it was really her."

Molly gave her a weary look and took the rucksack full of supplies Taz handed her.

"Good point. Be safe and keep the tower standing. Do what Milo and Beryl tell you."

Sammy pulled a face. "Fine, if I have to. You really should employ me officially you know."

Molly nodded. "Consider it done."

She pulled out her orb with the maps from Mulberry on and set off toward the double doors. A flash of white whooshed over her head as Aurora took the lead into the labyrinth tunnels, and Molly flinched as pressure hit her leg and Arrow scampered up her limbs to perch on her shoulder.

"You know, don't you?" she asked.

He chittered in her ear as Kainen and Taz once again settled to walk either side of her.

"A bit like old times, isn't it?" Kainen said, far too cheerfully.

Taz grunted something under his breath, but Molly found the map they needed and focused forward.

They traced routes that Molly almost found familiar, but she couldn't shake the irritation that each turn and tunnel seemed far longer than she remembered.

"The route we should be taking will skirt around the-"

"Shhh!" Taz hissed.

Molly twisted around, looking for potential threats, but Taz had his head tilted sideways, his eyes wide.

"I can hear her! Oh thank Faerie, she must be out of whatever iron they had her trapped with."

Molly surged forward. "Ask her if Talie's with her!"

She waited, her heart pounding until she felt like it would leap right out of her mouth.

"Yes, she is, and they're working their way back to the centre. Demi says they'll keep walking and let me know if there's any landmarks to guide us all together."

Molly lifted her hand up, palm out and waited for Aurora's claws to drop around it.

"Can you find her?" she asked. "Can you find Talie?"

Arrow chittered indignantly as Aurora took flight. Before Molly could say a word, he was off into the tunnel.

"Will he know to come back for us?" Kainen asked.

"I have absolutely no idea." Molly set off after him. "He's a barrel-rat, knows directions like Fae can't even imagine. Aurora too, and she'll be faster even if she isn't able to track them. We just have to keep walking toward the Night Tower."

Taz had fallen silent but the relief on his face almost made Molly dizzy by sheer proximity. She wanted to put a million questions out for him to ask Talie, but she let him have his time.

"Demi's concentrating on keeping them warded for a bit," Taz said, the grouch back in his tone. "I've given her as many directions from that map as I can. Also, Talie said to tell you that she would do it again if she had to, but if you're going to be mad at her then do it once she's had a chance to sleep."

Molly's laughter snorted out loud enough to echo off the walls.

"When you next check in, tell Demi to tell her no promises."

CHAPTER SIXTEEN

TALIE

Talie choked down a relieved shout as the cell door finally swung open. With Demi guiding her hands, she'd managed to finally breach the lock and the wards, but even that had taken energy.

"What now?" she asked.

Demi waved a hand at the doorway and sighed.

"You go."

"What about-"

"There's still a ward stopping me from getting out but you can pass through them. The first person you see, glamour into them instead. Get yourself either out with others or into the tunnels."

"I'm not leaving you after all that," Talie insisted.

She glanced around. Her gifts were on almost non-existent as it was, but then so was her patience, and she'd had barely any rest since leaving the citadel to go and see Kainen in his court days ago. She couldn't remember the last time her stomach wasn't growling at her.

I don't know how long it's been since I saw Molly last.

She searched the doorway and the hall outside for

something, anything that might help her get Demi into the hall. Her gift sensed water rushing nearby, a pipe above their heads most likely, but she couldn't do anything with it.

Frustration, exhaustion and hunger brought tears to her eyes, and she couldn't bear Demi's sympathetic frown.

"Go, honestly," Demi said again. "I can hold my own."

Talie shook her head. "It's not fair! It's bad enough they're doing this, but they're *killing* people just to bring them back under control. And they want to kill you, he said so!"

"Ah, loads of people want to kill me. Hazard of the job."

Talie couldn't stop the growl rumbling out of her throat, so frustrated that it kept rumbling long after she was still again. The doorframe shook around her and she looked up to find the stone wall quaking. Tiny cracks appeared, then fissures, and she shoved her hands over her head as the water in the pipe rushed fast enough to burst free.

Demi was already on the far side of the room but she was grinning wide.

"I regret telling Kainen off for gifting you now to be honest," she said. "Don't tell him that though, his ego won't take it."

She strode through the newly gaping hole in the wall that had water gushing down the side of it and off down the hall.

Talie hurried on stumbling feet to keep up with her.

"He's actually a lot more fragile deep down than you think," she replied. "But don't tell him I said that either."

Demi clicked her fingers and summoned the arrow into

her hand. The wound had scarred over but Talie caught the tiny wince on Demi's face as she transferred the arrow quickly to her good hand.

"What now?"

Demi frowned. "Well, that little burst of joy has ruined your glamour for a start."

Talie looked down to find own arms and her longer, skinnier legs back in place.

"Oh. I don't have the energy to do that again I don't think."

"No matter. They'd have figured it out soon enough and the others are already on their way. I can't realm-skip out because of the covenant still in place on the other towers, and I can't make a first move against them either."

"Well I can."

Demi shook her head. "Probably not. You think I was lying when I called you family? That wasn't just to throw them off the scent of the glamour. Faerie and the nether know these things, and you're Molly's family now, which makes you ours."

"Not sure how I feel about that."

"Irrelevant, it's just the way it is now. Taz is all but ready to admit you to the group chat officially, and that's harder than getting crowned."

Talie snorted and the sound echoed down the hall.

"Can you run?" Demi asked.

"Not well, but I can try."

"Good, go."

Demi skidded around suddenly and Talie cannoned past her. She stumbled to a halt and twisted back to find

Phoenix racing toward them. Demi threw up a hand and Phoenix hit her warding so hard he rebounded back into the wall. Ru hurried into view behind him and stood with his arms hanging limp at his sides.

"Defence only, no harm done," Demi announced.

Phoenix glared at her, then at Talie.

"I should have known it was you."

"That's me, disappointing orb-munchers since the day I was born," she retorted.

"So, how's this going to work then?" Phoenix spat. "You ward until you're too tired to stand anymore?"

Demi shrugged. "Then we sit."

"I can wait."

Talie caught Ru's eye, which slowly slid to the door right behind where she and Demi stood. She lifted her eyebrows, a question. He nodded the tiniest amount and looked at the door again.

It might end up being a trap, or a cupboard. I don't look like Molly anymore either, unless he somehow can't tell in his vacant state.

Before she could doubt it, she nudged Demi's foot with hers and swung the door open wide. A long hallway sloped up on the other side, no sign of light, but Demi shovelled her straight through. She yelped as her shoulder pinged in agony and succumbed to the pounding of her pulse in the darkness as Demi slammed the door behind them.

"Now what?"

Demi muttered under her breath for several moments, then a flicker of pale blue light flared.

"Oh." Talie blinked back the burn of tears. "Molly does

that.”

She wiped her arm over her face as Demi started forward.

“I’ve warded the door to keep it closed but it won’t last long, so go as fast as you can. Any idea if we’re headed in the right direction?”

“No, but any way is safer than here right now.”

“True. I’ll try getting in touch with Taz as we walk.”

“That’s really useful, that mind link thing you all have.”

“It developed randomly. I know Kainen and Reyan use the shadows, but for me and Taz it was completely unexpected.”

Talie let the sound of their footsteps tapping on the stone fill the silence for a while. It was still weird to think she was wandering around with a literal queen, but Molly’s princess status had numbed her awe for royalty somewhat.

“Wait, I’m noble now, right?” she asked. “Featherdown gave me a title and a bit of land, so does that mean I can gift people?”

“Not unless you’ve sworn to one of the courts, no. I think that was why Celeste was so determined to go for gift replication, she was never allowed to gift as a princess and the citadel isn’t a Fae court governed by the rules of Faerie and royalty. It’s kind of more like a lawless land governed by the whims and wants of the nether.”

“Oh.” Talie frowned. “The nether gifted me though, but Molly thinks it was mostly to spite her because she was kind of rude to it.”

Demi chuckled. “Yeah, she’s fearless when she’s trying to save people from what I’ve seen. Being on the nether’s radar isn't all bad but it can get you into trouble too. Faerie court gifts are given with parameters, and courtiers are trained and warned to be sparing. The nether does whatever it wants."

"So Faerie is like the order and the nether is the chaos."

"It's a lot deeper than that, but kind of."

Talie ducked her head and focused on putting one foot after the other over and over with her heart sinking.

"Ah, there he is." Demi pulled a face. "He knows I hate it when he yells in my head."

"Taz? Is Molly with him?"

Demi cocked her head then rolled her eyes.

"Yes, and I've told them you're with me. They're in the labyrinth working their way here so we'll hopefully meet in the middle. Might not be heading toward the middle but I guess they call it a labyrinth for a reason."

Talie let that thought be enough, that Molly was safe on the other side. If she could get through the centre of the core and back beneath the Sunset Tower, Molly would stay safe.

"Can you tell her something from me?" she asked.

Demi nodded. "Make it quick. I need to conserve energy."

"Can you say that I'd do it again if I had to, but if she's going to be mad at me, do it once I've had a chance to sleep."

"Okay." Demi laughed. "That I can manage."

They soldiered on a few more steps before Demi chuckled again.

"She says no promises."

Talie grinned. It hurt, but she managed it and her mood lifted instantly.

"Tell her I'll use my title to buy her a Sticky Sap factory."

"I don't think that would sway her somehow. Try telling her you refused to leave me behind when you had the chance instead."

Talie shrugged. "We don't leave anyone stranded. We used to say as much in the gym back when everything was normal, not that everything's really ever been 'normal'."

"Normal's overrated. Not saying I wouldn't take a few weeks off if it was offered to me, but still. Maybe you could go visit this strip of land of yours instead."

"Featherdown said it was a like wasteland or something, not worth anything. I've never owned anything so a wasteland is still more than I had before, but I think if I'm going to take Molly anywhere it'd be somewhere nice."

"Fair enough. I'd visit it sometime though, let the land get to know you. Sounds silly but Faerie really does live through the land. You never know what you might unearth that others have passed by."

"Even if we do…" She hesitated. "Never mind."

Demi let her drop the subject. No doubt she was doing the mind-speak thing with Taz given the subtle quirks and changes of expression as they walked, but all Talie had were her own worries for company.

I'm the chaos and Molly's the order. Can we even make it work if we somehow survive all of this?

She flinched as a voice echoed into her head, different from her own but not much like the one the Omens seemed to speak with either.

Chaos and order can work together.

She frowned. *Okay, I'll bite, but only because I'm bored of this endless walking. What are you, Omens?*

There was a sense of amusement that wrapped itself around her in the dark, but it took a moment to answer her.

I am endlessly more infinite than the Omens. They were borne of my essence.

Talie eyed Demi, but she didn't appear to be aware of any shifts in the nether as they trudged along.

So, you're saying you're the actual nether, and you expect me to believe that?

Again that amusement wrapped around her.

Why would I lie? As Faerie takes charges and favourites among the Fae, so do I. I am perhaps more discerning, but I crowned the queen beside you.

Talie hesitated. *Prove it then. If you're the nether, skip us to where we need to go. Skip me to Molly.*

She expected some kind of ethereal slap in the face, but none came.

A mix of arrogance and foolhardiness. I can work with that. What would you offer the nether in return though?

And there it was. Talie sighed, which captured Demi's attention but she didn't say anything.

I have nothing to offer. Well, I have things but I'm not willing to part with them. All we have are our choices.

The amusement intensified until it seemed to cradle her body with energy.

Arrogant, foolhardy and wise. Very well. I gifted you the storms you weave to annoy Faerie's most recent irritant, and now I will gift you a shortcut through the nether in honour of your 'choices'.

Talie grimaced. That was definitely mockery, but she still had no idea who the voice belonged to and she hadn't promised anything.

"Ooh, look there's light ahead."

Demi sped up but Talie couldn't go any faster.

I'm supposed to believe that's your doing? she asked.

The tunnel opened out into a large cavern lit with faelight.

I don't control what you believe, Lady Rain. Only you control your choices.

Nobody except for Kainen knew about the Lady Rain thing. She hadn't received any documents about her land deeds or title from Featherdown yet, none she'd seen anyway, and she hadn't officially named a title for herself.

Before she could fully comprehend that the nether was merrily holding discussions inside her head, the sound of footsteps moving fast echoed behind them.

"Stop."

The monotonous male voice was loud even without any emotion behind it.

"Drat," Demi sighed. "No point in a bubble warding now to hide us now, and there's only one exit over there."

Talie clustered close beneath Demi's protection as they kept making slow shuffles backwards. She held onto her fraying nerves as Ru stomped after them.

"You tricked me."

Talie sighed. "Yeah, but Phoenix would have killed me otherwise. I had to let them think I was Molly."

"Molly…" He shook his head.

"She's safe, absolutely fine in her tower."

His gaze cleared a little. "Then there's no need for either of you. I promised to keep her safe, but not you."

He approached the edge of Demi's warding and reached out a fist to punch it.

"Okay, even if he is undead, the arrogance is still astounding," Talie muttered.

Demi winced as his landed, but when it didn't breach the protection he drew a small iron pipe out of his pocket instead. The moment he swiped a hole in the warding with it, Talie dodged to the side on wobbling legs and waved her arms to draw his attention.

"Oi! I think that and the threat before counts as first blood, don't you?"

"Yeah, you know what?" Demi rolled up her sleeves. "I think it does."

CHAPTER SEVENTEEN

MOLLY

Molly lifted her head as Aurora swooped above and disappeared back into the darkness. She wasn't sure where Arrow had gotten to, but he was fiercely devoted to Talie so she could only assume he was off in search of her.

"You can't fight the undead, little princess."

She shook her head as a familiar voice whispered into her mind.

"Is anyone else hearing things?" she asked.

Taz frowned. "No?"

"Kainen?"

"Um… I mean I tend to talk to myself, not sure if that counts."

"No. You can't hear the Omens whispering?"

Taz stomped on ahead, his wings lighting the endless walls of bare rock, but Kainen slowed his pace.

"What are they saying?" he asked.

Molly shrugged. "I can't fight the undead, apparently."

"Well, we should have maybe done more research before coming down here, but time sensitive and all that."

"Do you think they're literally invincible?"

"Nothing is invincible. Ridiculously hard to kill, maybe but we're not here to smash our way through to victory. We're here to get Demi and Talie back to safety."

Molly stayed at his side as they walked faster to catch up with Taz. He had taken over control of her orb and the maps but whether he was still communicating with Demi or not through their mind-link, she hadn't dared ask.

"You'll need a show of power to defeat the Night Tower. They have grown strong in their affluence, but victory can be yours."

Molly bit her lip and temptation warred with sense.

"How do we do that then?" she thought back.

"Let us free, let us help you to greatness, and we'll show you."

She snorted. *"Yeah, that'd be a no."*

"Don't engage with them," Kainen warned. "I'm not sure why I can't hear them, but they won't be able to help you."

"I know."

She walled up her mind against the endless whispering but the voices fractured her thoughts until she was dizzy. The cavern at the edge of the well of power still had signs of the previous fight with Phoenix chipped into the walls, and she almost stumbled over a rut in the ground.

Now that she stood in front of the Omens, their white smoke roiling behind the invisible boundary between the five pillars that Demi had walled them in between, they were utterly silent.

"I forgot she blocked it off physically," Taz muttered. "Milo!"

Molly eyed the crumbled rock covering the mouths of four other passageways leading further into the core. There'd be no shifting that amount of rubble by hand, not unless she wanted to be ancient by time she found Talie again.

Anxiety clawed through her chest and she rubbed her hands over her arms as Milo appeared.

"Go get Beryl," Taz said.

As Milo disappeared again, Kainen looked Molly's way.

"She has an elemental gift," he explained. "She can shift this, or crumble it, or something."

Molly folded her arms and edged toward the nearest pillar. She didn't grumble about Kainen keeping pace with her, never more than one step apart. The Omens puffed up in answer.

"Get away from there," Taz snapped. "Bad enough we let Demi and Talie get taken."

Kainen placed a soft hand on Molly's shoulder and guided her away again, but a subtle whisper that puffed after them.

"You won't defeat the undead or their maker without us."

She followed Kainen across to Taz as Milo and Beryl appeared. Beryl swiped a hand over her messy purple hair, and given the questionable state of her pyjamas, she'd been having a rest day.

She's meant to be upstairs helping Sammy. How long have we been down here?

"Right, what am I doing?" Beryl asked.

Taz waved a hand. "We need that rubble cleared."

"Ah, easy. Milo, go back and sit with the baby for a sec, would you?"

Milo sighed. "Okay, but if she cries I'm not getting sicked on again."

As he disappeared, Kainen leaned closer.

"Ace is the one who handles baby duties when they have to babysit," he whispered. "I've already petitioned Demi to have Milo as our court's official Baby Liaison Officer but she said no."

"He'd never do it in a million years. He'd quit."

They both winced as Beryl flicked out a hand and the top half of the rubble blocking the tunnel disintegrated into a huge puff of dust and debris. It hit Taz's warding and bounced off, but Kainen had shadows taking the brunt of the rest before Molly could even ward.

He grinned. "Maybe, but everyone at Demi's court has started bets on what who's going to be named Protector."

"Protector?"

"All noble and royal babies have someone named as Protector, usually before their first birthday. It's largely ceremonial but if something happens to the parents, the Protector is charged with ensuring the kid gets properly looked after."

"Does that work?"

The remainder of the tunnel blockage exploded and Beryl wiped her hands on her pyjama trousers.

Kainen grimaced. "For Beryl's kid? It absolutely will."

"She asked Demi?" she guessed.

He nodded. "I'd ideally want queens for when I have

kids, but that might be overkill. Say, if it ever does end up happening, you wouldn't-"

"Let's go," Taz barked, already halfway into the tunnel.

Beryl rolled her eyes. "A thank you isn't unheard of you know. Milo!"

He reappeared to ferry her back up to Baby Aurora, and Molly trudged with Kainen after Taz.

"Will Milo still be able to come to us when we're past the core in Night Tower territory?" she asked.

It was mostly curiosity but also due to nerves hastily redirecting the conversation, because she barely had control of her own life let alone having to be responsible for potentially protecting a future baby's.

"If the way stays clear, I'd imagine so. The covenant doesn't appear to be in place or we wouldn't be able to enter their tower at all."

"Does that mean they've drawn first blood then?"

Kainen nodded. "Faerie and the nether know things without having to be told, so yeah, I imagine the councillors being involved in kidnapping the queen of Faerie is enough to bring it down."

"Which should be a comfort, but if we can get into their tower then they can get into ours just as easily."

"They don't have the protection your tower now has from Demi though. Don't forget you also have your own backing. There's power in titles and in respect. Being a princess of Faerie is no small thing, if only you'd embrace it."

Taz had stopped up ahead with the orb-cast of the map splayed out in front of him.

"There's no way of knowing where exactly they're keeping them," he muttered. "Demi's not answering either but I can feel her energy, so it can't be far away."

He ducked with a curse as Aurora swept past him, and Molly bent low as Arrow scampered toward her and up her outstretched arm. Aurora hovered overhead and made a determined chirping noise, which Arrow backed up by chittering loudly in Molly's ear.

"I think they know already," she said.

Aurora wheeled around and set off along the tunnel, so Molly settled into the soft weight of Arrow clinging to her shoulder with his sticky front paws on her cheek. They followed an intersecting tunnel veering right and soon enough Faelights appeared on the bare walls.

One more turn and Taz halted.

"Voices," he hissed.

Kainen waved a hand to veil them in shadow and Molly flinched against the nearest stretch of wall. Taz joined them as the sound of footsteps drew closer, steady and unhurried.

"Veil your flaming wings for orb's sake!" Kainen hissed.

Taz grimaced. "They respond to my mood."

The footsteps grew louder.

"Well cheer up, or down, or whatever. It's taking all my effort to keep them from breaking through."

Molly held her breath with her sunshine gift ready in her fingertips, but the steps grew quieter until they faded to nothing again.

"That was close," Kainen said. "King of all of Faerie

and you can't even veil your wings."

"I'd like to see you try it."

"Will you two stop bickering like an old married couple," she muttered. "They've moved on but we'll have to be careful."

They only made it a few more minutes before another glow flickered up ahead. Shouts punctured the air and Molly pulled her protection warding tight around as her as she rushed after Taz toward an archway. As he stopped at the edge and peered out, his shoulders sagged.

Molly peeked around his shoulder even as Kainen did the same around hers.

Demi had her hands raised and Talie looked half-dead on her feet. Molly winced as she swayed and crunched lower to hold her balance steady.

"We should be careful," Taz muttered. "There's only one of them and Demi's got it covered."

The sheer relief in his voice seemed to be affecting his urgency, like he needed a moment to breathe. Molly's insides didn't get the message when Ru reached out with a small metal pipe and slashed at Demi's warding.

As a group of Fae spilled out from the other side of the cavern behind Ru in an ordered line, Kainen grinned.

"Nah, punch first and ask questions later I reckon."

He darted through the archway and launched toward the enemy in a merry whirl of glittering black shadow.

"Only a ridiculous person would punch first and ask questions later!" she shouted as Taz charged after him. Then she saw someone else throw their fist into the side Ru's face. "Crud, that's *my* ridiculous person. Talie, wait!"

She ran forward as Ru attacked again with the metal pipe, but Talie dodged and drew her dagger. More Fae spilled out from the tunnel on the opposite side of the cavern as Taz reached Demi's side, and Molly went for Talie while Kainen held the enemy back with shadow.

Talie swung around, dagger ready even though her hand was shaking around it, and her eyes lit up.

"Molly! Wait, you shouldn't be here."

Molly glared back at her. "You are in so much trouble."

Talie managed a weak smile.

"Hello to you too, Princess."

"You look like crud."

"Oh." Talie staggered sideways. "You look beautiful."

Molly sighed. "Are you still concussed?"

"Nope. Promised myself if I saw you again, I'd tell you more often, that's all. Oh, by the way, he's undead."

She nodded to Ru as Molly slipped an arm around her waist. Ru saw the arm and shook his head, but the movement was jerky.

"Molly," he said her name softly. "You shouldn't be here."

She frowned. "People keep saying that. I'm here to rescue my friends."

"I'm your friend." He hesitated. "I promised to keep you safe."

"The undead thing has him confused," Talie muttered.

"You belong in the other tower. You shouldn't be here. You wouldn't leave her."

"He means I wouldn't leave Demi when he thought I was you," Talie said. "But he's right, we need to get you both out of here."

"We need to get us all out of here," Molly insisted.

She led Talie toward Demi and Taz with one eye on Ru as he rotated to face them with a frown deepening his face.

"Ready to go?" Demi asked.

Molly nodded. "More than. The core isn't far but they'll be right behind us."

"We don't want them realising that though."

"I'll get Milo to come in and get us."

Demi shook her head. "We need to close the path again. We'll get him to get Beryl to bring the rock down again, then I'll go and re-ward."

"As much as I'm enjoying being the hero right now, it's wearing a bit thin," Kainen called out.

Molly bit her lip and lifted a hand to let her sunlight flare as he staggered back. Talie winced as the light flared bright enough to dazzle, but Molly held it steady as Kainen ducked back behind their line and held it with shadow.

"What's the plan?" he asked.

Talie tensed a second before silence fell on the other side. A small window appeared in the curling shadow wall, just enough to see out through.

Phoenix stood with Betula, Oak and Argon, and what looked like half the fighting force of each tower behind them.

CHAPTER EIGHTEEN

TALIE

Talie rubbed a hand across her chest the minute Molly wasn't looking. She massaged away the lingering ache amid the fluttering exhaustion and relief as Molly shuffled her across the cavern toward Taz and Demi. Her mind swayed out of focus as Demi said something, but she forced herself to blink the haze away. Until they were back under Sunset Tower, Molly wasn't safe.

She tried to straighten up, but Molly clung on and it was too easy to succumb, to slump against her again.

The sound of chaotic footsteps brought her head up and another flare of anger give her the strength she needed to glare at Phoenix as he stood with the other councillors and a host of guards behind them.

"This is bad," Molly muttered.

Taz glanced over his shoulder as the sound of even more chaotic feet moving fast echoed from the tunnel they'd emerged from.

"I say we play for time," he said. "I took the liberty of calling for reinforcements."

Demi's jaw dropped. "You brought the FDPs into this?!"

An explosion of arms and legs and jeering voices cascaded from the archway. Talie froze next to Molly, helpless with awe as the most disorganized defensive line in all of Faerie gaggled together in front of them.

"They stole you!" Taz huffed. "That definitely counts as drawing first blood."

"We did warn them earlier." Kainen jogged into place beside them.

Demi sighed. "I still can't believe you brought the FDPs all the way here just for this."

"He didn't technically." Ace strode among the ranks like a general marshalling an army. "He stormed into Queenie's office, yelled something about royal abduction into the Arcanium-wide comms, and the entire atrium was swamped by time we got back down there."

"Well what took you so long?" Taz asked.

Ace grinned. "They need a lot more training."

A chorus of outrage waved across the clustered Fae, but given the subtle thrum of wardings all around them, it was mostly for show.

Phoenix and the rest were clustered by their closest exit but turned in unison as Demi strode to the front of the line.

Talie tensed as Molly shook her head, then nodded.

"What, what is it?" she asked.

"Demi says this is still my arena," she murmured. "You can go-"

"Don't say it. Where you go, I go."

Molly sighed. "Stubborn."

"So I've heard, Princess. Let's go."

She wriggled free so that they were walking side by side, but the subtle brush of Molly's arm against hers gave her the tiny jolt of energy she needed to stay upright as they joined Demi.

"Your arena," Demi said quietly. "I'll lead if you need me to, but it should come from you."

Molly nodded and a mask of determination settled over her face.

"Well then," she announced to the waiting crowds. "You've got numbers but so have we. I don't want this to result in fighting, but you drew first blood by kidnapping the queen and a lady of the royal courts."

Talie stared at her in horror as Molly turned and gave her tiniest of winks.

"What goes on in our towers is no concern of the crowns, or the Sunset Tower's temporary leader."

Molly cocked her head and looked at Ru. A shiver of regret passed over her face as she lifted her hand and pointed.

"He was a member of my 'temporary' tower. Did he get a choice to be resurrected?"

A fervorous muttering started up on both sides. Talie eyed the wary glances on the faces of the councillors, then reluctantly she looked at the vacant glaze in Ru's eyes and the slack tilt of his head.

"Ru has worked for me for a long time," Phoenix said smoothly.

"Maybe, but you're taking people against their will without consequence." Sunshine burst from Molly's skin to halo her amid the gloom. "You were in charge of Celeste right? The puppet pulling the strings all along. Well, then that makes her actions your commands. The gifts she stole, the fairies she kidnapped from the royal realms, were all on your orders one way or another. Do you deny it?"

Even Demi gave Molly an admiring glance, but Talie didn't need to. She stood proud at her side with one hand ready on the handle of her dagger as she scanned for threats.

Phoenix smiled. "I think we're all getting a bit-"

"Go on, deny it," Molly pressed. "Word it properly, otherwise we all know you're the one behind the kidnappings, the gift theft, and all the poor Fae that have been resurrected against their will."

"There are many-"

"Not a denial," Molly snapped. "And given all these awkward looks, you councillors are well aware about all of it. What if it were your wives or daughters, or husbands or sons? How long until they come for your families next? It started with the artificers in Sunset Tower, and stolen fairies from the royal realms, and it ends here."

Given the violent cringing a second later, Molly wasn't expecting a rousing cheer from the group behind them. Talie couldn't stop the grin spreading across her face as she watched the doubt rippling through the enemy crowd. Amid the worried looks were far too many vacant stares, and her heart sank again.

"Pretty words, but I don't think you have the upper hand here," Phoenix said. "We'll be in control of Sunset Tower by morning, and you're not the only royal family outside the citadel either. Advance!"

The vacant faces moved first and everyone turned to look at Ace.

He shrugged. "Well? Go!"

Talie ducked against Molly as the FDPs surged forward as one crashing wave, wardings and gifts splurging out in astonishing coordination.

"They can't stand in a line but somehow their gifts are in complete compliment to each other," Molly muttered.

Talie grinned. "Just be glad this beautiful mess isn't against us. Are we fighting?"

"You look half dead."

"I'm fine."

"Can you use your rain gift?"

"Probably not."

"Ward?"

"Barely."

"Then what are you going to do?"

Talie rolled her eyes. "Don't need gifts to stab people."

They staggered sideways to avoid getting swept up in a maelstrom of gifts pinging and sizzling across the cavern.

"No stabbing," Molly warned.

"Oh come on!"

Molly barely ducked to avoid a thick piece of wood flying above her head but Talie already had her blade out to swipe it aside.

"Okay, no stabbing unless absolutely necessary," Molly amended.

She let her sunlight gift free and Talie shaded her aching eyes as Kainen hurried past. She didn't even have time to react as he grabbed her hand and slammed a kiss onto her wrist.

"I gift you with immunity to Molly's sunshine gift. Oh for orb's sake, stop pulling faces!"

Talie laughed, the pure hilarity of it choking back any hope of gratitude she might have managed as he darted away again. She could see through the sunlight clearly now, enough to see Molly already halfway across the cavern with hordes of Fae between them.

Talie started forward only to stumble back as Ru loomed in front of her.

"Out of my way," she shouted.

He shook his head, his face contorted with confusion.

"You're the enemy," he announced.

Talie gritted her teeth and summoned a weak warding.

"I'm on Molly's side," she said.

"She doesn't belong here. Once you're gone, she'll go back. It'll all go back."

"No, she won't. She won't leave me."

The truth of it slammed through her the same moment Ru lunged. She darted back on wobbly legs.

"She'll never leave me," Talie repeated. "She's mine. You can't have her."

Ru lunged again and his fist dented the edge of her protection. She winced at the blow and staggered under the weight of it. He hit again and again, and all she could do was keep moving away.

She sought for Molly in the carnage but amid the smoke and the worrying amount of dust crumbling down from above, she couldn't find her.

Her attention slipped and her foot hit something. She had no hope of knowing what, a body, a loose rock, but it was enough for her concentration to fracture.

Ru's fist came sailing through the gap in her warding with a flash of silver. The dagger in his fingers scraped across her cheek as she twisted her head away.

"TALIE!"

Molly's voice punctured the panic and the pain blossoming across her face, but it wouldn't be enough. She reached for her wrist anyway, for the dagger she kept there, and blinked. Her vision wavered, but given the minimal blurring, Ru had missed her actual eye.

Ru glowered down at her, a leviathan with no emotion on his face. He never saw the glow growing beside him, not until Molly body-slammed him to the side. She twisted with no grace whatsoever to put herself between them.

"Touch her and I'll kill you," she snarled.

Talie's heart found a rhythm again and she lifted her sleeve to her face. The blood soaking through made her head spin, but she forced herself to her feet all the same.

"I'm already dead, Molly," Ru said, his tone immediately soft amid the clash and bang of the fighting. "It's not right that you're here. You belong in your workshop. Celeste, she wants you home. I promised to keep you safe."

Molly shook her head. "Celeste is gone, Ru."

"She said to keep you safe. Made me promise it."

"I am safe." Molly reached behind her and found Talie's hand. "I am now. I've got family and friends."

He blinked. "You're safe?"

She nodded. "I am with Talie, with my family, I promise. We can help you somehow."

"Bad idea," Talie muttered.

"Stop fighting for him." Molly ignored her. "Come to our side. We can figure out how to help you."

"Him?" Ru frowned. "Him… Marcus?"

He glanced over his shoulder and the flash of pain on Molly's face disappeared as quick as it appeared.

"Yeah, him. He hurt me, a lot. Hurt people I love. I'm not safe with him."

Ru's rigid shoulders lowered. For a moment, his expression cleared, as if there was still a spark of actual life in him fighting to get out.

"I promised to keep you safe," he murmured.

Before Molly could reach out with her free hand, before Talie could try to grab it instead, Ru nodded.

"I think I always loved you a little. I remember that. Was it real?"

Molly sucked in a breath. "Yeah, I think it might have been."

A mask of determination fell across his face and he squared his shoulders again. Gone was the vacant expression, but Talie refused to let Molly step forward as Ru turned away.

"Let him go," she insisted. "He was gone long ago anyway."

"I just… I wish things could have been different."

Talie nodded. "I know, but he made his choices. That's what we're fighting for, right? Choices? We need to make ours now."

Even though the fight raged on around them, FDPs fighting with skill while the undead fought the front line of the enemy with unfailing automation, Molly eyed Talie's face with a grimace.

"It'll be fine," Talie said automatically.

"I know, but it's still bleeding. Here."

She pulled a hanky out of her pocket and pressed it to Talie's face. Talie clamped her hand over Molly's.

"Going to look a bit gruesome when it scars," she said.

Molly rolled her eyes. "You're a fighter, aren't you supposed to want battle scars? Besides, I'm not just with you for your sunny personality, Sunshine. Scars don't change that for me."

It was as close to being called beautiful as Talie could imagine getting, and from Molly, in her own way, it was the balm to every doubt she had.

"Right well, what do we do now then?" she asked.

They eyed the carnage as Kainen jogged past like he was out for a morning run, a grin on his face as he made soldiers out of shadows that danced and blocked and seemed to laugh with him.

"I might have something to interest you, Talie. You wanted yours and Sammy's birth history, right? I'll give it to you for nothing."

Talie rolled her eyes. "Thanks but now's really not the time!"

Kainen stopped jogging to raise both hands indignantly.

"It's always the time when it's family."

Talie's chest crunched, emotion clawing through her exhaustion. That was the second time someone had said it so easily, that she was family.

She had no words for him, because it still didn't feel real, but she managed the tiniest of smiles. As she turned her head to find Molly, a flash of light caught her eye.

A metal plate with serrated spikes around the edges spun through the air. She scrambled to her feet, chest heaving under the effort of scraping in a breath. She lifted her hands as if she could pluck the plate out of the air in time, as if her gifts were somehow able to burn the metal before it hit its target.

He never saw it coming.

She screamed as the plate hit Kainen's chest, spinning a lethal line across his black t-shirt. He froze, captured in surprise even as blood leaked through the slashed fabric, his protective leather jacket metres away on Molly's shoulders.

Taz lifted his head and saw her first, then what she was looking at. His face went almost as white as Kainen's, both realising the truth at the same time.

Taz's roar reached her as a dull echo, and she choked over a sob as Kainen hit the ground. Her legs buckled as she stumbled forward, the shattering scream echoing at her side as Molly ran faster.

Darkness exploded around them, and Molly met it with sunlight to keep the path ahead clear as the slash and swing of an ice blue sword tore through anyone mad enough to still be in its path.

"Do something!"

Talie faced the pit of roiling darkness, fists clenched as Molly dropped to her knees beside Kainen. She twisted around, searching.

"Fix this!" she shouted.

Choices.

The nether's voice echoed in her mind. It had warned her about choices, assuming it really wasn't the Omens playing tricks on her. She dropped to her knees with Molly at Kainen's side.

"We'll have to be quick," Talie said. "You need to trust me."

"Trust you to do what?"

"Kainen belongs to the nether, not Faerie. She can't save him, and neither can Demi or anyone else, but maybe I can."

Talie eyed the murderous carnage Demi was causing, Taz right beside her with bright fire crackling out of his entire body in retribution.

"How can you save him?" Molly asked with tears in her eyes. "Orbs, he's got the court, and he's... How?"

"You need to trust me," Talie repeated.

"To do what though?"

"Do you? Do you trust me? Let go of him."

Molly hesitated, then slowly retracted her hand. She must have sensed the warding that Talie raised between them to keep her out because her eyes widened and she reached out again.

"Talie! Don't! Stop!"

Talie lifted her head to look toward the swelling mass of darkness that was creeping down the hall, massing behind them. Demi twisted to face it, horrified, but Talie held its focus.

"Alright, nether. You said it's all about choices, so let's talk."

"Wait." Molly scrambled to her feet. "What!?"

CHAPTER NINETEEN

MOLLY

Molly screamed as Talie swayed and reached out with flailing arms to catch her before she hit the ground.

"Hold the line!"

Demi's roar echoed nearby as Molly settled Talie beside Kainen on the ground and clawed for a pulse with shaking hands. She couldn't find one and choked over a frantic sob when Demi knelt beside her.

Molly couldn't stop searching Talie's neck with one hand and her wrist with the other, determined to find some sign she was still in there. Boots thudded beside them but she didn't look up.

"Let her go, Molly," Demi said.

She sounded almost as distraught as Molly felt, but Molly couldn't make her hands move. She flinched when Demi prised her fingers free, and her sunlight gift pulsed uncontrollably as someone she vaguely recognised pressed his hands to Kainen and Talie's foreheads.

"Don't move them," he warned. "Don't change anything. There's death waiting, but something other is going on."

A loud cracking noise brought everyone's heads up as Taz joined them with his chest heaving and his eyes storming with retribution.

"They're holding too strong," he snarled. "We need to start withdrawing everyone back to the core."

Demi nodded. "Beryl and I can seal the tunnel behind everyone and ward it back up."

"Tyren, are they…" Taz nodded to Kainen and Talie.

The man still holding their foreheads grimaced.

"Holding on but we can't move them yet, not until we're sure. There's no guarantee whatever's anchoring them isn't fixed to here."

"I can stay here with Milo under a warding," Demi suggested. "If they wake, Milo can take them through."

Taz shook his head. "It's too dangerous. I won't let you."

"It's all we've got. Get everyone falling back first, then take Beryl to close the gap. When she's done, Milo can take me through to ward it. Maybe whatever's going on here will have sorted itself out by then. Molly-"

"I'm not leaving her."

"I know you're upset but-"

"I'm. Not. Leaving. Her. I can ward and I have gifts."

Demi sighed. "Fine. Taz, pull everyone back and get Beryl to wall us in."

"There's no guarantee it won't resurrect the covenant. Either all of us go, or none of us."

"This is going to be tricky." Milo wrung his hands as he surveyed the chaos. "Tyren, if I put my arms around you and hold onto them, we should be able to get through the nether without you letting go."

The man with his hands on Kainen and Talie's foreheads nodded.

"Do what you have to do. We just need somewhere we can bunk down for a while. They're both holding on but while his life-force is slipping and sliding because of the injury, hers is jammed somehow."

Molly watched as Milo surrounded Tyren. She opened her mouth to insist she go with them but they vanished before she could say a word.

The fractured lines of their forces were still holding firm but Phoenix seemed to have wave after wave of unseeing faces marching forward to attack over and over. A couple of them hit the ground barely even twitching with their eyes still wide open. The other councillors were gone, but Phoenix was still visible.

Molly surged forward and ducked under Taz's arm as it swung out to catch her.

He's going to pay for this.

She hit a wall of energy and stumbled back.

"Not happening," Demi insisted. "Come on, we need to retreat now. There are too many of them."

"I'm not letting him get away!"

She rounded on the warding holding her back with a fist, but Demi waved a hand and Molly got dragged along behind her on flailing feet.

"She's over-reaching her authority already." The voice slipped into her head. *"We could still help you, still bring them back."*

"Go away," she snapped.

"I know you're hurting, Molly, but-"

"Not you."

Demi slowed as they moved through the archway.

"The Omens? I hear them too. Just ignore them. Whatever they promise won't help any of us."

Molly wanted to shout that she already knew that, she'd been the one to fight them before, but she kept her mouth shut as Fae cascaded past along the tunnel and Beryl hurried toward them.

"Reyan found out," she said. "She's upstairs with them now so we need to get this done and fast."

Demi nodded. "I'll ward the last of our lot through and count you do- Please tell me you didn't bring the baby!"

Molly leaned sideways to see Baby Aurora in a baby carrier strapped over Beryl's back. Given the closed eyes and the little fist smooshed calmly against her mouth, she was used to the normality of Fae mayhem already.

"That would be a lie if I did," Beryl said placidly. "Sammy had a few things to handle for the tower so she couldn't watch her either, and obviously Meryl and Cheryl are here with Hutch. Besides, she's an FDP in training, you said so."

"She's not even one!"

"Well, start them early, that's what I always say. Are we doing this or what?"

Demi rolled her eyes and lifted both hands to send a wave of sheer power radiating out.

"She's holding on by the way," Beryl added. "Your Talie. Tyren told me. Whatever's going on, she's tough. She'll make it back."

"Beryl!" Demi snapped. "Three, two, one!"

Beryl whistled a piercing note. A loud rumbling started up and Molly flinched back as the rock overhead started to crumble. Beryl tipped her head back and pulled a face.

"Okay yeah, I hit the wrong note. We might want to run."

Molly twisted on her heel and fled with Demi beside her and Beryl already several paces ahead with Baby Aurora still fast asleep on her back. Molly slipped and slithered over the ground under the shaking of the falling rocks behind them growing ever louder.

She lifted her head, lungs ready to burst, to see Taz airborne with his fiery wings flared. She didn't even slow her pace, knowing he'd go straight for Demi first, but even as he pivoted in midair between them, Milo appeared beside her and snatched her arm.

The nether wound around them, her protests and laboured gasps lost in the swirl, until her bedroom bloomed around them and the light seared her eyes.

She lifted a hand and blinked through the dazzle until she saw Kainen and Talie on her bed with Tyren between them and Reyan kneeling at Kainen's side. Apologies frothed to her tongue and died unspoken as Milo disappeared.

He reappeared a moment later with Beryl, then Taz and Demi arrived together unaided.

"Milo, bring every healer you can get," Taz insisted. "Get Marvin, Marthe, and anyone from the Fauna Court."

Milo nodded. "I've asked for Marthe but the Oak Queen refused. Marvin's on his way via Lolly for any tinctures that might help, and Cerys is sending her best."

Molly wrapped her arms around her waist. Sammy would hear something any moment now, or find out they'd returned and come storming in. She'd see Talie pale and unmoving.

I can't let her lose her sister, not after everything else they've lost.

She noticed Taz and Demi slip into the hall and inched after them.

"It's warded but things are so unstable now," Demi muttered. "The covenant has fallen which means it's only my wards that are holding everything in, and I don't have as much sway here as I would in any of our realms."

"Yeah, and the only person who might have the power to pull them back from the brink is my mother, and even then it would require sacrifice."

"She won't do it," Demi said sadly. "Talie admitted that someone had contracted the towers to kill me, and until I know who, I don't trust anyone but our own."

"She wouldn't."

"Wouldn't she?"

Molly bit her lip and edged away from the door.

I'm leader of the Sunset Tower. That gives me certain powers. She dredged up her Fae connection and focused on her memories of the Oak Queen's court. *I can do this.*

She imagined the throne room of the summer court and let her energy spool out. A subtle breath of air brushed her face and she cracked one eye open only to find herself face to nose with an enormous wooden throne.

The marble pillars and dark patterns in the pale marble

floors looked even more imposing as she glanced over her shoulder, then back at the hint of brambles curling across the feet of the throne.

She flinched back down the marble steps until she was a suitable distance away, but the pink slippered feet belonging to the person seated on the throne were also covered with ominous looking thorns.

"Molinia, I am not expecting you."

There was amusement in her grandmother's voice, and a hint of warning, but absolutely no surprise, as if her unexpected arrival was inevitable.

Or planned for all along.

Molly pushed the thought aside and stared at the woman in front of her. The Oak Queen tilted her head with smile that had no warmth in it whatsoever.

"What brings you to my court unannounced?"

CHAPTER TWENTY

TALIE

Talie opened her eyes to more darkness, but it was the kind that had depth and meaning. She couldn't lift arms or legs, couldn't feel she had a nose to twitch, but her mind was sharp and there was a blessed relief that she had nothing to feel pain with for once.

"You are bold, I will give you that."

The voice came at her, echoing around her and through her.

"Are you the nether then?" she asked.

A ripple of amusement curled through her awareness.

"In a way. The nether, Faerie, the Omens, the Fae. All are products of the same system. You think darkness of the nether is evil, but the pearlescent swirl of its ability to carry you through realms is enchanting. You think Faerie is benevolent because it gives food and life, but forget to fear the very poison it creates. Why do you think Fae whisper about the nether and the mysteries 'it' holds, but Faerie, oh 'she' is all-giving warmth."

Talie opened her mouth but the sharp breath stalled in her throat. She had nothing to counter that with. It sounded like the kind of wisdom Kainen might have spit at her in one of his amused moods.

Orbs, Kainen.

"What price then?" she asked. "For the Lord of the Illusion Court? I'm here to ask you to save him."

"I find it hard to imagine you are in the habit of 'asking' anything. Is this a demand, Lady Rain?"

"No, but he's among the best of them and I will save him if I can."

"So are countless others at their end. Are you going to come and beg me for their lives too?"

"I- can't."

A knowing 'hmm' vibrated around her.

"Long ago, when the realms were pure chaos, when life and darkness would move together through the sway, all were to have a choice. The darkness, the life, the storms that would rage and the trees that would grow to withstand them. The Fae that would form into being."

"That's what Molly's been saying all along."

"Ah yes, the crown princess with the attitude."

Talie didn't snort, but the sensation of it echoed into the nether somehow all the same.

"She has her moments, but she's good where it counts. She believes that everyone should have a choice."

"They do."

"Not when others are using power to crush them they don't."

"So you take power to crush those abusing power?"

"I'm not asking for power! I'm asking for..." A favour? She wasn't even sure.

"A trade then? What would the princess of Faerie's summer blood offer the nether in exchange for one man? Perhaps a hundred years of service?"

Talie hesitated. "What do you mean by service? No offense, but I don't want to be stuck in darkness."

A lofty sigh rippled around.

"You assume that's all the nether is? Darkness? What fun would that be?"

"So again, what kind of sacrifice? Lose an arm or am I tied to a rock for decades or something?"

The nether's amusement danced around her like frissons of energy tingling over skin.

"Nothing so dramatic. The pit beneath your citadel has long been needing a custodian. Someone to manage it, let it grow. It's been hemmed in for far too long and the beings within are getting... restless."

"That's it?" Talie frowned. "Look after the well of power?"

"For a hundred years, yes. Too many wars have been fought over this part of me now. It's time I had some peace."

"I'd be tied to the citadel? I can't leave?"

"Perhaps you could, but you would be responsible for returning to it. It is your home, is it not? This is the cause of all the excitement that has the energy roiling, this building of stones and glass?"

"Fifty years," she demanded.

"You are in no position to make demands."

"If I'm tied to the citadel for a hundred years, that's my life all but over."

"And yet, if the princess is who you say she is, the one championing a choice for all, she will also have the choice to stay with you for the length of it. She's why you hesitate, no?"

Talie grimaced. "Molly… she wants to see the whole of Faerie. If I do this, I can't."

"Perhaps not, but you wanted a choice and there is always a price to be paid. Life in exchange for life, except I am offering you a chance to keep yours. Both Faerie and I have not always been so benevolent in situations past."

"Choices." Talie sighed. "They'd all tell me I don't have to do this, that it's not my burden to bear. He'd tell me not to do it, and for that alone it's worth the sacrifice. Okay, done. I can still leave the citadel now and then to visit people, right?"

"Who knows? Perhaps you will not even need to, if they choose to visit you instead. Very well."

"Wait, what does a custodian even do?"

CHAPTER TWENTY ONE

MOLLY

"What brings you to my court unannounced?"

Molly grimaced. "We need your help."

Her grandmother smiled, and it wasn't the smile of kin to kin, but of a queen surveying a pawn.

"Interesting. I can only imagine what trouble everyone has gotten themselves into." She cocked her head. "A moment."

Molly stood frozen as the queen descended her throne and swept through a door behind it.

Okay, that was weird.

Molly bit her lip as she waited. The rash decision was looking more and more idiotic with each passing second, but if the queen could somehow help Talie and Kainen then she had to at least try. She tested her connection to ensure it was still holding strong in case she needed to realm-skip away again, but a soft tapping sound echoed behind her before any hint of it materialised.

She just about managed a protection warding as Marthe hurried into the throne room.

"Oh, your highness." Marthe dipped into a small bow.

"Hi, Marthe. I'm not staying long."

"Now is really not a good time for you to be here," Marthe muttered, her words barely audible. "Her Majesty is not in a good mood and I can't intervene."

Molly's heart sank. "What's happened?"

"It's a mess. The family is all but broken. Even Princess Mayflower has even retreated her entire entourage to Arcanium to ask for sanctuary."

"That bad?"

"I'm afraid so." Marthe grimaced. "The court, the house, it's even refusing to allow her majesty access to Master Taz's conservatory."

"His… what?"

"His private conservatory. It was a gift for his birthday, a safe space away from the whims of his siblings, but the queen has always been able to wield over it where needed, until now. I only wanted to warn you."

She turned and scurried back out of the door before Molly could do more than part her lips in worry. She flinched as the queen swept back in and resumed lounging on her throne.

Molly tried to realm-skip away, failed, and faced the queen with her heart sinking.

This was a huge mistake, and I doubt I can even trade my way back out again either.

"So, what has happened to the Holly Queen in all this mismanagement?" the queen asked.

"That's your first question? Not 'is my son alive'?" Molly couldn't stop the instant laugh of disgust rippling out, all hope of diplomacy dashed to nothing. "Demi's fine and so is he. I'm here because they mentioned you might be able to bring a couple of people back from some kind of stuck living death they're in."

"Why would I do that?"

"One of them is Lord of the Illusion Court for a start, and the other one is my girlfriend."

"Neither of them are of much concern to me. We can get you another girlfriend easily enough, and the Illusion Court can be re-assigned."

"What- no! They're my friends, my family. The citadel needs help."

"So I hear."

Molly stilled. "From who?"

"From many people. It's not just Demerara's pet rejects that have titles you know. There are also several ancient lineages that still owe loyalty to *my* court."

"Would the councillors of the other towers be included in that?"

The queen smiled. "Perhaps."

"Great. So you installed Celeste as a watcher and a puppet, and given the contents of your library here, probably helped her with the whole gift extraction thing. Are you in league with the councillors to get the Fae duplication plant up and running as well? Are you on Phoenix's side? Is he on your payroll, or are you on his now?"

"Careful, Molinia. Accusations must be founded in fact by our laws."

"Well it's an orbing fact that you're not denying it!"

Her voice shattered through the air and a moment of

tense silence passed between them. The queen would likely blow her off the face of Faerie but she had no hope of escaping either so the whole thing was hopeless anyway.

She went for it.

"Are you the one that told Phoenix to have Demi killed?"

The queen tilted her head to one side, her lips pursing as she rubbed a forefinger back and forth slowly across them.

"I imagine many would have a vendetta against the young queen."

"Again, not a no, and you'd be right at the top of the list I reckon."

"I am growing tired of this attitude, Molinia."

More spiky thorns wound up the legs and edges of the throne, and Molly knew then that any indulgence the queen might have shown her was long gone, nothing more than a pretty illusion to veil control.

Definitely a mistake coming here.

She focused her connection on her bedroom instead, on home, willing with everything she had to be realm-skipped back.

Nothing happened.

"Oh dear." The queen laughed. "I might have allowed you in, but do you really think I'd allow you out again?"

Molly firmed her warding around herself with a shaking hand clenched at her side. She had no hope of holding it against a queen, but she couldn't stop the retort slipping from her lips all the same.

"I guess not after May managed to escape. That's five

kids either defected or incarcerated now, right? Leaves you with zero."

The queen didn't move but Molly buckled as a sudden splash of agony clawed over her skin and down to rattle her bones. It tore a scream from her lips as her knees smashed against the marble floor, her hands too, and she crunched in on herself further as the pain receded.

Stupid, stupid, stupid.

Tears leaked out but she lifted her head the moment she managed to catch her breath. With a snotty inhale, she clambered to her feet.

With the queen's laughter echoing in her ears, she ran.

She stumbled out into the hallway and toward the stairs in her panic, but the staircase whipped away from her and she slammed into a wall instead. Her nose throbbed from the impact so she twisted in the direction of the kitchens next. They wouldn't hide her from the queen, or be able to help her, but they might miss snatching her if she made it past them.

"Where can you go?" the queen taunted. "This is my domain."

Molly stumbled over an enormous plant pot that fell in front of her, half-expecting the vines inside to reach for her legs. The hallways twisted as she staggered on and her mind swam as she ended up briefly running along the ceiling dodging ancient chandeliers.

She came to a halt at the end of a hallway with no doors or windows, just a tapestry.

Even if I hide under it, she'll find me.

The tapestry fluttered a corner as if in answer. Footsteps

tapped an unhurried rhythm behind her and she tensed herself ready to fight.

The tapestry lifted again, little more than a breeze ruffling through, but Molly caught the flicker of light from beneath it.

With the queen still advancing at a mockingly slow pace, Molly twisted under the tapestry.

A short length of stone corridor stretched ahead with light and the scent of earth at the far end, so she stumbled toward it.

"How is that possible!"

The queen's furious shout rattled the stone but Molly kept going until she burst into the brightness and all hint of noise fell away. Warmth wrapped around her and a strange sense of familiarity, of peace.

She remembered what Marthe had said before, that nobody had been able to get into Taz's conservatory, the safe space he'd been given for his birthday. She had no doubt the queen would be able to, but perhaps there were safeguards against her too, wards wrapped into the gift that kept her out.

She'd be in here already if she could. Either that or she'll wait it out to toy with me.

Molly eyed the abundance of plants towering overhead, hues of green, blue, purple and red all around her. A small cluster of cushions waited nearby, along with a pile of books.

As she approached the cushions, an extremely unimpressed looking lizard blinked at her.

"Er… okay. Hi, lizard. Are you poisonous?"

The lizard blinked again and she flinched out of the way as he plodded toward the nearest tree with a black and red striped trunk. Molly watched him clamber up it and disappear into the foliage.

"Weird," she muttered. "Okay Molly, think. This must be Taz's secret place, but even if the queen can't get in, that means I can't get out. So first step, see if there's anything safely edible in here."

She wandered through the unorganised cluster of plants until she found a bush full of white oia berries and a yellow apple tree nearby.

"Okay, if anyone's listening, Taz or whoever, firstly come get me, secondly, I'll pay you back for these when I can."

Nobody answered, but it was more to stem the sudden surge of hysteria that was bubbling up in her chest. She took a couple of apples from the tree, along with a handful of oia berries, and went back to the cushions.

I guess I'm stuck here. She threw the oia berries into her mouth.

A loud crash tore the air and she almost choked on the berries when the ground juddered beneath her. The sound of shattering glass came next, and she raised her warding as several of the plants were blasted aside by a wave of heat.

The conservatory warped into a swirl of disorientation and Molly landed on her knees back in the throne room with the queen several paces in front of her.

"You will come to heel, or I will make you." The sugary-sweet voice was at odds with the storm raging in the queen's eyes. "You are my granddaughter, blood of my great lineage, and above all you are Princess of Faerie. I can use that to make you obey me for that if nothing else."

Molly stilled. Every part of her ached and she wasn't sure she had any energy left to wield gifts, but that didn't change who she was.

Choices. That's what Talie had said to the nether. *All I ever wanted was the choice.*

"I abdicate my title of Princess of Faerie."

She said it quietly but clearly. Even the air seemed to hold its breath as the queen stared down at her.

"I refuse to accept it."

"I abdicate my title as Princess of Faerie, and of the Royal Oak line." Molly wobbled to her feet with her blood roaring in her ears. "I am leader of the Sunset Tower in the Grand Citadel of Faerie. Any move you make against me will break the ancient covenants."

"You dare dictate to me covenants that I oversaw made?"

"Yeah. I allowed Demi's court freedom in my tower because she's family, and the other towers broke the covenant today, but we never extended any of that to the Oak Court or your branch of royalty. You attack me, you break the covenant."

The queen lashed out a hand and one of the marble pillars exploded to infinitesimal shards. Molly flinched but her warding held against them. She pushed the surprise aside as the queen stalked to stand toe to toe with the edge of it.

"Then I shall send you back to the other councillors to

deal with. They want your head as it is. It was mostly *my* influence that has kept you safe thus far."

Molly let that sink in, but she couldn't find it in herself to be in any way thankful.

"Maybe, but don't forget you as good as admitted that you're behind all of this, the threat to the Holly Queen's life, the plant of Celeste in the citadel in the first place, your involvement in the gift extractions and the resurrection of the undead, all of it."

The queen's anger roiled around her like a cloud and the vines growing up around the edges of the wall quivered, as if even the queen's power was afraid of how she might choose to wield it.

"That would violate the very laws of Faerie, surely?" Molly pressed. "The very entity you supposedly align your rule with, and you're picking and choosing which bits of her you obey."

She knew the queen would kill her. It was inevitable, but then it might make it into the Book of Faerie that Milo had mentioned a lot. At least Demi and Taz would know from it that she went down fighting on their side.

Talie will know, assuming she's not waiting for me in the dark already.

She folded her arms across her chest and faced her grandmother down for one final shot.

"The Fae that Faerie cares for, loves, nurtures and provides her life for, are being mined like metal for ridiculous wars that none of them want. It's only the greedy few who would benefit from the sheer deviance of cruelty that are fighting for this. Kind of makes you the villain in the whole thing really, doesn't it."

"They are nothing without me," the queen raged, debris and vines whirling around her. "The nobles, the courts, the citadel, they are all nothing."

"They are *everything*, with or without you, and I'll die fighting for them if I have to."

Her vision flickered, or perhaps it was the lights in the room as the queen snapped and lifted a hand.

"You could have been so promising. Now I'll have to start the family dynasty afresh. Then again, what is another twenty or so years of waiting."

She threw out the lifted hand, fingers splaying, and Molly thought of Talie. The sheer power radiating toward her should have lifted her off her feet at the very least.

Should have.

She looked down at the arms she'd lifted automatically to defend herself with, and at the willow branches wrapped around them. They wavered in front of her like angry tendrils, as if she'd cast the wall of willow holding firm against the queen's fury all by herself.

Dizziness crashed against her forehead and bubbled up her throat, burning her chest as her limbs gave out. Only the willow binding her held her in place, but the bubbling and burning and dizziness morphed into an astonishing rush of air, like freefalling from the highest level of the tower.

She lifted her head, bemused as some unseen entity dashed the Oak Queen to her knees.

"What will you do with her, Queen of Oak and Sunshine?"

Molly gasped as a soft voice echoed in her head. The willow branches around her limbs pulsed against her skin, a gentle caress.

"I don't-" The words slithered on her tongue. "I…"

I don't want to be queen, but if I reject this now, if I somehow get back to the citadel to fight for it, we may well lose. As queen, I could save so many.

"Do I have a choice?" she asked.

A rustle of laughter echoed behind her, but the voice that answered was still in her mind.

"Of course. Choices are all Fae have."

She nodded. "Good, that's what I've always asked for. But, if I did say yes, can I move my court to the citadel? Or nearby at least?"

"Oh child, what does it matter where a queen sits, as long as she rules fairly? Kindly?"

Molly flinched as something wrapped around her wrist and she looked down to find a crown of real oak leaves woven with white daisies.

"Treachery!" The Oak- *old* queen shouted. "After all the centuries I've ruled, kept the balance!"

The willow branches receded but the reminder echoed in her mind.

"What will you do with her, little queen?"

Molly bit her lip. "She's still technically family. It doesn't feel right to kill family. I'm not like her."

The old queen lunged forward and Molly's hand lifted on instinct. A spasm of power flew out from her fingertips, not fire but a whip of pure sunshine that circled the old queen and had her veering back from it to shade her eyes.

"Okay, this is bad." Molly reached into her pocket and pulled out her orb. "Please work, please. Demi? Holly Queen? Um, Demer- oh, hi."

"Hi?! Where the hell are you?"

Molly had no idea what 'the hell' was, but it sounded like some kind of curse word the way Demi was snarling it. Her face loomed into pearlescent clarity in the middle of the throne room.

"WHERE IS SHE?!" Taz all but screamed it in the background.

"Is Talie okay?" she asked.

"Seriously?" Demi sighed. "Yes, she's still the same, but where in the name of Faerie are you?"

Molly choked over a hysterical snort.

"Name of Faerie, funny thing that. Um… I'm kind of a queen now? And the old one's still here, so I could really use your advice."

Demi stilled for several seconds, long enough that Molly worried the connection had frozen.

"Wow. Okay, do I have permission to enter your court then?"

"Of course." She nodded frantically, which made her head pound. "Oh, as long as you mean no harm to me or mine. And assuming I'm even in my court. None of this makes much sense."

A ripple of air flickered a moment later and Molly flinched as Taz launched past Demi to grab her shoulders.

"What's going on?" he demanded.

She couldn't summon a suitable answer, not sure what even counted as one, but his eyes widened as he looked around and saw his mother on her knees in a circle of sunshine.

"That's... not something I ever thought I'd see," he said.

"I don't know how any of this works." Molly fought the sudden emotion in her voice. "She kept me here, then tried to attack me when I wouldn't play along. Then I abdicated, I think, and she tried to kill me but Faerie surrounded me and now she says I'm queen. Faerie says it, I think. It's a voice in my head, kind of like the Omens except it's different."

Demi sucked in a sharp breath. "Will you tell me your full title, please? The name you were given?"

Molly tensed at the formality, but the echo of it danced through her mind.

"Queen of Oak and Sunshine. And look, I have this oak crown but it has daisies in it."

"It's very nice," Taz said gently. "This must be a huge shock for you."

Molly turned around but any hint of willow was gone from behind her. She stood with the crown still in hand and her grandmother seething inside a boundary that she was holding without even having to focus on it. When her knees buckled, Taz caught her.

"Can I go home?" she asked.

Demi nodded. "There will be a lot of paperwork I'm afraid, but I can lend you Milo on a diplomatic temporary basis."

"Okay. Have him deal with Sammy, and maybe if he can train her a bit? They didn't get on the best last time but she was grieving then and she wants to be part of things. Orbs, Talie!"

Taz still had a hold of her shoulders so she couldn't wriggle away. As he eyed his mother again, still in her sunshine prison, Molly got the unnerving impression that he was trying not to grin. A lot.

"How about we say anything that is offered by our court to yours over the next three days is a diplomatic gift," he suggested. "That way you don't have to worry about whether your court would owe ours or not. That okay, Dem?"

"Of course. Three days and then we'll have a sit down and sort out any treaties you might want. What do you want to do with the situation here though?"

Molly grimaced. "What do people usually do when this happens?"

"It doesn't." Demi shrugged. "I guess the last time it did happen was when she deposed the old king and killed him. Then he got brought back and that was a lot of hassle, but it's your decision to make. I can offer you space in the Forever mountains as they're my domain. She did try to kill you without cause after all."

"Oh, and you. I almost forgot. She all but admitted dealing with Phoenix to have you killed. Or maybe it wasn't him, it might have been the councillors. She's definitely been pulling the strings, the citadel, Celeste, all of it."

Demi closed her eyes in torment as Taz went ramrod straight. His wings flared out in a crescendo of flames and he stalked to the edge of Molly's sunshine boundary.

"You did *what*?!"

His mother eyed him with contempt, a queen reduced to a person as she rose to her feet in one swift movement. She had centuries of power, of practice and experience, but Molly couldn't ever imagine developing that level of grace even if she had forever.

Before any threats could spew from his lips, the throne room door slammed open and Marthe ran in.

"I'm getting all sorts of conflicting informa- Oh, Master Taz, Mistress Demi, you're here. Communications were down. But it's…"

She slowed to a halt and her words fell away as she saw the old queen, then her gaze narrowed on the crown still in Molly's hands.

Without a word, she dropped to one knee with her head bowed.

"My queen."

Molly looked at Taz for guidance but he only shrugged.

"She's a bit overwhelmed right now, Marthe," he said. "Are you saying your shifting your allegiance with the crown rather than sticking with its previous owner?"

Marthe sighed. "It pains me to do it, but things haven't been right for a while now. The sun has been setting for a long time, and then attempting to kill Mistress Mo- the- orbs, which title do you prefer to be addressed as?"

Molly cringed as Demi and Taz did their best not to laugh.

"I, Molly's fine?"

"Hmm." Marthe's gaze sharpened even though she hadn't yet lifted her head. "Perhaps 'my queen' will suffice for now then. I swear my service to you, your court and your rule. If it suits, I will continue to operate the court in your best interests until such time as you see fit to release me. It would be my honour."

"Okay, um, thanks? But I'm hoping to move back to the citadel. Faerie said I can move the court wherever I like. It's still not fully rebuilt yet, and they might not want me anymore what with the whole royal thing-"

"Nonsense. May I rise, my queen?"

"Oh orbs, yeah, you don't need to bow or kneel or anything like that, please."

"Hmm." Marthe stood up with a frown. "It shouldn't take me long to dissolve the court, petition the nobles to re-swear allegiance, and of course we will need to pack."

"Pack?" Molly asked.

She didn't argue when Taz discreetly joined her side and slipped a reassuring arm around her waist.

"Of course pack. The Royal Oak Court is ancient, and with that comes the wealth and antiquities accordingly. There may be some trifling quibbles with nobles who wish to remove their service but I wouldn't worry too much. The courts serve the queens after all."

Molly blinked. "I think I need to sit down."

"Good idea. You go have a rest, my queen. I'll handle everything. The citadel, you say? Hmm. We already have a host of nobles with patronage in various towers. About time someone shook them up and gave them something to do. Might I suggest I reach out to the Nether Court and the Fauna Court on your behalf? Oh, and the Revels and Flora Courts of course."

Molly eyed Demi, who gave the tiniest hint of a nod while staring with dedicated determination at one of the nearest statues.

My statues now, orbs.

"Okay, yes please. But when we get to the citadel, do you remember Sammy?"

"Of course. Exuberant young girl, very friendly."

"Right. She's been helping me a lot while I've been ruling the Sunset Tower, for all of three weeks. Can you involve her please? Train her maybe?"

"And make it seem like her idea no doubt. Of course, you only have to command, my queen."

"Marthe?"

"Yes, my queen?"

"I know there's meant to be a way of doing this, but if I ever command rather than ask, at least in private or among family, let me know."

Marthe's lips twitched. "Yes, my queen."

She hesitated as her gaze drifted across the old queen still mutinously silent inside the boundary.

"It was an honour once," Marthe said softly. "I really mean that, but my loyalty will always be to the family, not the head wearing the crown."

With that ominous confirmation lingering in her wake, Marthe swept from the room and Molly sagged against Taz.

"So, Forever mountains?" Demi prompted.

She waved a hand at the old queen and Molly nodded.

"If you think that's best for now. I just want to go home. If- When Talie wakes up, I want to be there."

Demi strode forward and Molly sensed the warmth of her sunshine give away to the icy chill of Demi's control. She allowed it as the sunshine around the old queen turned pale blue, and Demi realm-skipped away with the old queen in tow.

Molly clung onto Taz as he took another lingering look around the throne room.

"I really need to learn how to do that now, don't I?" she said wearily. "The realm-skipping thing."

Taz smiled. "One step at a time. I won't miss this place to be honest. It's no secret that my mother's been a pest for a long while now, even since before Demi took her crown, so it's a relief to have someone kind to work with again."

Molly didn't reply as the nether wrapped around them, but she sensed a subtle wariness about it, as if it didn't want to wrap too tightly or delve too deep.

Only when her Menagerie bedroom reformed around her and she saw Talie and Kainen on her bed, with Tyren slouched between them still holding their foreheads, did she look at the crown in her hands.

Reyan was sat beside Kainen and looked up with swollen eyes.

"Demi will do an announcement," Taz said.

"Announcement of what?" Milo asked, then cocked his head. His eyes grew wide and his mouth dropped open. "Oh orbs, that… I need to issue statements!"

He disappeared, only to reappear and bob a weird half-bow, half-twist in Molly's direction.

"I will need to ask you to sign some things, reaffirm some treaties," he gabbled. "I usually deal with Marthe, but-"

"Marthe has sworn for Molly already," Taz said. "Whatever you need, continue dealing with her, and if not her then go to Sammy."

"I… do you want me to call you by your title?" Milo asked.

Molly grimaced. "No I orbing well do not. Not in private anyway. I still haven't processed any of it as it is."

Milo disappeared again with another frantic mini-bow and Molly settled herself on the bed beside Talie.

"I'm not going to ask," Reyan said, her voice raw. "I know the other queen might have been able to tether them to Faerie and draw them back, but I won't ask."

Molly bit her lip and passed a fingertip over Talie's cheek.

"I don't know how. I would if I could for both of them, in a heartbeat."

Talie's skin was too cold and her chest squeezed tight.

All this power and I don't even know how to use it. She sniffed as the tears fell down her cheeks. *Come back to me. Come stomp around and glower at everyone and grumble at me. Just please wake up.*

CHAPTER TWENTY TWO

TALIE

"Tell me again, what does a custodian have to do?"

Talie sensed the nether's impatience even without any actual hint of body to sense it with.

"You guard the well. It is a vortex of power, one of the few places I am pure and potent still. The last time the custodians failed, the Omens were born out of the greed and malice of Fae. Your role would be to stop them managing it a second time so I can exist in peace."

"Ah, and getting the Omens out first no doubt?"

"Well, it would be a nice goodwill gesture on your part."

"But I'd go back to my normal life, just tied to the well? Can I at least be in the citadel?"

"I don't see why not, but the boundary of the citadel walls will be your boundary. Things are changing and evolving fast even now."

Talie nodded, her exhausted mind struggling to think through the countless loopholes.

"And Kainen will live, as he was before he got cut down?"

"In all his delightfully wicked glory, yes. He is one of my favourites but in these matters, even I am unwilling to intervene."

"Unwilling or unable?"

The cramped silence suggested she was toeing a very thin line so she let that one slide.

"One hundred years tied to the citadel," she muttered to herself. "Not like I wanted to go anywhere else much anyway, but Molly did. She might visit though, or even choose to stay with me. And Kainen will be around, I probably owe him that much."

The nether was suspiciously silent and the sense of patience echoing around her was driving her mad already.

"Alright. I'll be your custodian for a hundred years, in exchange for returning him back to his life the way he was before, and me to mine the same."

The amusement returned. *"I am delighted. You have the makings of greatness, and I do need to ensure there is adequate balance on all sides."*

"Er yeah. So you're going to send me back now, I'm guessing."

"Unless you have more you wish to discuss?"

Talie hesitated, the no tilting on the tip of her tongue.

"I don't, but maybe there's something you would? I mean, maybe send me back now because Molly's going to be flipping tables, but I could come and see you at the well now and then, if you wanted."

She couldn't work out the sensation that radiated around her that time, but the nether had said that Faerie tended to get all the attention.

"That would be... sufficient."

Awkwardness threatened to choke her, even though she still didn't get the impression her conscious mind had a throat to choke. She hoped that wouldn't be a regular part of the custodian job, but thoughts of Molly had her desperate to get back.

"Wait! Can I have one thing?" she asked.

"What would that be?"

"A day off." She hesitated. "A day to leave the citadel, maybe once a month?"

"Once a year."

"Okay, a week then, a week a year."

"Five days per year, to be taken whenever you choose, and be grateful."

Talie nodded. "I get that Faerie and you are all powerful and stuff, but I reckon you'd be pretty bored without us."

"Well the queens will be delighted to hear that."

Talie frowned. "Demi maybe, at a push, but why would the other queen care?"

Amusement rippled, powerful and loud.

"Remember that we can get bored, Lady Rain. No doubt you'll be visiting Faerie with the belligerent one soon enough. Tell her that it's her move."

"Er... sure. Do I just close my eyes then? Will he be awake or do we need to have the healer come for him?"

The nether didn't answer but the sensation of arms and legs and scrapes and agony slammed back into existence with enough clarity to confirm she was in her body again.

"TALIE!"

"Let her breathe."

She didn't recognise the second voice but Molly shouting her name through sobs was enough to keep her gasping air into her lungs. She tried to open her eyes, then managed a garbled mumble.

"K- Kai-"

"Orbs, what in the name of Faerie is going on? Why is everyone clustered around my bed? Wait, this isn't my bed."

She recognised Kainen's voice, weak and shaking but still there, and the warmth that radiated over her limbs.

"Talie, answer me."

Molly's compulsion slithered over her body and she choked out a laugh.

"I- oww."

"Can you open your eyes?" Molly asked.

There was a demand in Molly's voice that sounded deeper, more ancient, even though that was ridiculous.

Maybe she has Faerie princess powers she hasn't used on me yet that I don't know about.

"Let her go, Molly." It sounded like Taz that time.

"No."

"Orbs, why am I surrounded by so many stubborn women. Fine. Hold on then."

Someone else grabbed her other hand and a whisper of amusement wound around her again, shortly followed by the communal rumble of voices.

"Lips open," Taz said. "You need a tonic quickly, and I don't trust Molly not to choke you with it right now."

Molly huffed, the most delightful and thrilling noise Talie could ever remember hearing.

"I wouldn't. Give it to her by all means, then I am going to kick her. A lot."

Talie grinned as something pressed against her lips and she struggled to drink down whatever liquid someone was giving her. The fruity taste of the purple tonic hit her tongue and she let it swim through her system for a minute before she risked opening her eyes.

"Hi, Princess."

Molly scowled even as tears streamed down her cheeks. Talie had a vague memory of the core and dark rocky ceilings before the nether, but her mind was still clinging to the one person she needed who was currently dripping tears all over her face.

"Don't you 'hi, Princess' me!" Molly sniffed loudly. "What were you thinking?"

Talie settled back and closed her eyes with all-encompassing relief.

"I took a risk, but it worked. Kind of."

"What do you mean, kind of?!"

She winced. "Well, he's alive which is good, and I'm alive which is also a relief. I just had to promise the nether I'd be the custodian of the well of power for a hundred years."

Silence. She cracked one eyelid open to find Molly staring down at her wide-eyed, jaw hanging open.

"You WHAT?!"

"I had a choice, and I made it."

"Talie! You only just got those choices to make! You can't sacrifice your freedom now."

"I can."

"You can't!"

"Literally can. It's my choice, right? Or are you speaking for both of us now?"

"No, but-"

"There we are then. Do I need to get up yet?"

Molly grimaced and closed her eyes tight. It took a long while before she opened them again and sucked in a sharp, purposeful breath.

"Can you get up?" she asked.

"I don't think so."

Talie twisted onto her side with a grimace, only to find Kainen staring at her.

"Why does my chest feel like it's been sliced open?" he asked.

Talie sighed. "Because it has. You died, but the nether brought you back."

"From what vague memories I have of it, you saved my life."

"Orbs, you were awake?"

"Not exactly, but there's a sense tethering us together, and I know I owe you big for it."

"Forget it, and don't start getting weird on me just because I saved your life," she muttered. "You still need the actual wound patching up properly as well, so I wouldn't look down."

"It does look really grim," Reyan said. "You want to do it here or at home?"

"Said the lord to the laundry maid," Kainen mumbled.

Reyan sighed. "Yeah, he's back to normal. I'm going realm-skip us home if that's okay with the queens?"

"Yeah, we should be fine for a bit," Demi said from somewhere nearby.

Talie frowned and turned her head to look around the bedroom. Kainen and Reyan vanished, along with another man who Talie vaguely recognised as the one who'd given her the vial of iron in the Rose Tournament, which left her with Taz, Demi and Molly. She couldn't see the Oak Queen anywhere, not that she'd recognise her.

"Queens?" she asked.

"Never mind that now. What happened?" Molly demanded.

Talie sighed. "The nether kept whispering to me while I was under the Night Tower. I don't know, it spoke to me, and it didn't sound like the Omens. So I called to it and everything went dark. Then I made the deal to save him."

"What is the deal exactly?" Demi asked.

"One hundred years as custodian. I'm tied to the citadel for a hundred years. But I get a five days outside every year."

She waited for the inevitable. Molly stared, her jaw slack and her eyes wide, but she didn't say a single word.

Talie's heart plummeted.

She wants to see the world, to travel. She ended up leading the tower because they voted her in but she never wanted to stay here forever.

"So, yeah." She grimaced. "What was that about queens? The nether said something about queens as well, but I don't think I've ever met the other one."

A look passed around the others and she used the residual strength from the tonic to sit up.

Molly hesitated. "Yeah, about that. You've missed a lot with that mad stunt."

Talie stared in absolute horror as Molly held up a crown, intricately woven with oak leaves and white daisies. When she didn't say a word, too stunned and confused, Molly reluctantly put the crown on her head.

"Surprise."

# CHAPTER TWENTY THREE

MOLLY

"Talie?" Molly sat on the edge of their bed as Talie continued staring at her. "Say something."

"You're the queen."

"Well, one of two, that I know of, but yeah. It's a long story-"

"You're the Queen of all of Faerie."

"Queen of Oak and Sunshine technically, but yeah."

"And the other queen? Your grandmother?"

"Replaced."

"By you."

"Yeah."

"Right." Talie inched back down on the bed before wincing back up to sitting again. "Are you hurt?"

"A bit, but it's fine."

"Is she needed right now?" Talie demanded.

"We can hold everything off for an hour maybe," Taz said. "But the other towers will be regrouping and we need to announce Molly's appointment and discuss what needs to be done about the well and the Omens and... yeah. You have maybe half an hour."

"Half an hour then."

Molly's chest warmed as Talie took her hand.

"I'm not sure who's meant to be shouting at who anymore," she murmured.

Molly smiled. "Me at you, definitely, but I won't. Don't ever do that again though, promise me."

"We'll leave you be for-"

A loud bang cut Demi off, and Molly's sunlight exploded on instinct.

"Orbs Molly, turn it down a bit!" Sammy lifted a hand to shield her eyes in the doorway. "What's this about a royal court here? And apparently Milo of all people is now my personal liaison? No offense, but he's already filled half the office with random papers. Oh, and there's a summons from the other councils as well, and can someone explain to me why Marthe is here measuring the entrance hall?"

Molly groaned. Loudly. She managed to tamp down on her gift but she had no idea how to even begin.

"Right, new plan," Demi announced. "Molly, brush your hair and put the crown back on. We get the jump on the gossip first-hand. Sammy, Molly's now the Oak Queen of Faerie, but we need to sort the other towers out and the well's safety before we celebrate. I'll call Cynthia now and we can get the gossip part over with."

Sammy stared at her, then at Molly.

"She's finally speechless," Talie muttered.

Sammy frowned. "Do I bow now?"

"Not in private." Molly sighed. "Milo's going to advise you on how courts run. Marthe's heading up the royal household. Talie's looking after the labyrinth and the core. Assuming you want to help still?"

"Of course I do! This is amazing! Now it makes sense why Milo was muttering about the size of the office." She turned to leave then raced across to give Molly a hug. "My sister is the queen of Faerie!"

"I- that's not- wow, she moves fast," Molly said.

Taz handed her the daisy crown. "Let Demi do the talking, okay? Oh, and whatever you do, when Marthe mentions a coronation, tell her you only need the symbolic version."

"When's the real coronation then?" Talie asked. "Won't she need that for it to count?"

"Faerie crowned her so no, but in the eyes of the nobility a big show will be expected eventually."

Molly wiped a hand over her face and put the crown on, then held still when Talie reached up to adjust it.

"You'll make a great queen," she said softly.

Molly frowned. "We still need to discuss all this. You're tied to the well now, and I have an entire court to consider as well as the tower, so-"

"Showtime." Demi strode back through the doorway with an orb ready in hand and a silver circlet of holly and ivy on her head. "Talie? You in or out?"

"What?" Talie's eyes widened.

"Taz stands at my side for stuff like this."

Molly bit her lip as Talie hesitated.

I can't ask her to, it has to be her choice.

Talie stood slowly and Molly let herself relax as they all stood side by side with her and Demi in the middle.

A subtle sheen of green flashed over Demi's orb and a woman's overly excited face loomed into the middle of the room. Then the dots connected and Molly froze at the sight of the most famous host of *The Faerie Net*'s most popular news orb-cast.

"Thank you, Cynthia," Demi said. "We're bringing you the breaking news live from us personally so there's no chance for confusion. Less than an hour ago, the Oak Queen Tavania conceded her crown, title and rule. As of now, Faerie has claimed and crowned her successor. I have every faith that Queen Mol- Molly or Molinia?"

Demi glanced her way and Molly couldn't say a single word, her throat frozen in horror.

"Molly," Talie muttered.

Whether she was prompting or making the choice for her, Demi nodded.

"Fair enough. I have every confidence that Queen Molly will prove herself in the coming days and years, and I look forward to the future we can all build together. So yeah, thanks."

"Well that certainly is astonishing! And that, dear viewers, is our breaking exclusive, brought to you of course by-"

Demi swiped her thumb across the orb to silence it and lowered her arm with a ragged sigh.

"Was that live?" Molly asked.

Demi nodded. "Yep."

"And I look like this."

"Yep."

"And I didn't say anything."

"Nope."

"Oh. Marthe's probably not going to take that well."

"Neither does Milo when I do public appearances, ever, but we move on."

"Your formal speaking is getting wordier though," Taz said loyally.

Molly turned to Talie in the absence of any sanity elsewhere and dropped her head to Talie's shoulder.

"What do you need from me?" she asked. "As in, what does a custodian need for the well?"

Talie's shoulder tensed beneath her forehead and a moment later she stepped back.

"The nether said the Omens came into being the last time the custodians failed, made from the greed and spite of Fae like us. It wants them gone and to exist untainted in peace."

Molly wrapped her arms around her middle in the absence of Talie's touch.

"Until then, we have to manage the councillors first and find some kind of stalemate to hold them off," Demi said.

Talie sighed. "There is one person who might know more. Why don't you lot sort out the councillors and I'll find what I can in the meantime."

"I can help," Molly offered.

Her heart sank when Talie gave a strange, sad little smile and headed for the door.

"You're still leader of this tower, Molly, even if you are queen too. The councillors will expect to see you."

Not Princess, but my name. I can't even remember if she's ever called me Molly before.

She watched Talie go with anxiety swelling in her mind, but she couldn't deny it either.

"She's right. Tower first. I guess we invite the councillors here then on safe ground?" she asked.

"I couldn't agree more, my queen."

She whirled around at the sound of Kainen's voice. He had a bandage peeking over the collar of his shirt and his eyes were ringed with shadows, but his grin was as feral as ever.

"Reyan said I was getting under her feet at court, so here I am to get under yours instead."

Molly didn't even hesitate as she crossed the room and threw her arms around his middle.

"Okay, oww. Also, seriously? Royalty doesn't hug! Haven't I taught you anything?"

CHAPTER TWENTY FOUR

TALIE

Talie walked up the lanes, awed to see the locals still going about their business without any clue that she'd almost died, that Molly was a literal queen, and that there was a war brewing deep inside the core of their home. The fragile signs of growth were flourishing, because of course in a few short weeks Molly had listened to what her people actually needed and let them do what they did best without trying to control them doing it.

She skirted around a cordoned off hole in the lane and headed across to Butch's shop. He lifted his head as she approached and hovered a few paces away.

"Hello, Young Talie. I actually have some wares to offer you this time."

His smile was tired and worn, but there was a spark in the depths of his eyes, a knowing that she'd seen before countless times but never understood until now.

"You know things," she said, in the absence of anything concrete to accuse him of.

He sighed. "And now so do you. I felt the subtle shift and wondered how long it'd take the new custodian to find me."

"Yeah, it's me, sorry."

"I'm not. You're a solid choice." When she pulled a face, he chuckled. "You love the citadel and you know what it's like to struggle for it. You can understand the dangers of power and greed, far more at such a young age that I and my brethren did at many years older."

"You were a custodian."

"Yes, one of five. They all succumbed to the powers or perished in one way or another, but I endured."

"So, the councillors aren't custodians?"

"No. They were Fae-appointed or installed by insidious masters over the years. It has been a long time since I've met another custodian, and now by the feel of the nether, I can finally hang up my hat."

"Wait, you can't stop now!"

He laughed. "Oh yes I can. I've given far more to hold the boundary, to manipulate minds and sway confusion to keep grasping hands away from the well. Celeste evaded me and I failed there, but then the nether sent me champions to carry on the job. You and your young friends have done more for this citadel in a few short months than I and mine managed in decades."

Talie wiped a hand over her face. The realisation of what she'd agreed to, the enormity of it, was beginning to crush what little resolve she'd built up.

"How? How am I meant to keep the well safe? How did it even go wrong in the first place? I don't understand any of it."

Butch eased himself onto the small bench beneath his

shop's window and tapped the space beside him. The bench was meant to be full of produce but rebuilding would take time.

Will Molly even be around to lead the tower now that she's queen? Her court is an entire realm away.

She sat next to Butch and did her best to shove away the rising irritation as she bounced her leg against the edge of the bench.

"It was supposed to be a new world," he began. "The Oak Queen had just decimated the old king and her power was fragile. We knew she would turn to the nether, either through fear of it overtaking the power of Faerie or to use it. If not immediately, there would come a time where she would want it for her own ends."

"Yeah, I haven't actually met her in person but she sounds like the type."

Butch sighed. "She wasn't always that way, but time comes for us all in one way or another. All we have are the choices in front of our feet."

Talie sighed. "Always choices. I'm not crazy about mine right now."

"Well, perhaps not, but you made them all the same, and for the right reasons clearly. Faerie grew powerful under the queen's control and the citadel was nervous, so we made the Omens as a protection. It was only meant to be a deterrent but they were far too powerful."

Talie thought back to the swirling white smoke and the image of Molly's dead body from a previous time they'd clashed flickered in her mind. She shuddered even as anxiety gnawed at her insides.

"We built a big stone prison over the well," he continued. "But some of the councillors refused to find ways to get rid of them in case we ever had need to use them. We never did, but they remained. They grew volatile and the nether stopped whispering to us. We'd failed in our duty to protect the well from the queen and the entities we'd made."

Talie stared out across the lane. Sunlight glowed outside the citadel glass but they were still keeping to the seasons and the air was chilly around them. People hurried up and down past the shop, wrapped in coats and scarves, the thud of heavy winter boots echoing on the stones.

"And I'm supposed to be the next line in fixing it?" she asked.

Butch nodded. "The nether has claimed you and my time is done. I'll be able to finish out my days here in peace. Any advice you want, it's yours, but it's your time now."

"Is there any way to get rid of the Omens?"

"We never found a way to vanquish them entirely, but they could be contained. It was an emergency failsafe we added into their creation, but every time any of us mentioned using it, others would insist we needed to keep them for our own safety. The citadel grew and the glass walled us to keep the outside out as much as the inside in."

He gazed out and Talie gave him all of a moment before pushing the issue. Every second spent away from the Menagerie was time away from Molly, and she still had to figure out how to guard the well while also finding a way to swear herself into Molly's new court without being able to be physically present in it.

"So, this containment..." she prompted.

"Oh, they'll slide into a small containment each as easily as a large one. Mind they are captured and separated though, otherwise they'll be unimaginably concentrated together. You'll need material from each of the five towers to craft a suitable vessel. Metal, wood, grain, glass and something organic. Once those are blended in equal measure, the Omens won't be able to choose which to break first and it'll confuse them."

Talie stood. "That simple?"

"And that difficult. Equal measures exactly isn't an easy thing to achieve."

Molly could do it.

"Right, thanks Butch. I'd better go and tell the powerful ones."

"You're the custodian now, Young Talie." He laughed. "You are the powerful one."

She grabbed a small bag of grain from the edge of the bench and held it up.

"Owe you?"

He nodded. "Call it a gift, because I'm so orbing *relieved.*"

Talie stared after him as he eased to his feet with a weathered groan, sauntered into the shop and shut the door firmly behind him.

Somehow, that's not in any way reassuring.

She set off back down the lanes, barely noticing the snatches of feverish conversation about Molly's new title and the citadel's exciting new future. Stuck in her

thoughts, she didn't remember that Molly would have
called a meeting with the other councillors, not until she
stormed into the entrance hall and interrupted it.

CHAPTER TWENTY FIVE

MOLLY

Molly surveyed the councillors as they realm-skipped into her entrance hall. With Demi on one side and Kainen on the other, she was beyond protected. That didn't stop a flicker of nervous anticipation amid the roar of fury burning in her chest.

"We don't bow to crowns here," Argon spat.

Molly smiled. She had refused to put a dress on despite Marthe's hissed insistence, and owned her sweatshirt and jeans as proudly as Demi did. There would be plenty of time to establish herself in finery when the nobles inevitably came courting. Their whispers and favour was the true currency of Faerie, and she would need it in order to build her tower back up until she could leverage enough coin from the royal court to share around.

"Nobody said you had to," she said. "Yet. But Faerie has crowned me and this is still my tower."

"Barely. We'll be rescinding any claim you have on it through the covenant."

Molly eyed him up and down. Slowly. Dismissively.

"The covenant you broke by kidnapping a queen? That

bond was obliterated, so let's not waste time clinging to it." She lifted a hand to her head and removed the daisy crown. "If you prefer, I'll talk to you as leader of the Sunset Tower only. I'm surprised you don't have Phoenix with you though. You all seemed so cosy before."

Betula sighed. "We do what we must to keep the balance of our towers safe. Phoenix has influence with many of the initiatives we've been working on for years now, and we can't negate that."

"You mean he tricked you all into being beholden to him?"

Nobody answered, not a sound present other than the grinding of Argon's teeth.

"So, you tried to summon me, and now here we are," she prompted. "What do you want? I won't be conceding my rule of this tower, at least not until the situation is calm and most likely not after. Either we agree an impasse and continue to trade, or you declare yourselves openly against us and my tower will function alone."

"How will you manage without our trade?" Oak demanded.

"She'll have trades with the rest of Faerie," Demi said smoothly. "Nothing set in stone yet, but I'm more than willing to treat with my fellow queen now there's no covenant blocking us, citadel or no citadel."

The councillors exchanged a fleeting glance, but Molly thought of Talie half-dead under the Night Tower and let the retribution flow sweetly through her veins.

"The choice to trade or retreat is yours. I'll let you return to discussing it behind my back, assuming you've no other threats to issue for the moment? Not planning on kidnapping any more of my family?"

She headed toward the staircase with Demi and Kainen at her side, but turned back at the bottom to face the rest of the council again.

"Tell Phoenix if he wants to concede, I'll have a cell waiting for him. Any allegiances he ever had with the Oak Court are now so far beyond dead even he won't be able to resurrect them."

She strode up the stairs with her pulse pounding, trusting Demi to keep the containment on the entrance hall until the councillors were gone. She peeked just once at the top of the stairs and sagged to see it empty.

"It never gets any easier," Demi announced cheerfully. "Well done though."

Molly stood at the top of the stairs with her hands welded to the banister as Demi lifted the containment and sounds of the Menagerie and the wider tower outside filtered in.

She held in the groan as Sammy rushed up to her waving a small scrap of paper.

"This just came from one of the councillors. I thought they just left?"

Molly took the scrap and eyed the hurried scrawl.

"Tulip wants to return with a few 'trusted confidantes',", she said. "She didn't say a word when they were here, but she wasn't with them in the Night Tower."

"Doesn't mean she's trustable though," Demi warned.

"I know, but I get the feeling she's not happy about the way they're doing things. I'll see her and make sure I find out the truth."

"I can compel them if they're unwarded," Kainen said.

"Thanks, but I can compel myself if needed."

Demi shook her head. "Mistake. Don't turn down help from people you trust. When they offer to share the load, I'd advise you to take it."

Molly hesitated as the urge to refuse bubbled up, to insist she could handle it all herself. Then Talie walked up the stairs and her mood lifted.

"Yeah, okay. I doubt they'll come unwarded but you never know."

Her nerves tilted as she caught the frown on Talie's face.

"How was the council?" she asked.

Molly sighed. "Huffy. No resolution though."

"Right. I spoke to Butch and it turns out he used to be one of the custodians of the nether. I figured he might know something considering he's ancient, but turns out he just wants to throw the cap at me and retire."

"Orbs, I never even considered that, but he has been here a long time."

Talie nodded and stuck her hands deep in her pockets with a moody shrug.

"He also said we can't get rid of the Omens but we can contain them. We'd need something from each tower though to build a vessel, and the vessel has to be made with equal amounts from each tower."

Demi frowned. "Urgh, not this again. Okay, I'll check in with Milo and get him looking for any suggestion of how we do that."

"I'll stick around and assist her majesty, your majesty," Kainen said with a grin.

Molly rolled her eyes. "Do you- oh."

In the few moments she'd turned her head, Talie had disappeared.

She must have moved fast. Realisation hit her. *Or she used stealth, which means she didn't want to risk me going after her.*

Demi realm-skipped away and Molly looked to Sammy next.

"Can you send an invite back to this for me?" She waved the bit of paper. "Add that it's conditional on them meaning no harm to me or mine."

Sammy raced off and Molly covered her face with her hands.

"You're doing really well," Kainen said.

"I don't know. I just want the Omens gone so the nether is safe and Talie can mind it while I deal with court stuff up here. I don't even know what court stuff is!"

"If you're sensible, it's mostly smiling and waving. Build a court you trust and do it early. Let them earn their place through loyalty. Pick people based on what they want. No sense asking someone who hates people to charm nobles, that kind of thing."

"You're thinking of Talie," she mumbled.

"Orbs, she'd be a disaster at diplomacy. You'd have to rename it the Royal Court of Bruises and Stabbings. But let Marthe take the brunt because she loves it, let Sammy challenge the old traditions for you, and when you think something is simple, assume it's not."

"My head hurts."

"Welcome to leadership. It sucks, but it can be okay sometimes. Ah, showtime."

He indicated with his hand to the entrance hall below and Molly dropped her hands quickly to her sides. She couldn't do anything about Talie going off on random disappearances, but she could deal with the problems in front of her.

She walked down the stairs with a warding around herself to find Tulip with three other Fae she didn't recognise, two women and a young man.

"I won't bow, but congratulations on your crown," Tulip said.

"Thanks. I'm here as leader of my tower right now, so what did you want to see me about?"

Tulip hesitated. "What happened last night, I had no idea about until it was done. The other towers don't trust my morality not to get in the way apparently."

"How awful for them."

"Indeed. I and my companions here are tired of being glossed over. This is River, head of the Forestry Guild of the Morning Tower."

A young woman with a brisk air, large brown eyes and brown hair with tints of green that Molly assumed was good for camouflaging gave her a tentative smile.

"Briar, who unofficially runs the metal plant in the Sunrise Tower."

The brisk-looking woman with a sheet of black hair tied back from her face, stiff overalls and a blue shirt with the sleeves rolled up, nodded in greeting.

"And Allium, leader of the Glass Refinery in the Night Tower."

The young man with his head shaved had a black suit on with the hints of gold that marked out the Night Tower colours, but his pierced eyebrow winked at her readily enough.

"You're all welcome here as long as you don't mean me or mine any harm," she said. "But that still doesn't explain why you want to see me."

Tulip sighed. "I'm not even sure at this point but we're worried about how things are turning out. We'd like to see the towers opened to the rest of Faerie. Trades suffer and we're at the whims of the nobles no matter how prettily the current leaders spin the narrative."

"And you think I can help with that?"

"You've clearly done more than any of us have managed, and in a short time. Our leaders were dealing with Celeste's dramatics until recently, but by many accounts Phoenix has been even worse."

Molly smiled. "I had a lot of help. I'm not sure how much you know about the citadel's history or why it was made, but I'm hoping to fix the rot inside, or try to at least, and open my tower to the wider realms for trade. If you're all in agreement with that, then perhaps we can keep talking."

"How are you planning to do that?" Allium asked.

Molly hesitated. "How much do you know about the current state of things?"

"We know the Omens are powerful," Tulip said. "I've read that they're ancient and likely to cause untold damage if released. One tale I've had from someone I trust is that if they were somehow removed, the citadel might be able to settle."

Molly nodded. "And from someone I trust, I believe that we'd need an item from each tower in order to achieve it, but how I'm still not entirely sure."

Kainen shifted beside her, nothing more than a subtle change of his stance, but a warning all the same. She'd forgotten about the compulsion possibility, but she had to trust he would try it without her asking him to.

"We could source the necessary items," River said quietly. "We each of us run the real parts of our towers."

"That would be a start," Molly said.

"Perhaps we could send you a few gestures of our craft from our respective towers," Tulip suggested. "We'd want your word though that if a new dawn were to rise, a united citadel to move into the future with, the restrictions on our people would be done with."

Molly smiled. "Everyone should have a choice over their own life. It might not always be the right ones we make, but we should have the right to make them as long as they don't harm anyone else. At least, that's what I'm building my tower on. I'd expect nothing less from any other tower I were to work with."

The others exchanged a look but Molly caught the soft smile River quickly smothered, and the subtle sagging of Briar's slender shoulders. Allium gave Tulip a nod, and that appeared to be it.

"We'll be in touch then, but this must stay between us," he said.

Molly caught the wary glance he gave Kainen.

"Nobody but my closest will have any idea," she insisted. "I would hope that perhaps this new dawn might even welcome me bringing my royal court to my tower."

"That is a big ask," Briar said.

River nodded. "The covenant was to keep us free of royal control."

"The covenant is gone and royal control seeped in through the cracks anyway. Celeste was a princess of Faerie and the old queen used her to pull enough strings for long enough to let Phoenix attempt to assassinate the Holly Queen."

Tulip grimaced and Briar exchanged another indecipherable look with River.

"How would it work then?" Allium asked. "What's your vision?"

Molly hadn't even thought that far but she could see it unfolding with enough hope to put her whole confidence behind the words.

"The citadel would be like one free tower, governed by the different counterparts as before, but it would be given the privilege of hosting one of the two royal courts. That would bring in fresh nobles too, but we would need to agree certain new covenants and treaties that outlaws any suggestion of gift extraction, resurrection process or anything that goes against the natural laws of Faerie and the nether."

She laid it all out despite Kainen shuffling closer to her side.

Tulip sighed. "Yeah, that I can absolutely get on board

with. We've all lost people to this awful greed machine in some way or another. Enough is enough."

"Expect our gestures of goodwill immediately," Allium said. "The quicker we move, the better."

"I'll run interference where I can," River offered.

Briar nodded. "And I can tangle all manner of nobles to keep them busy a while."

"Until we need to meet again," Tulip said.

They realm-skipped away and Molly wrapped her arms around her middle.

"I need to lie down," she muttered.

Kainen clicked his fingers and summoned a cup. Molly took it and downed the tonic inside.

"I need to figure out where to get these from as well."

Kainen grinned. "Marthe makes them, your royal kitchen bottles them, and your court sells them at extremely high cost to a very select few buyers."

"Oh. Well, that's something then."

"Indeed it is. I do hope you'll agree to continue letting us be one of the select few."

Molly opened her mouth to agree automatically, then smiled.

"I'll consider it."

He grinned. "Finally, she learns! Seriously though, I only get about two bottles a quarter, and I should at least be down for four with all this espionage. Demi gets a whole eight bottles!"

"Well she is queen."

"Absolutely not the point."

She handed the empty cup back and her pulse picked up

as Talie walked in from the lane. She had a small brown sack in one hand and held it out as she approached.

"Figured you'd need this."

Molly frowned. "What is it?"

"Grain. You'll need something from each tower, right? Well, this is from yours. I got it from Butch but forgot to give it to you just now."

Molly took it with a hesitant hand, unsure about the gruff distance in Talie's voice, even as Sammy raced up with a bundle of parcels in her hands.

"These have just been delivered," she announced. "From the other towers apparently. Are they likely to explode?"

Molly sighed. "Orbs, I hope not. I suppose I better take these to the workshop and start figuring out how to make containers."

Her heart sank as Talie released her lingering hold on the grain bag and muttered something under her breath.

She walked away but Molly ignored Kainen's not-so-subtly lifted eyebrows and set her mind on her task.

Five items into three containers in equal amounts. Getting back into the workshop was going to be the easiest thing she'd done in a long, long time.

CHAPTER TWENTY SIX

TALIE

"What do you mean the nether is talking to you?" Molly asked.

Talie didn't slow her pace, still weary as she stomped through the core tunnels with an entire entourage of royals trailing behind her. Demi and Taz were squabbling in silence, Kainen was whistling to himself even though Taz had threatened to send him home twice already, and Molly had the instructions on how to cast the containers for the Omens clamped in her fist.

"It's speaking to me, I can hear it in my head."

"Are you sure it's not the Omens?"

"Yeah, I'm sure."

She frowned as Molly ducked her head down and slowed to walk alongside Kainen instead.

I still haven't had a chance to figure out what's going to happen now that she has a whole royal court to consider. Can we really last on five days a year and whenever she has time to drop by and see me?

She bit her lip. While the nether was guiding her through the labyrinth toward the well, and being unnervingly conversational about the whole process, it was refusing to give her any suggestions on how she might do anything else, like get rid of the Omens.

"Explain the boxes to me again," Kainen said.

Molly sighed. "It's the only thing I can think of based on what Milo unearthed at the Nether Court archives. The Omens aren't solid so we need to channel them into the containers. The container needs to be made from items the Omens were created with, so I've made an hourglass from the Night Tower's glass and our grain, surrounded it with Iron from the Sunrise Tower and stone from the Morning Tower."

"Well I get that bit, but how is it going to work?"

Molly dropped her hand to the three small boxes that looked more like lanterns hanging from her belt. She picked up a fourth box made of glass that glowed and held it up.

"The Day Tower sent faelight and fae-water. Together they make this pearlescent liquid. We'll release it as the fifth equal part and use it to channel the Omens into the boxes."

Talie still didn't understand it either, but Molly had been hunched in her workshop overnight and had emerged with her shadow-ringed eyes. She'd apparently barely eaten the food Talie had insisted Sammy take her either, although Marthe was already making herself busy enough for an entire realm and had probably force-fed her.

"We'll have to get the wards down to let the Omens through," Demi warned. "That could make us vulnerable to attacks from them but also from the other towers."

"We'll be quick," Taz said.

Talie sensed the subtle worry rippling through the group but continued ploughing forward at the front. The nether was guiding her on the quickest route, and she was almost certain it wouldn't involve taking Molly past the big cavern with all the bats.

"Ah, there they are," Molly muttered.

"Yeah, I hear them too," Demi said. "Ignore them."

Talie slowed her pace. She hadn't heard the Omens since being able to hear the nether, and it was a relief not to have to focus on their poisonous whispers.

"We're almost there, just down this last tunnel," she said.

"We should stop and regroup then."

Talie held in the groan and halted. The entrance to the Omens cavern glowed up ahead and she could feel the nether nearby like a jolt across her skin.

"Are you okay?" Molly asked.

Talie nodded. "Fine."

The irritation leaked out without her intending it, and her heart sank at the hurt crunching over Molly's face. She couldn't even bring herself to apologise as Molly turned away and fled back to the others.

I'll sort it out once we get this done. The promise to herself didn't ease her guilt any.

"So, once I bring the wards down we'll have to let the Omens play their hand," Demi announced. "Then it's up to Taz, Kainen and I to challenge them while you two manipulate them into the containers."

"Can't we pick a better name?" Kainen grumbled.

"For what?"

"Well, containers makes them sound like food."

Demi gave him an unimpressed glance.

"What would you call it then?"

"Vessels of eternal damnation."

"Er… sure. Any other objections?"

The moment heads were shaken, Talie set off again without waiting for the others.

Quicker we do this, the sooner I can get Molly back on side and figure out if we can make this work. She'll have to come visit me, but perhaps she can realm-skip in every evening.

It didn't seem fair somehow, but she was tied to the citadel so it would be Molly's choice to make.

Always orbing choices.

The moment she stepped foot into the cavern over the well, the white smoke swelled angrily. She couldn't hear them, but given the doubtful looks on everyone else's faces, the Omens weren't happy to see them.

"Everyone ready?" Demi asked.

Talie didn't bother to nod, aware of Molly holding the glass box of faelight and water in front of her. Even with her recent moodiness, Talie closed the distance between them until their wardings merged.

"Are you mad at me?" Molly asked.

Talie grimaced. "No."

"Right, sure."

"I'm not, I just… things have changed, and now's really not the time to be discussing them."

Molly bit her lip as Demi let out a wave of icy blue

power and the wards keeping the Omens penned inside the five stone pillars crumbled.

The nether swelled like a darkness mass behind the white smoke as the Omens billowed out, but Talie knew there wouldn't be any help coming. The nether was impartial, not willing to choose between the Holly Queen it crowned and the Omens that had been borne from it.

If you did have any advice, now would be a great time, she grumbled in her mind.

The nether answered her with silence but she could feel its tension all the same, expectant and still.

Molly shook her head violently.

"What, what is it?"

"I'm not doing it," Molly snapped. "You had your chance and you failed."

Talie clenched her fist at her side as her rain gift beaded across her skin and a rumble of thunder echoed overhead. This close to the nether, her power felt magnified and she struggled to keep her mind calm enough to stop it roiling out in one enormous wave.

"We didn't think this through." Kainen appeared beside her with shadow whirling around him. "They're going for power so Demi and Molly are swamped."

Talie reached out and grasped Molly's hand, horrified to find it ice cold. Molly's gaze was narrowed, her expression pinched with effort, and nearby Demi didn't look to be faring much better.

"You open the faelight water thing then, and I'll channel it," Talie insisted.

He shook his head. "The faelight doesn't respond well

to shadow, we checked, remember? We need Molly's sunshine gift."

A loud crash tore the air and Molly sagged as the Omens' focus fractured. Talie clung to her hand tightly, her tiny shred of hope crashing under the boots of the Fae spilling in from various tunnels.

Vacant faces fanned out in droves, as though they'd been posted at the tunnels to wait it out however long it took.

"And now the orb-munchers are here," Kainen cursed. "Right, new plan. Taz! Get Milo to initiate protocol Jelly Butter."

"Is that the one with the-"

"The everyone one! Orbs, why do I have to put up with this?"

"Then stop choosing ridiculous plan names!"

Another loud bang shook the foundations of the cavern and whatever Taz said next was lost, but Talie saw Kainen's plan before he could explain it.

"Get the Omens focused on many not few?" she asked.

He nodded. "Overload. While they're busy, you and Molly do what you need to do. Demi, help me hold the line until reinforcements arrive. Molly, take five, you look half-dead."

"Who put him in charge?" Molly grumbled.

Demi managed a pained smile. "I did. Still can't quite believe it to be honest."

"Hey!"

Demi lifted a ward of protection that fell over them before anyone could strike. Talie stood inside the bubble as the white smoke curled around the outside, obscuring their view. A couple of screams had Talie clenching her fists, but Demi and Kainen stood silent at the edge of the protection.

"We can't stand in here and let them attack," she muttered.

Demi shook her head. "Who are they meant to be attacking? We're all in here. No, it's a trap. We wait until we have reinforcements. Our FDPs are trained against mind-tricks."

"Let me out there then," Talie demanded. "I'll fight."

"No, we need you. Think of the bigger picture. Oh, never mind, Taz is nearly here. Ah, Molly, I forgot, you need to give us retrospective permission to bring a realm-skip into your tower."

"Er… yeah, this once is fine."

Kainen grinned. "Girl's finally learning, I am so proud."

"Okay, ready?"

Talie stood tense as the sound of crashing and the thrum of gifts exploded into a crescendo and the smoke roiled in as Demi lifted the warding.

Bodies slammed into each other from all sides and Talie had no way of knowing who was on their side and who wasn't. Even with the undead on the opposing side, there were Fae also fighting through the thick of everything in tower colours.

"Ready, Princess?"

Talie lifted a hand as the white smoke came rushing toward them, but Molly didn't answer. Her face was contorted and sunshine was sputtering out of her fingertips.

As Kainen appeared next to her, Talie had forgotten about the Omens, even as they domed around her and funnelled past like she didn't exist.

"The Omens will go for Demi and Molly." He grimaced. "And I have one in my head now too. Taz has FDPs controlling the… you need to use the nether."

"How do I do that?"

She tensed even as the whisper danced in her mind.

I could help, for a cost.

The nether wanted a trade but she didn't have anything left she was willing to give. As Kainen whirled away with his shadow sparking against the smoke, Talie closed her eyes and warded. The edge of her protection couldn't cut through the smoke to join Molly's, but she guarded herself and focused harder than she ever had before.

It was like preparing to face an opponent in the ring. Calm. Purpose. Assess their weaknesses.

Beneath the panic, her storm gift answered the stillness and she sensed the pull of the strange pearlescent liquid shimmering inside the lantern-like containers hanging from Molly's belt.

Faelight and water.

She bit her lip and took the shot. The white smoke roiled against her protection as she shoved her way through it, but when she reached Molly her heart seized.

Molly lifted her head, her face pinched and her gaze unfocused. She didn't even flinch as Talie bent low and swiped the buckle to pull her belt and the lanterns free.

Talie popped the cap on the smaller box and let her gift flow free. The water inside the faelight concoction leapt to meet it and she held the lantern aloft.

"Molly, how does this work?" she shouted.

Molly shook her head. "I… what?"

"The lantern container thing. How do I get the Omen inside it?"

"Wrap the water, drag it."

That didn't help, but Talie summoned every essence of moisture from the air around her and lent it to the faelight now bubbling out of the container and bursting into a multicoloured spray that glimmered in midair.

The moment the Faelight touched the smoke, the water hissed and dryness burned across her skin. She winced and focused on Molly's words, wielding the spray like a net as the smoke writhed against it. The faelight inched toward the container under her will and she closed her eyes against the effort as the smoke roiled and fought against her.

"It's okay, I've capped it."

Molly's voice filtered through the haze and she let her shoulders drop with exhaustion. As she opened her eyes, Molly's weary face appeared.

"One down. Milo!"

Talie didn't have the strength to ask as Milo appeared, grabbed the container full of white smoke and vanished again. She also didn't ask when Molly waved a sluggish hand over their heads, but she did drink the entire cup of purple liquid that was shoved in her hand moments later.

With the tonic stitching over the worst of her aches, she looked for the next fight.

"Over there." She pointed. "Go stand with Kainen. Help him confuse them."

"Are you okay? That looked like it took all your effort."

Talie frowned. "We're all at the edge of our effort, I'll be fine."

Once again the sharp tone slithered off her tongue before she could check it, but she didn't have time to apologise as Molly turned on her heel and set off through the chaos toward Kainen. He stood hunched with his arms above his head, an entire shield of shadow rioting against the white smoke that fought it.

Talie followed with her warding firm around her, but she noticed with a sinking heart that when it brushed the edge of Molly's, it didn't get the choice to merge anymore.

CHAPTER TWENTY SEVEN

MOLLY

"Kainen, let me through!"

Molly called out and his head twitched in her direction. He had his eyes closed but she sensed the subtle gap in his iron-strength warding and whirled through it.

"One down," she told him. "Stand with me and we'll work together on this one."

He grimaced and reached out a hand. She took it and let her sunshine gift spill out, illuminating his shadow until the dark danced with the light.

You can't best us. The voice slipped into her mind, sharp and insistent. *We are free and gaining strength. The amount of avaricious minds here alone will be enough to sustain our full release.*

She stared through the haze of their gifts with her pulse pounding. Taz was fighting to hold the line even as he struggled to reach Demi's side, but on the opposite end of the cavern Phoenix was directing wave after wave of bodies with unseeing eyes. The white smoke seemed to be skimming over them, as if their fractured minds weren't deep enough to prey on, but that left their side to fight the whims of the Omens as well as Phoenix's army.

"We can beat you, and we will," she shouted. "Those undead minds aren't any good to you, are they?"

Irrelevant, little queen. You could rule the world at our side, with us you would be all-powerful, no other queens or enemies to contest you.

"Where's the fun in that? Besides, if you think I'd go against my family for mere power, then I'm way more powerful than you think."

Kainen's fingers squeezed her hand tight, but she couldn't hear what wars he was fighting beside her.

Let this be a lesson to you, queen. She held on as the white smoke started to recede. *There will always be greed in Fae, and the time will come when you need us.*

She shook her head even as Kainen sagged beside her. He kept the shadow around them as protection, but she let her sunshine gift dim enough to see Talie wrestling the cap onto another lantern.

"Milo!"

She flinched when he appeared beside her to grab it, but all eyes turned to Demi, encased in a crackle of icy blue lightning. Molly ran forward with Kainen holding the warding over them to join Taz, who had one hand out to send fire flashing at anyone nearby and the other stabbing indiscriminately with his sword.

"She's trying to save the FDPs and fight the Omens," Taz growled. "Why can't she just follow a simple plan? She knows she can't manage both, even if she is a queen!"

Kainen cocked his head. "Have some faith in her. She's survived more than this before. Okay, kind of arrogant, I grant you, but we're Fae. It's literally what we stand for."

Taz shot a glare his way but Kainen only rolled his eyes and held his hand out to Molly.

"Shall we?"

She had no energy left to fight with but she nodded anyway and took his hand. As he led her forward, she glanced back at Talie already fiddling with the cap on the final lantern.

Molly let the dregs of her sunshine gift spool out again and meet with the shadow, the air dancing toward the lightning like a maelstrom of power.

Demi looked their way once, enough to let them in, but she was still wielding her lightning against the enemy in jagged flashes as the final cloud of white smoke slithered between their gifts.

"Stand strong," Demi warned. "We don't know what desperate trick it'll try."

Molly clung to Kainen's hand even as a subtle spray of water lurched past them. She grimaced, knowing Talie's gift was faltering as badly as hers was.

The white smoke began to recede again, and she sucked in a laboured breath.

It must be easier with only one of them left.

She twisted around to check on Talie, but the final lantern was open and still entirely empty.

"It's changing allegiance," Kainen called out. "Defence!"

Molly stumbled as he dragged her backwards but she managed to snare Talie's hand on her way past. Demi backed away with them, her lightning crackling around her body and lifting her hair on end as the white smoke billowed away over the crowd.

Molly groaned as it immediately wrapped itself around Phoenix's outstretched hands.

"It'll be weaker without the other two, but we can't let it possess him," Demi insisted.

Kainen nodded. "Agreed. Plan?"

"We get Talie as close as we can to grab it and make a last ditch offensive to keep everyone else busy."

"On it."

Demi shook her head at Taz, a warning in her eyes almost, as if she knew he was about to tell her off for overstretching herself.

"Molly? Talie?" she asked. "You good?"

Talie huffed. "No, but we're here. We'll do what needs to be done."

Molly didn't answer, just took a deep breath and lifted her hand. Almost instantly Marthe was beside her to pass out tonics, the same way Milo seemed to be able to reach Demi.

"Orbs, do I have to pay for this one?" Demi asked, then necked the tonic Marthe handed her.

Marthe opened her mouth but Molly pre-empted her.

"Not that one, no. Consider it a goodwill gesture in the hopes we actually survive this."

Demi smiled. "We'll survive, don't worry. He's powerful and experienced, probably gifted to the hilt, but remember we're strong together. No sense being queens if we can't beat the bad guys. Kainen and Taz will hold the line and keep the FDPs moving, while you and I take on

Phoenix together. That should give you time, Talie."

Taz and Kainen yelled out a random string of words between them, each one darting in opposite directions. A sea of Fae parted like sand around a stone, except the stone was Phoenix's forces that massed like an impenetrable wall of the undead.

"They're going to box us in," Talie shouted.

Demi nodded. "They are, and we're going to fight from the inside."

She threw out a hand and a whip of blue lightning cracked through the air. It cleaved the white smoke into two but the final Omen billowed back toward Phoenix just as quickly.

Molly raised her free hand and let her sunshine flare, but Phoenix's eyes were turning white too fast, and Talie's storm gift was faltering as the smoke evaded the edges of the lantern. Her lips were cracked, her eyes red with dryness, and Molly panicked.

"Snow!" She pulled Demi around. "Give her snow to melt, or the frost thing you do."

She wrenched her hand free of Demi's and eyed Phoenix.

"What are you going to do?" Demi asked.

She grimaced. "Something dim."

Before Demi could ward or stop her, Molly darted forward.

Her gifts weren't working but she'd learned at least one thing from Talie and barrelled through the white smoke to land her elbow in Phoenix's gut while he too was busy being possessed to notice.

The white smoke raged against her warding, whispering and seeking entrance as much as it tried to crush her.

I just need enough time.

She blinked but the white haze had covered her completely. A dark shadow loomed closer and she scrambled to get to her feet without memory of a single fighting stance left in her head.

The shadow lunged, arm outstretched, then doubled as a second figure barrelled the first sideways. She pushed her sunshine gift out and stumbled forward until she reached the edge of it and a horrified gasp left her lips.

Phoenix stood beside Ru's unmoving body, his eyes narrow and mouth pinched as he lifted his arms to welcome the white smoke back again.

Molly dropped to one knee at Ru's side. He was out cold, or worse, but she didn't have time to find out if the undead had a pulse.

Anger tore at her insides and she lifted both hands as heat coursed through her limbs and exploded out of her.

"STOP!"

The sheer fury wrapped in compulsion stilled most of the FDPs. She wasn't their leader but she was a queen of Faerie, to be obeyed on command. Even the undead Fae seemed stunned into inaction, glassy eyes focused in all directions, as the last wisp of the white smoke was tugged roaring into the final lantern.

Demi slammed on the cap and Molly broke into a weak-kneed run toward them.

"Duck!"

Talie's scream had her doubled over but without

balance she hit the ground and rolled to one side instead. Her jaw throbbed from the awkward impact but as she lifted her head, a familiar round of metal frisbeed through the air.

Talie stared as the metal swung toward her, Phoenix's hand still outstretched from throwing it, and Molly knew she wouldn't reach her in time.

The metal glinted as it arced on perfect form and struck with deadly accuracy as Talie toppled to the floor. She patted her shoulders, then her chest, confusion flashing across her face to find no obvious injury.

Molly froze as Ru looked down at the metal embedded in his chest, even as Talie was fighting to get back to her feet.

Molly sensed Demi's warding closing behind her, but the lantern whizzed past her head before she could focus. She twisted, stuck between problems, immobile with despair as the lantern landed on Phoenix's outstretched palm.

"Orbing summoning gift," Demi muttered.

Molly ran her gaze over Talie thoroughly, then approached Ru.

"Can we pull it out?" she asked, her throat burning and her voice raspy.

Ru blinked at her. "Even undead have hearts, Molly. Mine is... leaking."

"We can fix this-"

"Don't heal me, please. I don't feel like I know I should. I promised to keep you safe. That includes your heart. No heart left if she's dead."

The heart in question broke at the sound of his emotionless tone.

"There must be something," she insisted.

She tried to steady him as he dropped to his knees, wisps of what looked like dark brown gunk oozing past the metal in his chest.

"I'm not truly in here anymore, Molly. I'm a stack of limbs and potions and someone's scrambled memories, and it hurts. Let me go."

She bit her lip as Milo appeared beside them.

"Okay, I'll let you go." She lifted her head as Ru's dropped.

"Save him if someone can," she mouthed.

She would let him go emotionally, but if there was any kind of cure, she would find it.

Milo laid a hand tentatively on Ru's shoulder and Molly choked over a sob as they disappeared. She let Talie take her hand as the tears fell.

"Phoenix still has the last one," Talie said.

Demi nodded. "Yeah. Regroup and attack."

"The lanterns are protection locked," Molly mumbled.

"It won't take him long to smash through it," Demi said. "We take him now."

Molly shook her head.

"No."

"No?"

"There are laws as infinite as Faerie itself. We fight his forces with ours but if he gets the lantern open and the Omen possesses him, it's over."

"It took a few minutes at least before with Celeste,"

Talie argued. "If we-"

"It's in its concentrated form so not hard to swap the lantern for him."

Molly wiped a hand over her face and strode to the edge of Demi's warding with one thought echoing in her mind.

Talie is really going to kill me this time.

She clung to that in the hope she might survive long enough for Talie to try, then she lifted her voice as loud as she could.

"I challenge Phoenix Whatever-His-Family-Name-Is to single combat."

CHAPTER TWENTY EIGHT

TALIE

"What are you doing!" Talie shouted, then glared at Demi. "What is she doing?"

Demi grimaced. "I have no idea but it can't be good. She's worse than me for stupid stunts, and that's saying something."

Talie strode to Molly's side as Phoenix cocked his head.

"Nice try, but we all know that wouldn't be a fair fight," he called back. "You might have been crowned recently but you also have the young king consort's protection over you from previous altercations. Would you truly ask a man to face you directly when he can't fight back?"

Talie sagged. She'd forgotten about Taz's protection over Molly, but it was exactly the reason she would be thanking him profusely, straight after she gave Molly an orbing good shake.

Molly glanced over the waiting crowd, still apparently stunned by whatever compulsion she'd swept over them. It didn't appear to be holding inside Demi's protection, but Talie didn't have any clue whether that was a Molly thing or a Demi thing.

There is still so much I don't know.

A sea of worried faces watched them. Talie pressed a hand to her breathless chest as she spied Sammy and a bunch of her gym friends in the crowd too.

"I rescind the King Consort's protection over me then," Molly announced.

Talie closed her eyes tight and groped around to find Molly's hand.

"Will you stop doing absolutely idiotic things?" she hissed.

When she opened her eyes, Molly wasn't even looking at her, but words trickled from the corner of Molly's mouth for only her to hear.

"The alternative is conceding power to him by choice. He has the last Omen. If you get a chance, grab it. If I defeat him-"

"If?!"

"-then I win it by default. You asked me to trust you before, now I'm asking you to trust me."

Talie winced. "You're going to throw that in my face now?"

"Yeah. Focus on the wider danger, Sunshine."

Molly pulled her hand free and squared her shoulders.

"If you agree, we fight for that container you're holding and the contents," she announced.

Phoenix smiled. "Ah, the young queen is hoping her new title will give her the edge over experience when it comes to power."

"Nope. I'm hoping your arrogance chokes you so I don't have to."

Talie snorted hysterically as Phoenix nodded.

"Very well, I accept your challenge. We fight for this container and its contents. Shall we say one break to be called by either side, then it's to the death or concession?"

Molly nodded. "Fine. Ten minutes to prepare?"

"Agreed."

Phoenix sauntered off toward the waiting lines of vacant faces and a bunch of worried ones dotted in between.

Molly didn't saunter. She turned and the determination all but bled from her face.

"This is bad," she announced. "I couldn't think of anything else though."

Kainen approached with a sigh. "It's a risk, I'll grant you. Here, take my jacket. It won't hold out everything but there are protections in it."

Molly let him help her into the leather jacket but Talie couldn't stop her blood pounding. She eyed Phoenix marking out an arena between the five pillars at the edge of the abyss with purple chalk, but short of trying to kill him from behind, she had nothing.

"You can do this," Demi said. "Focus on him as an opponent, keep your warding strong and stick to what matters. You are leader of this tower. Remember that."

"I'm meant to be a queen. If can't even defend one tower, how am I supposed to protect the whole of Faerie?"

"Power is where people put it," Taz insisted.

Kainen nodded as he dabbed at a small cut on Molly's brow.

"Being crowned a queen means little if you don't have

anyone willing to swear to the court. You think the old queen got the power she did through being crowned? It's symbolic."

"It's being chosen," Taz added. "The gifts? Those were earned. She fought for every single one of them. Sure, her resolve was rotting through by the end, but she was a feared queen because she made people fear her, not because she had a title."

"But I can't do any of it!"

"You beat Celeste. You ousted Phoenix from your tower and fought the Omens. You were chosen by your tower by honest vote, and by Faerie itself."

"Those were just things that happened. I didn't plan any of it."

"We never do, but we keep fighting anyway," Kainen said. "There. One more tonic and you're ready."

"I'll never be ready," Molly muttered.

"Well, nobody ever is, but still. We'll give you a second."

Phoenix already stood waiting at the edge of the crudely drawn arena, but Talie grabbed Molly's hands and forced her attention back to her.

"No words of wisdom, Sunshine?" Molly said weakly.

Talie sighed. "If you exhaust your gifts, distract him until you can get a punch in. Here."

She slid the wrist strap holding her dagger free and attached it to Molly's wrist. Then she wound her arms tight around Molly's waist and held on tight.

"I'm scared," Molly whispered.

Talie nodded. "I know. I am too. Take a minute to get

yourself angry. Go in furious. He tried to take the citadel from your people. He helped your mother steal gifts. He undeaded Ru and countless others."

"Undeaded isn't a word."

"Yeah well, I'm pissed at you." She dropped a kiss on Molly's forehead. "Go kick him where it hurts so I can yell at you without feeling guilty."

Molly sucked in a deep breath and stepped away. With her head high and her shoulders squared, she approached the edge of Demi's warding and stepped beyond it.

"Ready to lose?" Phoenix asked.

Molly smiled as her sunshine gift warmed the air. It was a thing of summery beauty, of laughter and revelry and fresh green bounty. Beneath it, Talie could almost sense the poison growing strong, the briars and roots digging in deep and lethal. The comfort and the danger of a strong summer blending into one incomparable soul.

That's my girl.

She flinched as Molly stepped into the arena and the thrum of a warding burst between them.

"This is going to be tense," Kainen muttered.

Demi nodded. "She's got gifts, right? She's got stealth and sunshine and stuff?"

"Not enough," Talie said. "Never enough. She does these stupid things for the greater good and- orbs, that almost hit her!"

She gasped as Phoenix sent a wave of sparkling red power scattering across the arena without any warning, and Molly barely repelled it with her warding in time.

"Can't I just kill him?" she asked.

Kainen shook his head. "Not without retribution. They're in a duel. If you do that, your life will be forfeit and Molly would never forgive us."

Talie clenched her fists tight and set off to pace the edge of the boundary with Kainen following alongside.

"I can't believe I can't do anything," she hissed. "We're Fae, and you're telling me there's no ancient magic I can use to help her, no tricks? What's the point of being powerful if you can't use it?"

Kainen frowned. "Question should be what counts as powerful? What are the rules?"

She flinched as Molly sent out a wave of sunshine to dispel the red mist doming around her and hit the floor under the effort as Phoenix sent his metal plate through the air over and over to chip away at her protection.

"Who cares what the rules are?" Talie demanded.

"People who want to find a way of circumventing them might." Kainen gave her a meaningful look when she glowered at him. "Of course, we wouldn't dream of interfering, especially given that outsiders are not allowed to. Molly has to fight him with only the gifts and skills she alone has."

"So sunshine, compulsion and a crown? Is she supposed to dazzle him and throw the crown at his head?"

"Maybe. And maybe while she's doing that, people could try getting their heads out of their behinds and looking closer at the rules."

Talie froze. "What do you mean?"

He rolled his eyes and walked off back to where Demi was shredding the edge of her sleeve with her teeth and

Taz was muttering helpless suggestions under his breath.

What even are the rules? No outsiders, only one break which she's used, and fight until death or concession.

Talie eyed the pinch around Molly's eyes and the exhausted hunch of her shoulders.

Phoenix had played it well, she could admit it that much. After fighting the Omens, Molly didn't have the strength to fight with gifts much and didn't have the energy to consider the fight strategically.

She needs someone on her side to coach her through it.

She hurried over to Kainen.

"What do you want for a gift?" she asked.

He closed his eyes in momentary torment.

"Skipping aside how many traditions you just massacred with that request, it depends what the gift is."

"Link my mind up with hers."

His frown twitched. "I suppose I could. It would be unethical to do it without her permission-"

"Put a time-limit on it then, and I'll take any consequences if she's upset."

"I'd need to put a petition in with the powers that be-"

"Granted," Demi said, not once drawing her gaze away from the fight. "Taz, tell Milo."

Taz didn't answer but Talie guessed it was more about their dogged insistence on doing things fairly than an actual necessity.

Kainen grabbed her hand and pressed a kiss to the back of it.

"I gift you with the ability to communicate into Molly's mind, and have her communicate back, until the end of her duel. In return, you will support my court with new initiatives to reform the custom of hierarchy titling.”

“I have no idea what that is, but sure.”

Even Taz winced at that as she barrelled away from them, but she didn’t stop to ask what she’d just signed up for.

Probably should have done. Oh well.

She reached the edge of the fight’s boundary and tried to assess what exactly she needed to tell Molly to do.

As Phoenix sent out a jagged flare of bright yellow light, Molly hit the ground.

When she didn’t get up again, Talie screamed.

CHAPTER TWENTY NINE

MOLLY

Molly struggled to get her head upright, the ground swaying as she staggered a few steps over it. Phoenix grinned as he lifted a hand and she barely had time to brace for the wave of light that came at her, let alone dodge it.

Then it hit, a wave of pain so sudden she was almost numb with it, the shock fracturing any hope of sensation. As she closed her eyes against the jagged shards tearing her consciousness apart, it wasn't royalty she thought of.

No nobles, titles or riches.

It was family.

Demi being flippant and Taz rolling his eyes. Kainen saying something glib and Reyan laughing at him. Marthe and those from the royal kitchens that had moved to the citadel, and everyone who passed in the lanes with a smile or a joke. Everyone at the gym, Nia, Sammy, Beryl, Baby Aurora, and Talie.

Talie frowning and smiling and laughing like the brightest light in a dark world.

People that were worth dying for.

Molly closed her eyes against the pain, even as the smile

spread across her face.

The family she had made was worth dying for.

Molly. Get up.

Talie's furious voice echoed in her mind and she hazily wondered if she'd slept in again, until the pain clawed through her limbs, up her chest, unhinging her jaw as she screamed.

You're not done yet. Get up and fight.

Molly scowled. *Who made you queen?*

Nobody, and you won't be one either if you don't get up.

It hurts.

I know, Princess, but I'm here. Let's finish him together.

Molly opened her eyes to a haze of murky grey. Hearing Talie's voice in her head was a mixed blessing, but seeing her at the edge of the boundary with her fists clenched and her face torn with vengeful fury was enough to have Molly's instinct flaring.

I can't beat him.

Talie's lips thinned even further.

Yes you can. You're just not thinking straight. His weakness is vanity so put on a show. Ask him questions, lead him in circles to distract him. Attack with sunlight when you can and dodge when you can't. I'm not planning on training another girlfriend either way, so get to your orbing feet!

Molly snorted over a surprised laugh.

You say the nicest things.

It was worth the stinging in her eyes to see Talie roll hers.

Focus. Choose your moment to compel him. He'll find a way to avoid it so pick carefully. Compel him to use his gift, to tell the truth. If the people listening hear it then their allegiances will shift.

Molly swiped a hand over her face and faced Phoenix. He lifted one eyebrow, cocky to the last.

"You should have stayed down," he said.

She shrugged. "Never been too good with 'should'. I shouldn't have chased the gift extraction, but that's how I met Talie. I shouldn't have challenged the old queen to save her either, but that got me a crown."

Phoenix dodged as she sent out a wave of sunlight, one arm lifted to shield his face. Molly let the heat flow free along with the glare, but her energy levels were still faltering fast.

When he threw out another wave of pain, she ducked behind the nearest pillar and rode out the residual scrapes flowing over her arms around the sides.

Easy, Princess. It doesn't look like it but he's tiring too, I can tell. Keep him running around until you're ready to compel him.

Molly sucked in a laboured breath and clenched her fist at her side. As she slipped into her stealth gift and crept across the space until she was far to the side of him, she focused on the roaring silence inside the boundary and the frantic faces outside it.

I have people on my side. He has none.

"What's your plan then?" she called out. "You get rid of me, the Oak Court goes to my aunt and you start a war? The citadel can't afford a war, even if it hangs onto some of its nobles."

Phoenix whirled around and she let him see a glimpse of her before she slipped into stealth again and stumbled away from the flash of light he sent out.

"The citadel has long since defied the tyrannical rule of the royal courts," he shouted.

Molly reached a nearby pillar and let her stealth drop as she sagged behind it.

"Tyrannical under the old queen maybe, but with me and Demi not so much. Times are changing and you clinging to control is the real tyranny now."

She winced as his attack hit the pillar and shook it to the foundations. With her stealth gift once again tugging at her failing energy levels, she dashed across to the next pillar.

"This tower has been a beacon of hope for so many-"

"For who!?" She all but forgot to hang onto her stealth and keep moving as indignation leapt from her mouth. "Those walled inside with rising prices and their loved ones being stolen for Celeste's experiments? Those who got abandoned when my tower fell and no help came from the other towers?"

She ducked as the next flash of light went straight over her head and struggled to get up to her feet again.

"Or maybe it's been a beacon of hope for the rich who want to exploit hard-working Fae," she pressed. "Is that how you chose the ones to kill and resurrect? Did you care that many of them had families who would miss them?"

She stumbled as his fury caught the edge of her shoulder and another wave of pain scraped her back as she dodged behind the pillar.

You can barely stand. Remember the compulsion!

Talie's frantic voice screamed in her head and she dredged up every essence of energy she had left and walked out to face him. Phoenix stood with his chest heaving and his hand raised ready. Talie was right, he would want a show. She'd shamed him and he would want to make his dominance undeniable.

She cocked her head and imitated his arrogance as she straightened her daisy crown to keep him distracted.

Then she let herself fall to her knees.

Phoenix's laughter rolled through her ears, but she relied on his pure arrogance and smiled as she attacked with words instead of pain.

"Tell the people exactly what you've planned and what you've done to their friends, their family," she demanded, her fury rolling out in one feral spike of energy. "Tell them exactly what you plan to do with their futures, their livelihoods and *their* citadel."

Phoenix's face contorted like he was fighting the words frothing onto his tongue. He lifted a hand and she didn't have any energy left to dodge the strike. The pain crunched her into an impossibly small space but fragments of his voice broke through as his truth finally spilled out.

"This citadel is mine! Who would any of you be without me? I built it! Okay, not physically, but I orchestrated every single change and improvement."

Molly frowned, then realised that her eyes were shut tight enough to cause a headache. She opened them and struggled to her feet, unable to stay in one place without wobbling. She limped from side to side instead, keeping him in view as Talie's voice soothed the insides of her mind.

One last stand. Come on, Princess. You've got everyone out here raging, stand up and own it.

Talie sounded like she was crying, which was weird because Talie never cried.

"I manipulated every tower into answering to the Menagerie in secret, then every guild to answer to their tower," Phoenix shouted. "And the nobles? How easy it was to sway them with simple promises of land and wealth that we'd take from the people here."

Molly winced as she noticed her crown on the floor some feet away, but in that moment she understood. She couldn't remember who'd said it or if she'd figured it out on her own, but the revelation was enough to straighten her shoulders.

"I might be born a princess of Faerie," she announced. "I might have even been crowned queen by Faerie itself. But the people of my tower voted for me to lead them. That's what *I've* earned."

She dropped her hand to her wrist, to Talie's dagger that she had sworn to herself on the way into the arena she wouldn't use.

"Times are changing." She slipped the dagger free. "And I will not let you take our home from us."

Phoenix barely had time to lift his hands as she sent out a flash of sunlight so bright she dazzled even herself, but it was enough of a shock for her to move through. He didn't even see her coming as she drove the blade into his shoulder.

He dropped to his knees, panic mingled with hatred in his eyes, but she lifted her hand to the slender ropes that made up the decoration of her oak green shirt. She'd picked it out because it was nearest on the rack, but now she realised that every little gesture made by those around her was a mark of respect, from the easily detachable ropes on her shirt, to the fact River and Briar, Allium and Tulip had all conveniently sent her the exact same weight of their product, as if they wanted to help that little bit more.

"This shirt was made for me out of mutual respect I had for its maker," she announced, loud enough for all to hear. "Respect is sometimes the best protection we can have, and respect must always be earned."

She tugged the rope free and used her knee to push Phoenix onto his side. He twisted onto his front, but the rush of adrenaline was overpowering the exhaustion and she only had a few moments of untapped natural power before he gained the upper hand again.

She placed her foot level with the length of his spine and pretended to test her weight, just enough that he'd feel the pressure.

"I wouldn't," she told him. "Talie told me once that you can snap a neck easily from here."

Orbs, Princess, now is not the time to start channelling your inner me.

Molly heard the pride in her voice though, the hysterical amusement, and she smiled like a Fae queen about to finish a conquest. She leaned down and lashed one end of the rope around his arms, then wound the length of it around his neck.

"Do you concede?" she asked.

Phoenix twisted his head and tried to spit at her.

"Well that's disgusting." She sighed loudly. "From here I can tie the free end of this rope to your hands. Eventually, your arms will tire and lower and you'll slowly hang yourself. Not a nice way to go, but we did say death or concession, your choice."

Phoenix writhed for a moment longer, but the rope tightened and he stilled again.

"Yeah, I wasn't bluffing. I promised myself once that I'd never kill anyone, but for you? I'll give you the choice. I've always said everyone deserves a choice, so here's yours: kill yourself slowly or concede."

Okay, I definitely didn't teach you any of this, Princess.

Molly wanted to laugh, but it might send her too far into maniacal, so she settled for giving the rope a little tug.

"You could probably go to the Forever mountains with Celeste," she suggested, just to sway his choice that little bit. "Discuss where you both went wrong. Live to fight another day, that sort of thing."

She ducked down again and swiftly tied the end of the rope to his wrists, then stepped away so he could make the choice. She felt the wave of power before he released it, but she twisted aside as exhaustion clawed back in.

She almost missed the subtle mumble of sound.

"Sorry, what was that?"

Phoenix struggled to lift his arms and the rope tugged against his throat.

"I concede."

Molly huffed over a ragged breath as a cacophony of

sound slammed in around them. The boundary had shattered and she barely saw Talie before the familiar arms were tight around her.

"First order of business, get him out of our sight," Talie snapped.

Molly couldn't see who she was snapping at because her face was firmly welded to Talie's shoulder, but she could let everyone gathered see her emotion. Couldn't avoid it really considering it was pouring out of her eyes and, if she really thought about it, probably her nose as well.

"I have no words," Kainen said.

Taz snorted. "That'd be a first."

Molly choked over a laugh and lifted her head. Demi already had Phoenix in her power, but Molly caught her eye and a grim look of understanding passed between them. There would be talks and discussions about laws, right and wrong, and all sorts of serious things in the coming days.

"What do we do about you know, the vessels of eternal damnation?" Taz asked.

Kainen grinned. "I heard that. Permission to suggest we hold the preliminary containments at the Illusion Court? We have cells strong enough to almost rival the Forever mountains and we'd be happy to assist."

"Yeah, thanks." Demi smiled at Phoenix, wicked and full of dark promise. "Welcome to royal captivity. Unlike you, we still treat people as people. Kind of."

As she disappeared with him, Taz glanced around at the feverish crowd.

"Right, we need to disperse this lot," he muttered.

Kainen sighed. "Good point. Greetings everyone! For those that don't know me, I am Lord Kainen of the Illusion Court. For those who do know me…"

Molly tuned out, content to stay in Talie's arms. She guessed Sammy would be bursting by any second, unless Marthe had managed to stop her somehow, but she still had the other towers to deal with, and then she had Talie's deal with the nether to consider as well.

"You did it, Princess," Talie soothed. "I'm so proud of you."

Molly gulped down the sob that bubbled up but Talie stepped back before she could cling on.

"Orbs, you had me scared to death!" Marthe hurried in between them to pat Molly's cheeks down and smooth her hair back. "Let's get you to rest now."

Molly glanced over her shoulder at Kainen firmly chasing away any remaining gawkers in the crowd, and at the notable absence of the other four councillors.

Then she looked hopefully at Talie. Helplessly.

"Go on, I have something I need to sort out," Talie said.

Molly couldn't decipher the look on her face, her mouth quirked with some wistful, faraway thought even as she pretended to smile.

Milo appeared to take Kainen away first, then Taz insisted he and Demi would secure the core.

"Yeah, I'll help," Talie said. "I'm getting instructions coming through apparently."

Molly bit her lip as Marthe led her away like an oversized exhausted child.

"Straight to bed, yes?" Marthe asked.

Molly bit her lip. Talie and the others had the nether and the core sorted, and that was technically Talie's job now. Sammy had joined them and Talie showed no signs of sending her away.

"Okay, yeah." Molly nodded. "My place is upstairs now I think. Can you realm-skip then?"

Marthe laughed. "Oh my dear, can you not feel it? This tower has accepted the court so readily. The bounds stretch all the way here. I can realm-skip us anywhere you like within the tower, assuming you wish to let me keep the privilege?"

"Well, yeah. I don't know how to realm-skip yet."

"Well there's plenty of time for all that. But first, a nice long rest. Then food and a bath."

Molly let Marthe cling to her as the nether wisped around them, a sense of quiet acknowledgement radiating through it until her Menagerie bedroom materialised around them.

Talie's just sorting her side of things out. I have to believe that's the only reason for the distance.

Her heart still sank at the thought, but Demi appeared in the room before Molly could wriggle free of Marthe's grasp.

"Molly, you okay to talk for a second?" Demi asked.

"She needs rest," Marthe insisted, even as Molly nodded.

"I'm fine. I could do with one of those tonics though."

Marthe muttered under her breath and clicked her fingers to summon tonics, but Molly clung onto her cup instead of drinking it as Demi downed hers.

"Milo reckons the Omens will dissipate into nothing now they're separated," Demi announced.

Molly frowned. "What will you do with them?"

"Me? You won them by conquest. They're yours."

"What am I supposed to do with them?"

"Well, if you like my court could take them into safekeeping." Demi shrugged. "They'd be kept separate in different realms to avoid any contamination, one at my court and one at Reyan and Kainen's, and I suppose-"

"One should be kept here," Molly said, surprising herself with her firmness. "We'll need to decide how we go forward in the coming days, but I'm not warding the citadel beyond protection anymore, so perhaps we should share the load."

Demi nodded. "Absolutely. Who do you want me to give one to?"

"I…" Molly hesitated. "Sammy, under Talie's guidance. She's young, but the person I would ask I need to actually ask, so Sammy for now. What do we do with all the Fae that have been resurrected though? Orbs, I didn't even think to ask what happened to them, and the councillors are still in place even if Phoenix isn't."

She sank onto her bed with her elbows on her knees, head in her hands. Demi settled next to her.

"Taz has been speaking to the Fauna Court. There are hundreds of undead still, alive? Undead? I'm not even sure what to call it, but either way we have a place where the best healers in all of Faerie are trained, and they can be taken to recuperate there."

Molly thought of Ru and blinked hard against sudden tears.

"I want to make sure the families have the chance to go with them then," she insisted. "They can decide between them what to do under the Fauna Court's care and protection."

"Wise choice. I'll have Milo coordinate it between our courts. I still can't really be seen interfering in your citadel councils, that's down to you, but if you need any help I'm always here."

"Thanks. Orbs, I still have to deal with the council. Without Phoenix I think they're mostly leaderless, but they kidnapped you and Talie, they worked to overthrow my rule of this tower, and they knew about the resurrections and all of it."

Demi stood and wiped her hands on her jeans.

"I can't tell you what to do, but what I would do in your position is send out letters to the other towers. Introduce yourself to the guilds, their nobles, anyone with sway. Set out your position and let the discussions go from there."

Molly sighed. "I know who to start with but I'm so tired."

"Then let this be advice from queen to queen. Trust those who give you loyalty. Learn to lean on them. Pick someone you trust to do the conversations for you. Take today to rest and tell the other councils you'll be in touch in the coming days. Keep it vague. Do you want me to cast the protections for you for the time being? It can be a 'welcome to queenhood, it doesn't entirely suck' kind of gift."

Molly opened her mouth to refuse, to insist she'd already taken too much, but then Demi's advice settled around her.

"Yes, please."

Demi nodded. "Consider it done. You can take over now, Marthe, before you start plotting mutiny against me."

Molly managed a weak smile as Marthe gave Demi a fond shake of her head, but the door banged open before she could succumb to exhaustion and lie down.

Taz strolled in and gave her a relieved smile.

"You gave us all a massive fright, Molly. Nobody would blame you if you wanted to vacate to a neighbour court for a while until you get things sorted."

Molly shook her head. "I have to stay. This is my home, always has been, and a royal court renting space here could be exactly what it needs. I'm still in shock I think, but it beats languishing in a ballroom playing lords and ladies for all my years as a princess."

Taz pulled a face. "That sounds awful."

"Exactly, whereas here I can do some proper work, and I actually feel I've earned my place as well."

"I absolutely get it. I'd still be throwing a tantrum about abdicating if a fairy hadn't exploded everything around me and got herself crowned queen."

"You did abdicate technically for a while."

"Yeah, funny how things work out." He smiled. "But you're wrong about one thing."

"Probably wrong about most things but do tell. You sound almost like Kainen when he does his wise man of the woods thing."

He chuckled. "Ouch. No, I mean you've earned everything you're being offered. I'm so proud of you. Stay in touch as family too, not just as a fellow royal. We're family, titles or no titles."

"Okay, *Uncle Taz*."

His face contorted. "WEIRD. Oh, and I promised I'd ask you before anything else: have you named a successor yet, because May is determined to be the first person to swear to your court. That would put her back in line for succession."

"Er… I'll consider it? I mean, sure, but I should probably say I'll consider it first, right?"

He nodded. "Wise. At least she won't have to hide who she is anymore, but I can only imagine what the nobles will be saying about the crown princess of Faerie being a tattooed menace who likes practical jokes."

Molly managed a smile but the thought of tattoos reminded her of Talie and she had to push the sudden swoop of sadness aside.

If she's somehow having doubts about us now she's got the nether to manage, she can orbing well come and tell me to my face.

"We'll leave you be," Demi said. "We're only an orb call away remember."

Molly nodded and flopped back on the bed as they realm-skipped away. As Marthe set to fussing around her bedding, Molly closed her eyes and let the exhaustion win.

Now I just need to figure out what's going on with Talie, fix my new relationship with the other towers, and rule all of Faerie.

There was time in the coming days to talk to Talie and be completely honest about how she felt, and to explain how she wanted Talie in her life permanently, side by side.

She would have plenty of time to learn the art of being queen in the coming years as well, and while she still had the councillors to deal with, she would force them to deal with her via diplomacy rather than fighting.

I will not let anyone treat me like a child anymore either. I will be regal and in control at all times.

"Do you want me to put some soothing music on, your majesty? I have just the lullaby in mind to send you off."

Molly hunched further into her pillow with a grumble.

Starting tomorrow.

"Yes please, Marthe, if you wouldn't mind."

CHAPTER THIRTY

TALIE

Talie approached Kainen in the middle of the Menagerie entrance hall three days after the Siege of the Citadel, as everyone was calling it, with irritation jangling in her limbs. She guessed he'd arrived to see Molly, but she couldn't see any sign of the queen around.

She'd kept herself down in the core for three days talking to the nether and working out some fragile understandings, but it would take a long time before she would feel fully settled with any of it.

"Can you take me to see him?" she asked.

Kainen raised an eyebrow. "Oh I'm fine, all patched up, so kind of you to ask. Who am I taking you to see now?"

"Phoenix." She pulled a face. "I can skip through the nether at will now but not into your court without permission. And I'm glad you're fine. I just want to see him once before they ship him off."

"I can invite you, sure, but why?"

"I just want to make sure he knows something. I won't do anything too rash."

Kainen grinned, a flicker of Fae wickedness sparkling

in his eyes.

"That could mean anything coming from you, but yeah, follow me."

He held out a hand for her to take and realm-skipped them through the shadows the moment she took it.

"The Illusion Court is famed for its cells," he said. "Demi wants to question him some more before we incarcerate him, but you can have five minutes. He's contained behind wards but I can only give you five minutes, okay?"

She nodded. "I only need a couple."

Kainen eyed her dagger fully visible on her wrist, then slipped a fingertip over the wooden door in front of them and pushed it open.

Phoenix sat shackled to the wall by cuffs of iron. Despite the wooden box and cushion he was seated on being comfortable enough, his eyes were ringed with shadows and his lip curled the moment he saw her.

"Come to gloat?" he asked.

Talie nodded. "And then some. Everything you've done is an abomination based on pride and greed."

"I wouldn't expect someone like you to understand," he scoffed.

"Someone like me? Someone with a heart? How awful it must be to assume your pathetic little world of dominion is better than one with trust and loyalty."

"Pretty words."

"Ones that mean everything. You know it too, don't you? Otherwise you'd be far cockier about it."

Talie smiled as she approached. Even if he didn't have

the cuffs on, even if he was strong, she had a message to deliver, but first a question to ask for Molly's sake.

"I'm sure the powers that be will ask the relevant questions, but I have one I want you to think about first." She drew her dagger from its wrist strap. "Is there any known way to get the undead Fae their lives back?"

His eyes lit with that startling brightness that she now knew was his innate opportunism.

"Which must be worth something to you," he said. "Perhaps we have things to discuss."

"Not worth anything to me, no. As I said, the queen and her entourage will ask the questions. I just wanted to know if you had anything they could use."

"Others will come for her you know," he snapped. "Your precious queen. Others will take great pride in tearing her down until she's nothing but a memory rotting in the ground."

She smiled. "I'll double the protections accordingly, thanks for the heads up."

"The ignorance of youth." He shook his head in disgust.

"The arrogance of greed," she retorted. "Like you said, pretty words. Except I get to walk out of here and the poison you spit is all you have left."

She spun the hilt of her dagger between her fingers.

"You saw her fire and want to possess it, harness it and eventually snuff it out in a tiny jar to prove you can."

She angled the blade and cocked her head.

"Me? I want her to see how brightly she can shine."

Phoenix hadn't finished screaming by the time she pulled the dagger free of his hand, the gouge going right through to the wooden seat.

She walked out and slammed the cell door behind her, her irritation settling as Kainen lifted his head from his deceptively casual lounge-pose against the opposite wall.

"Better?" he asked.

She smiled. "You have no idea how much."

"Is he still alive at least?"

"Sadly, yes."

She decided not to dwell on the relief that flashed over Kainen's face as she took his outstretched hand and they realm-skipped back to the Menagerie.

"It's a bit of a soggy end," she admitted.

"How so?"

"Well, we've managed all this but Molly's got to be a queen with no idea how to do it, and I'm sure I'll figure out the custodian thing, but that's here. She hasn't even spoken to me yet since it all kicked off. It's just… flat somehow."

"Well, I have no doubt you'll be fine, you've always got yourself up, and Molly's still learning. Don't forget that she had a loving family until a year or so ago."

"So?"

He sighed. "You grew up knowing life was harsh and you learned to trust yourself. Molly's only been in the thick of it for a while. She's still learning to trust herself."

"I said I'd be at her side but she's just gone off on her own since being queen."

"She's probably thinking exactly the same about you. Words are easy for Fae. We can tangle them into traps and break what they promise. Actions are the true communication. Have you made the effort to be at her side despite her rushing around since becoming queen?"

Talie eyed the entrance hall that had fast become her home since Molly had taken control of it. She couldn't imagine walking the corridors or dipping into the kitchen if Molly was gone. The nether had also told her she had to remain in the citadel, but it hadn't made any stipulations on how much time she had to spend in the core.

"Sammy's safe and better set up than I ever could have imagined," she said slowly.

He nodded. "She is. It's scary not to be needed, but you can let go now."

"Then what?"

"Whatever you want." He grinned. "That's the really scary part. You can do whatever you want. Sure, there are always responsibilities and restrictions, but if you really want a way around them, you'll find it."

"Still, she's a literal queen of Faerie now. She's got a whole royal court to manage, so she'll have to go and do that. And I have to be here, minding the well."

"So, you haven't asked if she's staying?"

"How can she?"

"Why can't she?"

Talie frowned. "Because she has to run the royal court. I remember when she left ages ago to work there and I didn't see her for a couple of months."

"So? The court follows the crown."

"Which means what?"

"Go and ask her. I'd stake your claim on anything you're attached to as well, especially now that Marthe's started talking about redecorating the Menagerie."

Talie stared at him until her jaw dropped and he winked at her.

"She's… can she do that?"

"Marthe? I think Molly lets her have a pretty loose rein to be honest-"

"Not Marthe, Molly! Can she move the court here?"

He rolled his eyes. "Duh. She's queen. She can do whatever she wants pretty much."

Talie stared at him in amazement.

Orbs, that never even occurred to me.

Talie frowned as a flash of heat warmed the side of her leg. She put her hand into her pocket and pulled out her orb, the one even Sammy didn't need to contact her on anymore. She'd all but forgotten it and was happy to leave it for emergencies only.

She swiped her finger across the surface and the orb-cast projected in front of her.

~Royals Group Chat~

Taz has added Talie to the ~Royals Group Chat~

Talie stared at the simple lines. It was an invitation that somehow brought home exactly what her life was now.

I have an actual noble title. I know the most powerful Fae in Faerie, and I'm beholden to the nether itself.

"Don't go getting a big head now," Kainen joked.

"Although Taz is obscenely possessive of his group chats so this is possibly the biggest accolade of them all."

Talie bit her lip as Molly and Reyan walked toward them and assessed the easy smile on Molly's face.

Has she actually considered moving the court already, or is she just happy it's all over now?

"I won't bow, your majesty," Kainen announced.

Molly rolled her eyes. "I wouldn't expect you to. Maybe the odd head bob in polite company, but not anywhere else."

"A head bob I can do, but from now on I will never bow to anyone but my soulmate."

"You bowed to me once," Talie said.

Molly frowned. "He did?"

"Satire, I assure you," Kainen said. "From this point on, I refuse to bow to hierarchy. I'm surprised you even remember that. You were rather frantic at the time."

Talie rolled her eyes. "Where do you think the Lady Rain title idea came from? I had to pick something."

"Wait, you chose the title I picked for you?!"

Molly snickered at the utter elation stretching his face obscenely wide and Talie smiled to see it.

Maybe we can make it work.

"Orbs." Reyan groaned. "What did you tell him that for!"

Talie grinned. "It slipped out."

"I made a difference," Kainen announced, mostly to himself. "Wait until Taz hears about this!"

"We'll go now while his head is still small enough to fit through the nether," Reyan muttered.

Kainen huffed indignantly even as he took her hand and gave them both a ridiculously flourished bob of his head.

"Your majesty. Oh, I'll be seeing you for the next court social then, Lady Rain."

Talie frowned. "Nobody said anything about socials, and I'm not even sworn to your court."

"No, but you are family."

She wasn't entirely sure what to do with that, or with the sudden catch in her throat. Luckily, he and Reyan realm-skipped away, which left her with Molly.

Orbs, I'm too tired for this.

Despite the endless exhaustion she hadn't fully faced yet, her heart began to leap as she eyed the gold imitation oak and daisy crown on Molly's head, as well as her faded jeans and a ragged t-shirt.

That's my t-shirt.

"Do I call you 'my queen' now?" she asked.

Molly shook her head. "No, never. What's your plan then? I don't know what custodian of the nether entails."

"Neither do I still, but assuming we figure out how to protect the well from eating people and we keep nobles from wandering down there, then it probably isn't too exhausting."

"Oh. So you don't have to be down there all the time or anything?"

Talie steeled herself. "I promised I was on your side always, didn't I? I meant it. Not sure how that'd work what with you being royal now and all that though."

"It starts with moving the royal court." Molly glanced around at the entrance hall, already showing signs of change in the form of several really weird statues. "Marthe will do most of it, and Sammy's determined to have her say, but still."

Molly's smile was literal sunshine and Talie sagged from sheer relief. She plucked at the worn leather strap holding the dagger to her wrist and ducked her head to hide her flushed cheeks.

"You'll be run ragged with those two."

"Maybe we can figure it out together," Molly suggested gently. "You thought I was going to leave, didn't you."

It wasn't a question but Talie nodded.

"I assumed you'd have to. Then Kainen said otherwise. I can't leave often at all now, but like you said before I finally get to make my own choices, kind of, so I'm making this my first one. Stay here. Move your court. Not for me but so we can at least still see each other."

Molly snorted. "So you're starting your first official choice with me?"

Talie reached out and took her hand. Tiny droplets of rain beaded above them as her emotions splurged out and Molly's sunlight rippled out to make rainbows.

"Starting, ending. Who knows?"

Molly cleared her throat. "Right."

"Besides, you can't fight. Who's going to defend you?"

"I can fight."

"You really can't."

"I'm a literal queen now!"

"Yeah, but queen gifts are not the same as being able to fight."

"Train me then."

"That would take *ages*."

"Hello, we have ages." Molly huffed loudly. "Come on, fight me."

"You only have to ask, Princess."

"I'm not a princess anymore though."

"Still Princess to me, no matter how many titles you have."

"Okay, *Lady Rain*."

"Don't call me that. It's a tiny spit of land in the furthest reaches of the Illusion Court. It's a dummy title."

"If you say so, Lady."

"Argh. I think I preferred Sunshine."

Molly's amusement faded and she nodded.

"Okay, Sunshine. Whatever you want."

Talie groaned as Sammy sashayed toward them with a pile of cards in her hands.

"These came through, Molly. I think you'll like what's in them."

Molly took the cards, swiped through them and held them out to Talie.

She released Molly's hand reluctantly and read the four cards, all written in varying degrees of neatness.

"This is amazing!"

Molly nodded. "I can barely believe it. Almost every tower has overthrown their councillor."

"And we didn't even have to do anything." Talie shook her head in amazement. "You'll have to meet with the new ones in the coming days."

Molly nodded. "Each of those is signed by someone I've met before. Tulip's keeping hers, but Allium says he trusts his new councillor, as does Briar, and River has taken over as councillor of her tower. These are people I can actually work with!"

Sammy grinned. "Shall I alert the other royal court then? They'll be pleased to hear about it."

Talie took a step back. Now that Molly was staying she instantly found it much harder to resent the crown.

Could have taken a holiday first though, not that I can for long. I should probably save my five days for emergencies until the end of the year as well.

She pasted on a smile as Molly nodded.

"Yes please. Let Demi know and Kainen, and ask Marthe to send the news with a few bottles of the purple tonic stuff as a goodwill gift from my court to theirs. Oh, and could you do me a personal favour?"

Sammy nodded and Talie's smile faded at the sudden wicked grin on Molly's face.

"Wait until I'm gone, maybe ten minutes, then let Marthe know I'll be away today, probably into tomorrow too."

"Ah, you need to clear that apparently with the royal guard."

"We don't have one yet."

"Oh. Well that's alright then." Sammy beamed and grabbed the cards back. "Leave it all to me. Go, have fun."

Talie shook her head as Sammy raced off up the stairs.

"Where are you going then, Princess?" she asked.

Molly took her hand again with that same mischievous look still tilting her lips.

"Do you need to do custodian things today?"

"Not that I know of. Why, do you need me to do royal things today?"

"Not that I know of," Molly echoed. "But it could be a good time to go and see your land."

Talie frowned. "That's what you want to do?"

"We don't have to. You only have five days a year, so you should use them on things you want."

Talie squeezed Molly's fingers tightly and shuffled closer.

"I'm not bothered about seeing it, but if you need a break we can go. And maybe when we get back we can barricade the bedroom door."

"Maybe." Molly laughed, the sound echoing beautifully around the entrance hall as a random spray of daisies burst up the banister. "Until then, I haven't had much practice with this so hold on tight."

Talie froze. "Wait, what?"

The nether wrapped around them and Talie felt it laugh at her tension, although she sensed a curious wariness angled toward Molly. The moment it faded away to reveal a soft, dappled light, Molly gasped.

"This is... Did you take a wrong turn?" Talie asked.

Molly frowned. "Um... I don't think so. No, this is definitely meant to be it."

"How do you know?"

"What do you mean, how do I know?" Molly sighed. "I've spent the last three days learning to realm-skip for this, and I made sure to get the details of this place from Kainen. Oh, your deeds are in the office by the way."

"But this is..." Talie gazed around again in amazement.

"It's absolutely beautiful."

An abundance of thick pink foliage shaded the air above them, vast blossom trees with pale brown trunks that let soft sunlight dapple down around them and the ankle-length grass they stood in.

"So, this is the spit of land you keep being mean about?" Molly asked. "It's perfect!"

Talie nodded slowly. "It actually is. Featherdown said it was worthless because it was far from court. I figured that meant it was a total dump."

"This is not a dump! You could slowly build here, a stone cottage or some kind of wood cabin. Is that a stream at the far end?"

Molly took a step forward but Talie clung on and held her in place.

"It's fine, Princess. I own it and can only spend five days a year here. A cruel irony I guess."

Molly smiled. "*Now* you can only spend five days a year, but you want to know what I've learned?"

Talie let the remaining tension drain from her shoulders as Molly placed her hands on them, and she tucked her hands in Molly's jeans pockets in return.

"What's that?"

"Everything is a negotiation. Faerie, the nether, Fae, all of it. I reckon give it time and you might even be able to change the terms."

Talie sensed the tiniest hint of tension in the nether, as though it could hear their voices. It was in everything, as was Faerie, but she decided she would focus on that another time.

She let the spirited smile drift across her lips instead.

"Who knows? All I care about is that I have today, so I want to make the most of it."

The moment Molly kissed her, she let the worries drift away.

There would be countless problems in the future waiting for a summer queen and a lady who owned a tiny spit of land with an abundance of blossom trees and was custodian of the nether, but she had the one thing that made all the difference.

With Molly at her side, the choices she'd made so far for survival didn't seem too bad after all.

Not too bad at all.

ACKNOWLEDGEMENTS

A huge thank you to every reader who has walked with me through Faerie and is still coming back for another visit! To those who've shared on social media, done ARC reads or just given me compliments about the book to keep me going, thank you!

To my family and also my writing family as always, your support means everything to me – Aerin Apeltun, Katina Wright, Estelle Tudor, Maria Oliver, Anna Britton, Sally Doherty, Marisa Noelle, Emma Finlayson-Palmer, writing Twitter, the amazing ARC readers (who have caught so many printing blips it's not even funny…), the wider writing community and everyone who joins #ukteenchat, WriteMentor, SCBWI, and especially libraries and schools who've taken a chance on the previous books, shops that are still stocking them and giving this indie author a chance to reach more readers *deep breath* and most importantly to the readers who will find these books in the future:

THANK YOU!

ABOUT THE AUTHOR

While always convinced that there has to be something out there beyond the everyday, Emma focuses on weaving magic realms with words (the real world can wait a while). The idea of other worlds fascinates her and she's determined to find her own entrance to an alternate realm one day.

Raised in London, she now lives on the UK south coast with her husband and a very lazy black Labrador who occasionally condescends to take her out for a walk.

Aside from creative writing studies, an addiction to cake and spending far too much time procrastinating on social media, Emma is still waiting for the arrival of her unicorn. Or a tank, she's not fussy.

For the latest news and updates, check the website or come say hi on social media:

www.emmaebradley.com
@EmmaEBradley